SEPTEMBER:
SABOTAGE

JAN FANCY HULL

A
TIM BROWN
MYSTERY

September: Sabotage
© 2025 Jan Fancy Hull

Cover design: Rebekah Wetmore
Editor: Andrew Wetmore

ISBN: 978-1-998149-93-3
First edition September, 2025

Moose House Publications
2475 Perotte Road
Annapolis County, NS B0S 1A0
moosehousepress.com
info@moosehousepress.com

Moose House Publications recognizes the support of the Province of Nova Scotia. We are pleased to work in partnership with the Department of Communities, Culture and Heritage to develop and promote our cultural resources for all Nova Scotians.

We live and work in Mi'kma'ki, the ancestral and unceded territory of the Mi'kmaw people. This territory is covered by the "Treaties of Peace and Friendship" which Mi'kmaw and Wolastoqiyik (Maliseet) people first signed with the British Crown in 1725. The treaties did not deal with surrender of lands and resources but in fact recognized Mi'kmaq and Wolastoqiyik (Maliseet) title and established the rules for what was to be an ongoing relationship between nations. We are all Treaty people.

Also by Jan Fancy Hull

Non-fiction

Where's Home?

Short stories

The Church of Little Bo Peep and other stories

Inquire Within

The Tim Brown Mystery Series

January: Code

February: Curious

March: Enigma

April: Sweetland

May: Façades

June: Trespasses

July: Confidence

August: Treasure

Definition and thoughts

sabotage
noun
sab·o·tage ˈsa-bə-ˌtäzh
early 20th century: from French, from *saboter* 'kick with sabots [hard wooden shoes], wilfully destroy'

All business sagacity reduces itself in the last analysis to judicious use of sabotage.

—Thorstein Veblen

Leaders who are kind of insecure or egocentric, they basically sabotage themselves.

—John C. Maxwell

Procrastination is, hands down, our favorite form of self-sabotage.
—Alyce Cornyn-Selby

There are countless horrible things happening all over the world and horrible people prospering, but we must never allow them to disturb our equanimity or deflect us from our sacred duty to sabotage and annoy them whenever possible.
—Auberon Waugh

To those who solve problems for the greater good.

September: Sabotage

Jan Fancy Hull

Prologue: Robert's news

Yesterday

What a night it had been!

It started with Robert's urgent call, asking if Tim would come to the city immediately, or sooner. Robert's future had just arrived in his mailbox, and he desperately wanted Tim to be with him when he learned what it would be.

So Tim cancelled everything he had planned to do for the rest of the day, which was nothing at all, and zoomed up Highway 103 from South River to Halifax. As soon as he arrived at Robert's tiny bachelor apartment, barely an hour later, they tore open the big brown envelope and read the news.

The cover letter began: "Dear Dr Kirk: After due consideration, it brings us great pleasure to offer you..." and went on to describe everything Robert had ever hoped for, and more.

Tim had the presence of mind to call for a reservation at a posh downtown restaurant overlooking Halifax harbour. It was only Tuesday, so his earnest request for a table for two by the window was successful. What this letter was offering could not possibly be discussed over peanut butter and crackers or whatever leftovers Robert might have had in his tiny refrigerator.

Tim had brought along a bottle of goodish wine, not knowing whether it would be for celebration or consolation. It was only mid-afternoon, too early to start drinking celebratory toasts, and Robert was too excited to eat or drink anyway, so they put on their jackets and went out to walk and talk.

The apartment was on Oxford Street, on the border of the Dalhousie University campus. They set out toward the city's south end, along Oxford to Beaufort, left on Roxton, right on Robie, left on Gorsebrook, right on Tower and finally to Point Pleasant Drive. It led into the large, wooded Point Pleasant Park at the tip of the Halifax peninsula, with dramatic harbour and ocean views and a few preserved ruins of fortifications.

They noticed none of this.

Tim was publisher and editor of *The Times,* the community weekly paper in the South Shore town of South River, Nova Scotia. He had taken this year off to "delve" into newspaper stories or into his own life questions—he hadn't been clear about which. At age forty, Tim had already devoted about twenty-five years of full-time labour to the enterprise he had inherited. This year, he was gradually discovering that there really was a life outside of work for him.

Robert, the "Dr Kirk" to whom the letter was addressed, was organist and choir director at Saint John's Church in South River. He was also on the music faculty at the first of the two universities they had just walked past, where he taught organ, music theory, composition...anything he could get studio time and approval to do.

He occasionally gave ambitious solo organ performances. At his most recent one, part of a festival near Kensington, PEI, he met representatives of a widely-respected organ manufacturer from Quebec, Les Frères d'Orgue, who sold and refurbished their instruments all over Canada and the United States.

This letter was from them, inviting Robert to be their official organist at all corporate concerts showcasing their new or refurbished instruments. His affinity for their instrument in Kensington had impressed them, as had his willingness to consult with the builders on choices of stops and registers to enhance the program he was playing.

Robert's memory was famously sharp. As they walked, he recited details from the letter which he had memorized as he had read it.

"Five years, Tim! They're offering me this contract for *five years*! Who does that? I mean, is that done in business? That's almost like tenure. What if they don't like me after a while? What if I don't like them?"

"Easy now. Don't talk yourself into trouble before you've even discussed it with them. Yes, contracts can be for any length. There's usually an escape clause for both parties, describing how to terminate due to your inability to carry out the duties as described or as assumed or whatever, and guidance if you have to cancel due to illness, and how long before they'd terminate you if you became seriously ill. Or dead. Stuff like that. Also terms and conditions to renew, if it comes to that."

"They might not terminate me just because I died. I've heard of some old church organists that were suspected of having been dead for years."

"Well, that's not you. You have way too much life force. Anyway, let's not talk about that. I'll look over the contract for you, and tell you if there are any clauses I think you should challenge, okay? Let's talk about the concerts they've booked for next year. Starting when?"

"April. I can do April."

"And where?"

"Knoxville, Tennessee, first, then Boston. Oh my, I get giddy just thinking about it. Me, Robert Kirk, on tour! For pay! Performing on the make of organ I love the most! Because they 'admire my artistry'! Will you be able to come with me at all?"

"We will ask that and many other good questions, and we will find the best answers together. I'd like to go with you some of the time, at least, as long as I don't have to drive there. But right now, we'd better turn around. We've walked halfway to Tennessee already!"

~

Tim and Robert shared a fondness for many things, fine food and fine wine among them. This restaurant catered to diners who enjoyed the chef's extravagant creations. Robert's eyes shone as he recalled the mention of a subsequent recording contract in the letter. "I'll be able to pick up the tab for you one of these years, Timo."

"Oh, so there *is* an upside to all this upheaval! I shall look forward to those free meals. I'm not cheap, but I'm patient. I hope you'll reap big financial rewards, Rob, as well as artistic. You do deserve it. I suppose I'll be dining alone more often, poor me, but—"

"Don't remind me. Come with me the first few times, will you? I just feel more confident when you're nearby. You remind me to breathe and be calm when it matters. Like right now."

"I'll write breathing instructions on a piece of paper for you. But sure, if it works out, we'll see the world together. Maybe not the kind of world those so-called friends were talking about in July, but it's a big world, and it seems you've got the world you want by the tail right now."

Tim raised the last of his wine to toast Robert's good fortune, and then asked the *maître d'* to call a cab.

Back in the apartment, Robert spread the contents of the envelope on the sofa between them. Tim scanned the document outlining the proposed terms and conditions of Robert's work, and Robert studied the specifications of the organs he would be playing. Each read aloud when they encountered something of interest.

Both soon subsided into somnolence, so they relinquished the day and went to bed.

Jan Fancy Hull

September 1, 1999: Private booth

Wednesday

This morning, details of the envelope's contents and intentions were not so clear, partly due to the complexity of terms and conditions affecting Robert's professional career and his life with Tim, and partly due to the walking and fine dining yesterday.

"I wish Gloria was here," Robert mumbled. Gloria was their European queen of steam, which infused freshly ground espresso beans to make superb morning coffees. "She" was in South River.

"Mm. Not enough counter space. I found a place when I came to town with you last month, where I had a fine Americano, 'with room'. There's time for us to get quick showers and go there."

"What's 'room'?"

"Literally nothing, as far as I can tell, but you can put cream in it. It tastes like coffee and doesn't cost more."

They chatted briefly in the café, but not about Robert's mail. Contents of this Pandora's envelope needed to sit undisturbed in their minds before rising again, like bread dough.

Robert mentioned that he'd be back in South River in plenty of time to help with the party.

"What party?"

"Come on, Tim. It's a holiday weekend, you love showing off your new back garden, and you love entertaining ten or twenty of your friends. You should read your mind more: it's interesting—and quite predictable. Call me when you know what you're planning. If you have any choice in the matter, I'd prefer to have Monday without a crowd. My work-train leaves the station on Tuesday, and I'd like to have one more precious day to lollygag around before that."

They soon said goodbye and went their own ways, still a little rough around the edges from the late hour and such, but happy. Positive. Optimistic.

Robert's changes, should he accept them, wouldn't be in motion until next year, so now was the time to dream of travel and new audiences. Tim had some reservations about all that, but his life was going to change a lot in the new year, too, when he returned to regular hours at the newspaper.

They would talk much more about this.

~

Driving back down Highway 103, Tim wondered what he was supposed to be doing today. He wasn't "supposed" to do anything work-related, because he was still on sabbatical, with four months to go. But—and it was a very big but—this weekend contained not just any old holiday, but Labour Day. He and his smart interim editor, Elaine Fong, had gingerly mentioned this aspect of labour and human resources a few times.

Do the staff of The Times *really want a union?* Tim wondered. *It's up to them, but I've always tried to support whatever they wanted. How to raise the topic? We talked a little about a company-sponsored picnic for staff and family, but when? Should we give them time off to attend it? Labour Day is already mandated time off. I hope Elaine'll sort this out.*

Tim and Elaine had both confessed to a lack of skill with this topic, and a corresponding low degree of interest in it. Perhaps they'd come up with some gesture that would let the staff know they were appreciated.

They're good people, and I think they're paid fairly for their work. I guess we should ask, but how to ask without implying that universal raises are in the offing? Some might be warranted, but...

He parked in the lot across the street from his building. "I'm here now. Angels might hesitate, but I will rush in as usual."

The current issue of *The Times* had gone to print yesterday, and the next deadline always seemed far away. Today, the office was quiet and sparsely populated. Those who worked overtime yesterday to get the paper ready would drift in when they felt like it, and nobody would say anything about it. This one aspect of employee empowerment made Tim feel like the staff were in partnership with him, and he hoped the feeling was mutual.

"Where's Miss Fong?" he asked the receptionist.

"Right behind you," Elaine replied. "Am I late?"

"I wouldn't know, and would never say. Do you have a moment for me this morning?"

"I believe I do. This job isn't as scary as it was when I was first in charge last winter. Now I can relax a bit between cycles, because I know how hard we work at the end. My, I sound a bit—"

"Don't worry, I feel like you sound. I had to dash to the city in a hurry yesterday—or should I use business-speak and say I was 'called away'?—to celebrate some good news, so I'm feeling a bit seedy. We'll recover. I haven't had breakfast yet, have you? Let's go and surprise Evelyn."

"Sure. Why would she be surprised?"

"Watch."

The Daisy Café was next door to the newspaper building. Evelyn Whynot, a schoolmate of Tim's, had worked there for ages. With Tim's intervention and support, she had become a partner in the diner earlier this summer.

Tim opened the café door and waggled it to ring the bell that hung above it. Evelyn looked up.

"Tim!" She laughed a hee-haw laugh across the dining room, bestowed only upon those of whom she was most fond. "Did you get lost? It's not Thursday. Hello, Elaine, nice to see you, too. Are you two gonna talk business? Wait here a minute. I'll clear the executive booth."

"I see what you meant," Elaine said quietly.

"Follow me, please," Evelyn said, and led them to a booth at the back, not Tim's usual spot. This one was the same as all the others, except for two-foot-high panels of plexiglass fixed to the back of both benches, making an effective sound barrier.

"Privacy, see?" She poured two cups of coffee.

"I do see," Tim said. "What brought this on?"

"Funny, but I was thinking, unusual for me. Whoever sits here, they're right back on to the kitchen, not that Kenny makes much noise himself but he's always bangin' that bell at me. And the washroom's right over there, so someone might be hanging around waiting to get in, right? I sat here one day for my break, and I thought how nice it would be if it was quieter, so I asked one of my regulars if he could put up these panels for me. Did it next day. Not a bad return for a free breakfast, hey?"

"Would you like a job at the newspaper, Evelyn?" Elaine said. "We could use your ingenuity."

"Now, there you go, talkin' Shakespeare like he does. Thanks anyway, but working here is almost more than I can cope with most days. Your jobs would confuse the heck outta me. So, did you have breakfast already, or can I feed you properly?"

Both nodded. "Feed us properly," Tim said, "but not too—"

Evelyn was already through the swinging doors to tell Kenny the cook what to make for them.

The plexiglass really worked. It kept the ambient noises down, and their conversation from leaking out.

"Do we need privacy?" Elaine asked.

"We do."

"Because?"

"Staff. HR. Labour. Labour Day. We overlooked this happy topic when last we chatted."

"Hmm. Have you worked it all out?"

"You kidding? I have done exactly nothing about any of that, not since we met with that stylin' HR expert, Mademoiselle what's-her-name, in June or May or whenever it was. Have you?"

"You know the answer," Elaine said. "It's not that I don't want staff to be happy at work and all that pertains to that, it's just that I don't feel I'm good at peopley things. And I don't like to do things I'm not good at. Now you know too much about me."

"Same here. But don't undersell yourself: you led the team when we prepared our big breaking news story in the spring. Everyone followed you and did whatever needed to be done."

"True, but I was *telling*, then. Human Resources is all about asking, and feelings. 'How do you *feel* about this?' 'What do you *think* about that?' 'When would you *like* to have your work ready?' Talk about feelings: that kind of talk makes me feel like I'm drowning. I'd fear the ship would sink while someone who isn't qualified to make a decision makes the wrong one, or too late. Ugh!"

Elaine lowered her voice, which had risen a little. "Thank goodness for these baffles!"

"Did you say waffles?" Evelyn had arrived with two plates on each arm, and placed them on the arborite table top without mishap. "We don't have waffles on weekdays, but be sure to come back for brunch on Saturday or Sunday and you'll get 'em. Come early, though. There'll be a crowd once word gets out. Enjoy."

Tim had gotten up very early in the city and had only a latté at the coffee shop, so the eggs, bacon, and hash browns were welcome, and a diversion from this uncomfortable discussion topic. Discretion kept him from asking where and when Elaine had developed her appetite, but she, too, ate with gusto. Evelyn returned to top up their cups with her dark roast option.

Tim kissed his napkin to remove some of the grease from his beard, then spread a little jam on the final piece of toast.

"I'm waiting for you to tell me what to do next," he said. "You already know how I *feel* and *think*. I would not *like* to get into the weeds of any of this. But because you don't either, and I admire your work ethic and skills without reservation, I feel that our inadequacies are a sign of greatness."

"That's no help. Where are we on this?"

"Facing the abyss. Come on, we have to do something."

Tim took an ever-present notebook from his pocket and flipped it open to a blank page. Elaine handed him a pen.

"I usually use pencil," he said, "but I seem to have misplaced it."

"Be bold," she said. "Write this down: one, Labour Day picnic question mark; two, Human Resources issues; three, possible union question mark. We'll address these in that order, and in short order, too."

"Good. Right. Yes. I like using ink. It makes it look like the decision is half-made already. Now, Labour Day picnic: what about it?"

"I did ask informally around the water-cooler. Got a few smiles and one or two said that'd be nice, but nobody grabbed it."

"Of course not. They were likely mirroring your hesitancy. It probably frightened them to see you so hesitant. Let's decide something."

"Such as?"

"Like the day: are we talking Labour Day, i.e. Monday, for the picnic?"

"Let's say we are."

"Okay." Tim wrote that in his notebook. "It's in ink, so it's decided. Now, what do we mean by a picnic? Sandwiches on gingham tablecloths spread on the ground?"

"People don't eat on the ground these days, do they? When I see an historic photo of outdoor events, the hair and clothing are different, of course, but what I notice is that they're all reclining on the ground, not a table or folding chair in sight."

"Moving along..."

"Sorry. I'm finding it hard to focus on this. Listen, I support the concept and all that, but, in case you haven't noticed, I'm not an experienced host or party planner like you. Why don't we ask one of the—?"

"Cindy Martin?"

"Yes! Cindy would be the perfect planner, I think. She's been so busy selling advertising that maybe she'd want to spend Labour Day with her feet up. That's what it's for, isn't it? Resting from labour? Or is it celebrating labour?"

"The latter, I think, *ergo* the parade. Okay, here's my decision: it's Cindy Martin or nobody. *The Times* hasn't done anything special for Labour Day in a century, so if we miss the opportunity in 1999, so be it. We can always say we're open to it. Is she in today, do you know?"

Elaine took her mobile phone out of her purse and called Cindy. She didn't answer, so Elaine left a short message to call her as early as possible, important but not urgent. A few minutes later, Cindy called back.

"Are you downtown or near, Cindy? Oh good. Listen: Mister Brown and I—yes, he's with me now, and we—yes, I know, we all do. We're in the Daisy Café at the moment. Could you join us for a brief chat? We'll wait for you. Good."

She returned the phone to her purse.

"Cindy'll be here in a moment. She misses you. This booth is going to get a lot of use from us, I think. Perhaps Evelyn will let us reserve it."

Evelyn had been keeping an eye on things in the executive booth. Seeing her guests sitting back instead of hunched over their plates, she came by to remove the debris.

"Will that be all for today, folks?"

"We're starting over, Ev," Tim said. "We have a guest joining us in a few minutes, so we'll need fresh coffee to be sociable, and some of your muffins *du jour*. Excuse me, I must use the loo."

"Who's your guest? Is she a regular?"

"I don't know: it's Cindy Martin, our ad sales executive."

"Sure, I know Cindy, and I know what she likes. She brings a lot of your customers in here. I'll take care of her, no problem."

~

Cindy Martin entered the café with colourful scarves flying. She waved hello to several patrons as she sailed down the aisle to the back booth. Elaine had moved to sit beside Tim so their guest would have the bench to herself. She was as plump as Elaine was slim, and tended to gesture broadly as she spoke.

She had made her way into most of the shops and businesses in the county, frequently walking out with an advertising contract, or a promise of one. At more than one location, she had actually declined to accept their contract until they made improvements in their merchandise displays or other aspects of the customer experience.

It had been slow going at first, but, after she had been on the job only a few months, new money was beginning to flow in all directions: into the businesses, back to the newspaper and, to an increasing degree, to her.

"I'm so glad to see you, Mister Brown," she breathed. "I know you're off this year, but you've been so good to me. I can't wait for you to come back full-time so we can come up with more great ideas. Of course, Miss Fong has been a great leader—"

"But I'm not creative. I know." Elaine laughed.

"Miss Martin," Tim interjected, "it's nice to see you. Oh, thanks, Evelyn." New food had arrived. "Miss Fong and I had a topic in mind to discuss with you right now and we'll get right to it, if you don't mind. What would you say to a Labour Day picnic for the staff? And their families?"

"When?"

"On Labour Day?"

"Gosh, this year? I mean, what kind of picnic? If you want a caterer, it's a bit late. And if it's stuff from the grocery store, who would plan it and get it and set it up?"

"Not me," Elaine said.

"Nor I," added Tim.

"Me, neither. But let's think for a moment. Is a picnic what you want, really? What's it for?"

"Um, to show our appreciation...for the, uh, labour...of our workers?"

"Oh, dear, Mister Brown, I wouldn't buy whatever you're selling. It would have to be something you believe in, and something the staff want. Have you asked anyone?"

"We mentioned it to a few, maybe, in days gone by."

"And?"

"They didn't seem all that interested."

"So why do it?"

"We're not doing very well at this," Tim said. "Should we forget it?"

"No, no, I think you have a great idea," Cindy said. "Remember back a few months when you scattered that old fella's ashes off the old bridge and so many of the staff came and brought their families? They came for him, but it was about doing it together, too. I love that about this crowd. They are a lovin' spoonful, and you are the motivation for that—both of you are. So. Ed Garamond and his family like to spend time at my drafty old place, because of the acreage out on the point. They'll come over on Monday, most likely. Whenever they come, they always bring food— they're so grateful to get away from their tiny balcony. Anyway, there's room for a couple dozen more. And everyone could bring food. Yeah: potluck."

Tim and Elaine listened raptly to Cindy's out-loud thinking.

"Say, I know! Let's call a company-wide pot-luck picnic at my place, and ask each person or family to bring an outdoor game if they have one. Maybe not baseball, but badminton, bocce, tag for the little ones, horse-shoes, stuff like that. I like it! I don't have much outdoor furniture, but they can bring blankets. What do you think?"

"If you like it, we like it, don't we, Miss Fong?"

"We do. Is there something the company can contribute, like food or drink or games or blankets?"

"Off the top of my head? I'd say no, but if there are special expenses— like a broken window, ha-ha—we'll let you know. No, I think this should just be a party of the people, by the people, for the people, right? Just being happy together, like that other time."

"Why does this seem too easy?" Elaine asked.

"I know. I was expecting to contribute to this," Tim said, "to show the company's appreciation, you know."

"This is just my opinion, but I'd say to save your appreciation for Christmas bonuses, when every soul on staff will be grateful for actual money. Labour Day isn't about money, as I understand it. It's about work-ers' camaraderie. Big city businesses don't have this, I assure you. You can't manufacture it, and it's not made better by money spent the wrong way."

"You know, Miss Martin," Tim said, "listening to you almost makes me eager to come back to work—*almost*. So, how shall we proceed? What would you like us to—?"

"Do nothing. I'll take care of it. Don't worry, I'll tell everyone that it was your...no, not your idea, but you're in favour of it. This is employees for employees, okay?"

Tim saw Elaine nodding out of the corner of his eye. "Very okay," he said. "Just...how should we participate, then?"

"Hmm. You're always welcome at my house, both of you, but maybe this isn't the time to act as the organizers. Think about it. We have a few days yet. Meanwhile, I'll start putting the word out."

Cindy looked at her watch. "I have to run, sorry. I think we'll have a nice new advertiser. He just needs a little more attention before signing. Thanks for the coffee. I like this booth, too. I'll bring my downtown cli-ents here from now on. Sometimes these walls have ears. Lovely to chat with you both. Buh-bye."

When Cindy Martin and all her scarves had left the café, Tim let out a long breath, and Elaine moved back to the other side of the booth.

"High energy, that one," he said. "Is our problem solved?"

"I don't know. I really don't know. There will be a gathering on

Monday, as we sort of hoped, but didn't it seem that we're not invited? Unless I mis-heard her? I feel uneasy not going, but about going, too. I didn't see that coming."

"That's why we don't like personnel matters. There was likely a turning-point in the conversation where we lost control, but that just proves we're not sensitive to that stuff. Let's not prejudge it yet."

Tim picked up a few muffin crumbs from his saucer. "I know: let's invent potential prior arrangements that are waiting on someone else to confirm. We can look interested, even disappointed at the short notice, right? That way, we're neither going nor staying away. I'm going to try that, though Robert says I'm not a convincing fibber. Perhaps I'll just stay away from the office. That's legitimate."

"Easy for you. But I did plan a slim paper this week because of the holiday, so I'll do my best to stay out of sight. Shall we consult on Friday? We can play it by ear."

"Good. Speaking of playing by ear, today's Wednesday, music day at my house. Might you like to come over and sing through something fun this evening?"

"Already? I'm so sorry, Tim, but I have a potential prior arrangement that depends on someone else to confirm."

Tim looked up.

"Right," she said, grinning. "It does sound phony. Sure, I'd love to sing and forget about this slippery slope for a couple hours. See you after supper."

~

When Tim entered his house and tossed the keys on the kitchen island, he felt disoriented.

What day is it? Is it only Wednesday? Feels like it should be next week already. I went to Rob's only—he checked the big black and white clock on the kitchen wall—*twenty-three hours ago.*

Over-coffeed and well-muffined, Tim had no desire for lunch. He retrieved the mail and newspapers from the front porch and went to the sunroom. He sat on the sofa and looked out over his beautiful backyard and bountiful gardens.

When he woke, it was late afternoon.

Maybe I'm too old for late-night wining and dining. It was great, though. We were happy, especially Rob. Imagine, a relatively unknown organist being selected to be the ambassador of such a well-known establishment! I know he'll be away on tours, but starting next week he'll be away teaching most of the week anyway, so I'll get used to it.

He opened a can of soup for supper, thankful that Elaine wasn't coming until later.

I'll soon be back to the grind myself. So much has changed at the office that it'll be like going to a new job. I don't feel very qualified for it. Especially with Elaine gone to another community weekly up some mountain in Alberta or other remote place. I could call her for help: what's that, three hours difference? She'd love that, hearing from me at four in the morning.

He went upstairs to freshen up, decided to take a shower, and returned downstairs to soup boiling on the stove. It wasn't burned, but a thick layer was baked onto the bottom of the saucepan. He poured the remaining liquid into a mug and tossed the pan into the sink to soak.

He was still sitting at the kitchen island, morosely spooning soup out of the mug, when Elaine arrived for the evening of cheerful music-making.

"You look awful, Tim! What happened?"

"Do I? Nothing...nothing happened." He cleared the bottom of the mug with his spoon.

"Our meeting with Cindy got you down? Me, too, for a New York minute. But I have a different perspective on it this evening. Top up your glass and I'll tell you."

She looked around for Tim's usual wine.

"You're drinking *water*? No wonder you've got the gloomies."

She walked around the island and opened his fridge. She brought out a half-empty bottle of white wine, and took two stemmed glasses from the cupboard.

"Follow me," she ordered, and walked to the parlour. Tim meekly followed.

"Sit," she said, pointing to the piano bench. Tim sat. Elaine poured a half glass each.

"Drink. Good. Now listen to me. The gathering that may happen on Monday isn't happening to exclude you. Or me, either. But staff parties have always been initiated by you, correct?"

Tim shrugged. "I guess so."

"They were. It has always been your leadership, your bouquets of flowers, your bonuses, et cetera. I think that early-morning scattering of old GB's ashes in June was a turning-point for the staff. You were going to do it alone if need be, remember? You mentioned it to someone, maybe

Ed, and word spread quickly. When the moment came, the staff and their families stretched all the way across the bridge. Evelyn opened the café early on her own, without initiation by you. The priest came because he was curious, not because you asked him. Drink."

Tim had never been ordered to drink wine before, had never needed the prompt. Elaine's directions made him smile, just a little.

"So my theory is that your staff have begun to take notice of each other this year, with you around less, and me just a temporary figure-head. They do seem to genuinely like each other, and get along really well, for the most part, unlike some hornets' nests I've endured. So, when Cindy suggested that the picnic on Labour Day would not need you and me, she was just reflecting that remarkable trend toward staff solidarity. Appropriately. Her demeanour towards you was genuinely friendly, was it not?"

"It was."

"Right, then. You'll have to come to terms with the evolution of your business vis-a-vis relations with staff, but it's probably better this way. A little arm's length between management and staff is not a bad thing. I've enjoyed the friendly and respectful atmosphere you've cultivated in your office, but I don't see that changing with this."

"I like what you say. I want to believe it, and I hope it's true. I feel better already."

"Excellent! Now let's rip into a show-tune for the greater good of humanity!"

September 2: Grounding

Thursday

Tim stared at the ceiling for a few moments after he woke, reviewing the external and internal events since Tuesday. Robert's career, the looming spectre of Elaine's contract coming to an end, the staff planning an event without him, and Elaine's stern and effective counselling, which hadn't enabled him to meet the challenge of a book of unfamiliar English folksongs.

They had switched to "Sheep May Safely Graze", hoping a sweet Bach aria would give them a better sense of accomplishment. They ignored the lyrics about ruling with wisdom.

He hopped out of bed, grateful more than ever for Elaine, who had become a real friend as well as editor.

"Wouldn't that be fun," he asked Gloria as she squeezed out a thick espresso, "to have Elaine stay on as editor for life? Ah, well, let's not go there this morning. We don't want to be morose today. Mrs Mother Princess Aquino will be thumping at the back door any minute, and maybe she'll go to the veggie garden with me."

In the spring, as part of his quest to reclaim the backyard from years of neglect, Tim was tilling the round garden mounds when Mrs Aquino, his housekeeper, had seen him in action. Pretty soon, she was directing him to dig deeper, and wider, and to amend the soil with bags of this and that from the garden shops.

Robert had joined them when he could, as a trainee gardener. They were thrilled to be able to pull carrots, radishes, beets, and other edibles from the soil. Mrs A must have planted other seeds as well, as there were leaves and sprouts that Tim didn't recall planting. He took care to impress upon her that she had full rein—and reign—in the gardens, since she had room for only a few plant pots on the balcony where she lived.

Somewhere in all this, Robert had learned that her first name was Princess, hence her elongated name, a mash-up of Mother Nature and

Mrs Princess Aquino, all meant with affection.

Mrs A did arrive, carrying a small basket for her share of the harvest. She pointed here and there to direct Tim to "take, take" or "water, water". She was pleased, and that made him happy.

He helped carry her cleaning implements into the house, propped her cheque on the kitchen island and, to escape the constant running of the vacuum cleaner, drove downtown for his regular appearance at the Daisy Café.

He sat in his regular booth, too, having no secret business to conduct today. It was just Thursday, and Evelyn came over to give him her regular sass.

"No lady friends today? You had quite a crowd in our executive booth yesterday, didn't ya?"

"Yes, but don't be jealous."

"I might be if you weren't talkin' whatever you were talkin' about. My brain is stunted from working here. All I do is say, 'What'll it be?' and 'Will that be all?' a hundred times a day. And Kenny doesn't talk, thank goodness. Anyway, hon, I have a full house here, so *what'll it be* for you?"

She laughed her large, breezy laugh and walked away without waiting for Tim's response. What she brought would be exactly what it would be.

~

Tim preferred not to return home until Mrs A had left, because of the racket. He didn't have anything to do other than open the mail he had fallen asleep over yesterday, but that didn't appeal.

I need something to challenge my mind; not like that darn puzzle-box last month, but more like what came of it. Something of significance to humanity.

He laughed at himself. He was walking the South River loop across the two bridges. He had been walking on sandy beaches in recent weeks; now he felt like he had returned from far away.

He went for another loop, and when he reached the South River Library for the second time, he went in.

"Happy September, Tim," the chief librarian, Marlene Wentzell, greeted him.

"And to you, Marlene." He hadn't any idea why he had gone into the library, so he was stalling. "Do you—d'you know any poems that mention September? It seems there should be one."

"'Up from the meadows rich with corn, Clear in the cool September morn,'" she quoted. "John Greenleaf Whittier, if I'm not mistaken. Will that do? We don't have meadows of corn here in South River, but it's nice to visualize."

"You never fail to amaze, Marlene."

Then it came to him. "Say, I was wondering if you might have a book on legal contracts, terms and conditions, length of obligation, that sort of thing? I guess it would be in the reference section?"

"That's different, even for your eclectic tastes. We're a small branch, not much call for that kind of book here, but let me check for you. Be right back."

She needed only a few minutes.

"I found two volumes that might have what you're looking for. One's a law book, the other is written for laymen. Otherwise you'll have to go to the city. Or a legal office may have something. I left them out on the table back there. Enjoy!"

Yes, that's what I want to do today. I'll learn about contracts so I'll know what to look out for when Robert brings his envelope down.

He spent the day at it, taking breaks to pick up a lined pad at his office down the street, and one of Evelyn's wraps for lunch. He walked the loop again to clear his head. The reading material was dull, but he read with Robert's wellbeing in mind, and that made it a lot more interesting.

He left the library, finally, with photocopies of some pages of detail, and other pages of notes, satisfied with his initial "delving".

Timothy Brown, Private Researcher, is back in the saddle, and I couldn't be more pleased about it. I do like relaxing and all that, but I'm most com-fortable when I have some little nugget to ponder. It keeps my mind from feeling sorry for itself.

Starting next Thursday, choir practice would resume. Robert would drive down from the city after his classes, arriving just in time for a light supper before they went to the church. But that was next week, and Robert was taking care of other business today and tomorrow in the city. That meant that Tim could make a hefty dinner and take his time over it tonight. He hoped it would be grounding.

If the pork chop didn't ground him, the huge baked potato with broc-coli and cheese sauce certainly did, helped down with generous glasses of *Terre à terre*, a robust red wine.

He played a few pages of music until he felt ready for bed. It was early, but darkness came a little early on this cloudy night, and he was confid-ent of a good sleep ahead.

September 3: Lists

Friday

That baked potato was the pillow for a long sleep without dreams. Tim woke refreshed and ready to deal with the day.

"Good morning, Gloria," he said, carefully polishing the espresso machine's gleaming spouts and knobs. "Might I have one of your fabulous lattés today? I need to practice my artistry in foam."

"She" was in a compliant mood, infusing a perfect cup for him. He would have taken it out to his back garden for a stroll, but last evening's clouds were still misting, so he stayed inside and created the first To Do list of several surely to come in the month.

First, are we going to have our own gathering here this long weekend? Robert is willing, but said not Monday. That leaves Saturday or Sunday. I prefer Sunday, so that's when it shall be. Now, what kind of gathering and what guests?

He turned on the radio in the den to catch the weather forecast at the top of the hour. At first, he was concerned at what he heard: a post-tropical storm, formerly a hurricane farther south, would be passing between Nova Scotia and Sable Island this weekend, of all times. The announcer said that Nova Scotia's South Shore would receive "some" heavy rain by Sunday morning, and that the stronger wind would be on the Atlantic side of the storm, not on the Bay of Fundy side. Cape Breton would get a lot of both.

"Well, now, what do we think of that? Sunday will likely be a wash-out. Oh—Monday, too!"

What a shame it's a holiday. People will have planned picnics and outdoor games and such. Oh, well, sometimes it rains on parades, even Labour Day parades—or picnics. Well, I heard what Elaine said about letting people do their own thing. She's right. It's a change, and I will do my best to adapt to it. For almost all my life, the only people I spent time with were the staff...other than the choir, of course, but I only wanted to sing with them, not to discuss matters. Maybe that's why I felt left out when Cindy told us not to get involved in the party. That'll likely be cancelled anyway now, so I have a Get Out of Jail Free card. Good for me.

He made toast and another coffee.

Now, who for Sunday dinner?

He jotted down the names of his usual invitees, and a few new ones. There were couples, and there were singles. Who had met whom, and what kind of conversations would work with which mix?

He enjoyed this. He even considered prescribing the topic of conversation, as a twist on a dinner theatre or table-play. Previously, when thinking about certain subjects, he had said to himself that they would make good dinner conversations. Now, what were they?

Better pick the guests first, and then see if they need prompting, or would even stick to the topic.

He called Robert's cellphone and left the message that he was expecting him in South River tonight, to please advise *if* that was not the case and *if* he wanted something other than the usual for supper. And there would be guests for dinner on Sunday, but he didn't know who or for what yet.

He disconnected, then called back to tell the recording to be sure to bring along the organ contract for some intensive scrutiny.

He considered inviting Evelyn. What sort of dinner-table conversation would she enjoy? If she heard a multi-syllable word, she might just say, "You're talkin' Shakespeare," and check out of the conversation. That wouldn't work with the retired Anglican bishop, Mort Evers, though he thought Evelyn and Martha Evers would get on like a house afire.

If his Aunt Stella, the MLA for South River and the Islands, wouldn't dismiss Evelyn out of hand, she might admire what Evelyn had accomplished in her life.

Stella had invited Elaine Fong to take her little black dress to Stella's city condo last spring for a business networking event, and they had expressed admiration for each other's acumen, but this wasn't business.

Elaine and Evelyn would get along with each other.

In his backyard garden party on Canada Day, most of these people had shared the outdoor space very well. In the confines of a dining room, the oils and the waters might not mix as well.

And he had a hankering for a formal table, if not formal conversation. So he settled on just the bishop and his wife.

"Oh, Tim, how lovely!"

Martha called to her husband, "Mort! Are we promised for dinner anywhere this Sunday? He's upstairs at his memoirs, natch," she said to Tim. "What, dear? No? Well, we are now, so don't let anyone else ask us. There, that's settled. We'll be there with bells on. Will we see Robert, too?"

"Absolutely, he'll be here. It's his last gasp before regular teaching begins again. He loves to teach, but it does keep him away from South River. Shall we say five for six on Sunday? Or would you prefer earlier? It does get dark earlier now, and the forecast is for rain. Wait—tell you what, Martha, let's leave the time at five for six, and you watch out your window for your limousine at four-thirty. Okay?"

Martha made the obligatory faint refusals before gratefully accepting. She did drive with a lead foot, but not in darkness or rain. This way, she wouldn't have to miss a taste of whatever Tim might serve from his oven or wine cellar.

Done! If Robert wants to add someone, there are still plenty of chairs and elbow room available. Now, the menu.

~

When Robert arrived, Tim's usual Friday supper—takeout fish and chips, reheated until the batter was crispy and the fries had the texture of wooden pencils—was in the oven. Tim had taken the thoughtful step of covering Robert's portions with aluminum foil, for his more conventional taste.

They discussed possible menus for Sunday. They had enjoyed their summer meals, including the highs and lows of grilling, even of "jamming" ripe strawberries on toast when there wasn't anything else in the cupboard at the first cottage they'd rented.

Summer was a sauce that made any casual meal a delicacy, even more so with a beach nearby. Neither of them had ever before experienced days like those they spent in the out-of-doors this summer, and they reminisced about their adventures and discoveries through the evening while flipping through Tim's extensive collection of cookbooks.

While three weeks of summer still remained on the calendar, this weekend marked a turning point in atmospheric and emotional weather. The world seemed to have a back-to-school or back-to-work tilt, and that world included Tim and Robert.

They hadn't forgotten about the Big Brown Envelope of Potential, either. They agreed to save the review and discussion of the contents for tomorrow, after breakfast and chores were done. They would approach the discussion rationally and methodically, and with optimism.

September 4: Breathing

Saturday

The cupboard was bare. The steamed milk in their cappuccinos smelled suspicious. They dressed for the overcast day and drove down the turny road along the scenic South River to the bakery for breakfast, and a selection of breads and chocolatey chocolate brownies.

After giving fish, flesh, and fowl due consideration last night, they had settled on roast beef as the main dish for tomorrow. Robert was in charge, and every molecule would be under his direction. They drove back through South River to a small but reputable butcher. Having secured the "best rib cut ever", they scoured the shelves of the groceterias for the other ingredients. At their final stop, to peruse wine labels, they took the time this item deserved. Given the combination of flavours they had just planned for, they certainly would not want to serve the wrong wine.

Lunching at home on paté and Scandinavian crackers, they talked about the guest list, which still had only the Everses.

"I offered to send a taxi for them. I'd better set that up right now."

He called the three cab companies listed in the book, and got the same answer at each: they could bring the fare from Blue Rocks, but wouldn't guarantee that they would be able to return for them several hours later, no, not even for more money. It was a long weekend and everyone was going somewhere.

"Okay, Rob, we have a decision to make. Worst case scenario, one of us has to forego the delicious wine we've chosen, to fetch and return our guests. That's a one-hour round trip, twice, for us. Better scenario: why don't I ask Aunt Stella if Spencer is still chauffeuring for her, and if so, can we borrow him and her Jaguar for the evening? There's the risk that she might be at home, cooling her five-inch heels on a holiday weekend. If that's the case, we'll add a chair for her, not the worst outcome. What say?"

"I'm happy to have Stella anytime. She might liven up the conversation. Anything not to be on taxi duty. Give Stella a call."

Tim called Stella's private mobile phone. She answered on the third ring.

"Who is calling?"

"My, my, Aunt Stella, what's got you sounding so abrupt? It's me, your easily-concerned nephew. Are you okay? How are you?"

Stella gave a little laugh. "I'm fine, Timothy. It seems someone with nothing better to do has found this number and I don't care for calls with just breathing. I know who it is, and I will see that he is properly dealt with. That will be preferable to getting a new number. To what do I owe this pleasure?"

"Crank calls? Have you called the cops?"

"It's under control. I'm in no danger."

"If you're sure...but of course you are. I'm calling to offer an invitation and to ask a favour. Robert and I are planning a sit-down dinner tomorrow afternoon, with the Bishop and his wife—you met them at my Canada Day picnic, I think?"

"Yes."

"And you, too, if you're available."

"Thank you, and thank Robert, but I'm not available Sunday. I'm...out of town."

"Out of what town, may I ask? Your house is down the river as it is. For you, 'out of town' means either you're at your high-rise condo in the city, or a swanky country retreat within range of a cellular tower, which isn't everywhere."

"It is the latter, if you must know, and that's all I'll tell you. Mind your own business."

"You *are* my business, Aunt Stella. I care for your safety and happiness. Now: is Spencer still chauffeuring you in your Jag?"

"When I need him. He's not...he's not here."

"I wouldn't expect. I wonder if I can have him on consignment to pick up the Everses in Blue Rocks tomorrow afternoon and return them whenever they're ready to leave? I'd pay, of course, but I'd rather not do the driving."

"Let me confirm that he hasn't gone somewhere, since he won't be expecting my call."

She disconnected without further comment.

"Aunt Stella's in fine form," he said to Robert. "She sends her love, but I'd bet big money that she's with another love right now. She's checking with Spencer."

Stella soon called back with Spencer's phone number to call.

"Many thanks, Aunt Stella. I'll pay Spencer. Another time for dinner, okay?"

That done, Tim asked Robert, "Are you sure you're up for this meal? I know you can do it, but you usually prepare these complex recipes to calm your nerves before a concert. You don't have a concert imminent, do you?"

"In a way, I do: potentially three concerts a year for the next five years, and just saying that has made my heart beat faster. But none this weekend, or week, or month, thank goodness. Y'know, I've noticed that I'm feeling calmer than I used to be at the beginning of a new semester."

"Wonder why?"

"I think it's because I'm starting off looser than ever before. I spent lots of quality time with you this summer, just being and breathing, not always thinking and teaching. But even when I did think or teach, I was calmer, like when I taught here in South River last month, coming home to your dinners each night. Suddenly rushing off to choir camp with those kids took a ton of energy, but it wasn't worry-energy. All I had to do was show up and they were grateful. I did much more than show up, of course, and I learned so much."

He put their dishes in the dishwasher.

"This summer was very grounding for me. Perhaps the muses were preparing me for the year to come. I'm not saying I won't freak out ahead of the concert in Boston. They have three organs and a harpsichord there, and a bunch of organ scholars on faculty. Chances are I'll get to do a bit of teaching on the side, if all those scholars don't murder me in the organ loft first. The contract says I keep the money from any private teaching opportunities that arise. It's a nice perk."

"Well, Doctor Kirk, let's say the purpose of tomorrow's dinner is to wish you courage and vigour in all your future opportunities! Let's go have a look in this envelope while we ignore the rain. Can we tune in to the opera while we work? It's Handel's *Giulio Caesare*. I'll keep it low."

"Oh, sure, I love that one."

~

They worked steadily and methodically for the next two hours, guided by the material Tim had collected from the library. First, they reviewed Tim's list of points to watch for and looked for their absence or presence in the clauses. They made note of any questions. It was slow going because of the obtuse contract language, and also because this contract seemed to have been translated from French.

No matter what clause they were scrutinizing at the time, they stopped to listen to some of Handel's arias as they came along, especially *"Va tacito e nascosto"* sung by a counter-tenor.

"'Go silently and stealthily'," Robert translated. "His voice reminds me a bit of Maureen Forrester in her prime. The counter-tenor timbre is so rich. I'd kill to have a counter-tenor in our alto section."

"Please don't kill the tenor-tenors in Saint John's choir, because he would likely be me, and I'd like to stay alive."

Saturday supper was traditionally Italian, alternating home-made with delivery. They had shrimp at the rental cottage last Saturday, and couldn't recall what they had eaten the week before, so the choice was easy. Tim called the restaurant for pizza and they enjoyed it in the sunroom as rain ran down the windows.

Earlier, Tim had purchased an Italian red wine for this meal. *Buona fortuna* was the label. If it turned out to be drinkable, he thought he would get a case of it, because he liked the sentiment.

It was very drinkable, and because they talked so much and so late about the very acceptable terms of the Frères d'Orgue offer, there wasn't any need to put the cork back in the bottle.

September 5: Gravy

Sunday

"Guess what day this is, Rob?"

"Um, Sunday?" This from under the pillows.

"Correct! And guess what we don't have to do this morning?"

"Get up?"

"Oh, we'll get up. Gloria's downstairs waiting to steam some fresh milk for our coffee. But we can go slowly…one foot after the other…because…"

"Because we don't go to church today?"

"Correct! We get one final Sunday to ourselves before that season starts. Unless, of course, you'd like to go to church to see how your summer replacement has been getting along in the organ loft?"

"I would not, thanks. I'll drop in on Monday to check the organ and restore everything to my usual. Are you sure you don't want to go to join the last-gasp-of-summer choir?"

"Nope. I'll go Thursday evening and greet my fellow singers then. I'm looking forward to this afternoon, and I'm sure Mort will make us feel as if we've heard a sermon anyway, though he means no harm. Martha will keep him in check."

After breakfast, they began to assemble ingredients for the menu. Both visited the herb garden that Mrs A had created. Tim chopped some fresh mint leaves for a watermelon and feta salad that would contrast with his creamy potatoes mashed with goat cheese.

He arranged tiny chunks of pineapple and ham on toothpicks to accompany the pre-dinner white wine. Robert mixed ingredients that would season the roast, including grated orange peel, parsley, thyme, garlic, black pepper, shallots, and port wine.

Having all morning and most of the afternoon to prepare in the kitchen was a luxury. It also gave Tim time to dress the table with flair.

"Whoa!" Robert said when he saw the glassware and cutlery he had set out on the dining table. "Are you just cleaning the cabinets, or are we meant to use all this?"

"We'll use it all. We'll need a water glass and a wine glass, and the little glass is for port or sherry after dinner. There's a salad fork and a dinner fork, a butter knife on the side plate, a steak knife, and, at the top, the dessert fork and spoon. I think the charger plates look nice, don't you? We'll bring the salads already plated, and then the warmed dinner plates, which you will serve at table. The profiteroles are small, so maybe we won't need the dessert tools, but I'll leave them. Oh, and these damask napkins. They're big as tablecloths, but Mrs A does such a great job ironing them it would be a shame not to use them."

"Too bad we don't have a butler, like that Dan fellow at the posh hotel in Prince Edward Island. Would Stella's chauffeur be able to do it? That'd be fun."

"Spencer? Not a chance, though I bet he'd try. We'll use the boarding-house reach. This is not meant to intimidate anyone. I wouldn't attempt it with more than four or five of us. As it is, I'll be hand-washing the gold-rimmed dishes and silverware for a week."

"I'll follow your lead for etiquette. Oh, did you forget rolls?"

"Martha's bringing some. This basket's for them. Better take the butter out of the fridge now. What else?"

Gradually, answers to all the "what else" questions were identified, sourced, prepped, and ready for presentation. For lunch, they nibbled at Tim's hors d'oeuvres trimmings. They went for a quick walk in the mist, followed by a short snooze, before removing the beef from the refrigerator.

~

Hosting guests while preparing the meal, when the parlour and kitchen were many steps apart, required both chefs to take turns excusing themselves from the conversation at opportune times, hoping not to miss critical moments in the cooking. Tim and Robert checked on each other's tasks in the kitchen, and picked up on wherever the conversation seemed to be. With Mort, it hadn't always moved much farther along during an absence.

After they had executed this tag-team act a few times, Martha said she was more accustomed to being in the kitchen than in the parlour, and asked if they couldn't all go out there and watch the magic unfold.

That worked. Robert brought out a dining chair to accommodate Martha's short legs, and Mort found a stool perfect for himself.

Conversation roamed around the room like a sentient creature, touching this one or that, and soon the chatter sounded like twice as many people. Some of the extra voices were Robert's conversation with the roast through the oven door, and Tim's argument with a recalcitrant cork.

Martha, who had confessed to Tim that she dreamed of being a chef in a boutique hotel, watched Robert most carefully. She was intrigued that he was planning a sauce rather than traditional gravy.

In a large skillet, he melted some butter and then added shallots and thyme, cooking those for a few minutes. Port and the beef broth went in and were simmered down to half, and then he added cream and soy sauce.

There was more. When Robert opened a package of bittersweet chocolate and began to finely grate a chunk of it, Martha said, "Where the heck is *that* going?"

Robert grinned. He removed the skillet from the heat, swept the chocolate into the sauce, stirred it, and set it aside.

"Now I've seen everything," Martha exclaimed.

"Hey, what about my potatoes?" Tim said. "Creaming them with an electric mixer requires a delicate touch to avoid a disaster. As you will witness, I hope, they will be fluffy and creamy, not a stringy, starchy, gelatinous mess."

When it was time to move to the dining room, the guests helped to convey food to table. Robert brought in the roast, which had been "resting" to perfection under an aluminum foil tent. He carved and served it, and the other dishes were passed, hand-to-hand. It was very convivial. Butler not required.

At the very last minute, Mort asked permission to give thanks for the meal. Forks were lowered but not laid aside: he'd have to be quick.

"Heavenly Father, we give thanks for dear friends and family, and for all the blessings of the Holy Spirit. We are especially thankful for the skills and generosity of those who have presented this bountiful meal. I don't know how long it's been since I sat down to a table set like this, Lord, and I am counting on Your heavenly guidance as I try to use all the implements in their proper order. Amen."

Everything was delicious, of course. The meal might have been too rich if the servings had been large, but Robert carved paper-thin slices of roast and they served themselves small portions of everything else. And then took seconds.

When they rested their forks on empty plates, they were well-fed but not uncomfortable, and the cooks were well-praised, even by themselves.

"I'm certain I'll never make such recipes myself," Martha said.

"Are you sure, my dear?" Mort looked pleadingly at his wife. "I would search for a fatted calf for you."

"Yes, dear, I'm sure. Nor do I know anyone who would attempt it and succeed, other than these two wizards. But I'm sure glad I had it today. That sauce alone—with *chocolate*! I'd even pour it over pound cake and be happy."

"It's too savoury for cake, I think," Robert said with a laugh. "You can pour it over leftovers, though. We'll send you home with a container for your Labour Day supper. Don't freeze it; just reheat it slowly, or don't tell me if you do otherwise. I tried to get the timing just right; freezing and overheating would change all that."

"There you go, Mort," Tim said. "You'll have it again after all, just sooner than you expected."

They adjourned to the parlour for decaf coffees with the tiny cream puffs and thimblefuls of port wine, because it seemed futile to resist. Also, Mort had just begun a new anecdote that promised to be as amusing, and long, as the previous few; better enjoyed from a soft seat.

Food and conversation was just running out when Tim's phone rang.

"Hi, Spencer. Yes, I believe they're ready. You'll have two sleepy passengers riding back to Blue Rocks. Make sure you see them into their house, please; they might be a little top-heavy with all the food, ha-ha. We have a bag of Martha's dinner rolls for you and your wife. Oh, yes, I'll be there Thursday. Yes, it'll be great to see you, too, buddy. Yup. Okay. Okay. G'nite, Spencer."

"Besides all the great food and drink, thank you for securing a limousine for us," Mort said at the front door, seeing Spencer waiting outside on the porch, proudly wearing his chauffeur's uniform. "How thoughtful and kind you are."

He gave Tim and Robert both a two-handed handshake, and Martha followed with hugs and kisses. Tim handed Mort an envelope and asked him to please give it to Spencer.

"Can we tip him?" Martha whispered.

"No need," Tim said, "It's all taken care of. So glad you came tonight. I'll see you soon."

"Promise?" Martha said.

"I promise."

~

"That was just the best, Rob," Tim said, as they rinsed the pots and pans and put away leftovers.

"If we entered a cooking contest, we'd win."

"You cook to soothe your nerves. I'd cut my fingers off right at the out-set from nervousness, and I think that would disqualify us. But they were the right guests for that menu. They've dined high and low, and they know a brisket from a basket."

"They're fun. You'll miss them."

"I sure will! I knew they were in Blue Rocks only for the summer, but I hadn't expected them to leave this soon. I'll go over sometime this week to say goodbye. I just couldn't do it tonight. Anyway, they're only going back to the city. Still, I liked being able to call on short notice and pop over for a walk or a bowl of Martha's soup to keep my spirits up."

"You need a new project to occupy your fine mind. You get morose when you're not chasing down some bad guy like you did last month."

"Martha was such a help with that one! I don't know what I'll focus on now. Nothing comes to mind at the moment except closing my eyes. Thanks for today, Rob."

"Backatcha, Timo."

September 6: The alibi

Monday

They couldn't even reach the coffee-maker behind the heap of unwashed dishes and pans on counter and sink. The first action was to fill the dish‑washer with things it wouldn't ruin, and then hand-wash the precious pieces of china, stemware, and silverware.

With four hands on the job, they completed the task in much less time than they had expected, perhaps motivated by the desire to unearth Gloria. Robert carried the dishes to the dining room, and Tim put them away in their proper cabinets and drawers.

"Thank you for these, Mother," Tim said. "Or Grandmother, more likely. I have all this stuff because I inherited these huge cabinets to keep it in, and the large dining room to house the cabinets. When I'm gone, who will want any of it? Never mind, I'm here now."

He tossed the tea towels and napkins in a corner for laundering.

"There, all done. Thanks, Rob. Care for some humble toast and jam now?"

They didn't have any ripe strawberries to "jam" on the toast as they had done in the summer, but there was jam, and good bread, and hot cof‑fee. They sat in pyjamas and dressing-gowns, prolonging the morning.

Tim's phone rang. He hadn't been thinking at all about Labour Day or a picnic, but that thought flashed through his mind as he reached for the phone.

I hope this isn't an invitation to join the staff now, because I don't think I want to.

"Hello?"

"Good morning, Tim, it's Elaine, I hope I'm not disturbing?"

"Your call is always welcome, Elaine. To what do I owe the pleasure of your call?"

"I—oh, that's fancy talk."

"Isn't it? An old friend answered her phone like that a few weeks ago. I liked it and thought I'd use it from time to time."

"Nice. I'm calling because, I thought—that is, I—a rather large dinner was, um, cooked here yesterday, and I have a ton of food left over that will go bad before I can eat it all, so I was wondering if you'd like to share some with me? Today? Gosh, you'd think I had just learned how to talk. I guess it's odd for me to invite anyone to come here, especially for food. But it's really good, I assure you, not roadkill, the only recipe I make on my own. Shut up, Elaine."

She giggled.

"You're sounding jolly this morning. Who are you and what have you done with the real Elaine?"

"It's really me. I decided to take the holiday and let the chips and dip fall where they may. I'm not going to the office today, believe it or not, and neither should you. We should both be totally unseen today. As we said on Friday or whenever it was, we should have an alibi if anyone asks. If you'll come over, we'll both have a 'previous engagement'. Besides, I have all this food."

"I follow you." Tim looked out the window at the steady rain. "I doubt if there'll be an outdoor staff picnic, anyway. But I like your invitation on its merits. Robert's here; may he come, too? What time were you thinking?"

"Of course, Robert. Anytime. Whenever it suits you gentlemen."

"Hang on, Elaine. Rob, somebody else in the world has delicious leftovers. Is dinner at Elaine's possible for you today?"

It was. Robert wasn't enthusiastic about driving to the city in the rain, so he didn't need convincing to go early tomorrow morning instead.

They used some of this extra time together to mark on the calendar the days Robert expected to be in South River. Tim offered to spend an occasional night in the city, too. They both knew that Robert's tiny apartment was little more than a shelter, a convenience for Robert, not an attraction in itself.

They reviewed Robert's contract again, discussing things requiring clarification or more information. Neither saw anything really objectionable. It was unusually straightforward.

"Maybe it's what happened to all that talk of concerts in July that makes us untrusting," Tim said. "I keep going from pie-in-the-sky to the sky's falling, you know? That's too bad. Or maybe it has simply made us savvy. Oh, d'you know who might have some advice about this?"

"Who?"

"Jeremy Grillon, your impresario over in Kensington. He put these wheels in motion by inviting you to perform there to inaugurate the organ that Les Frères d'Orgue rebuilt. Then he hosted their techs and you at his inn. He set up that whole deal, I warrant."

"You 'warrant'? You sound like someone from a previous century."

"Do I? I must be channelling Sherlock Holmes. Well, Doctor Watson, there's no time to lose! Make haste! Who has Jeremy's phone number?"

Laughing, Robert dug in his briefcase and found the number. Tim pointed him to the phone in the small den, and closed the door. He was more than happy to support Robert in any way he could, but he wanted him to take care of his business decisions himself. It was his career, after all, and only he knew what mattered in it. Tim was there for support and advice, but not choices.

When Robert emerged from the den, he was all smiles. "Jeremy sends his best to you, and reminds you that he's waiting for us to invite him over here this fall."

"Excellent. I want him to visit, too. So…what'd he say contract-wise?"

"He said to go for it! I gather that he was aware of the whole plan, behind the scenes. He agreed about the points we wanted clarified. He thinks they're just honest omissions, nothing devious. It's all positive, Tim. I can hardly believe it!"

"Sure you can believe it. You've earned it. Why not sit down right now and compose your response to Les Frères? They'll be waiting, though I shouldn't be surprised if Jeremy is on the horn, telling them right now that he's heard from you. They're putting a lot of faith in you, so show them they're right!"

"All right, I'll draft a letter. Don't suppose you have a word processor anywhere? Didn't think so. Typewriter? A chisel and slate won't give the right impression. I'll type it up when I get back to campus. Do you have something to do now, too?"

"I have work things to ponder, yes. I'll ponder in the sunroom so I won't disturb you with my mumbling. You can use the study or the dining table."

"After I have that letter drafted, I want to run down to the organ loft. Won't take me long."

"Okay. We have some of Martha's rolls and a few stolen slices of beef for lunch, self-serve."

~

Tim's pondering began, as always, with a cloud of words and concepts, but eventually it devolved into the familiar form of a To Do list. The topic was to do with his business, *The Times* weekly newspaper.

The conversation with Cindy Martin last week had seemed to go so well at the outset. But it hadn't gone the way he had expected. Judging by Elaine's invitation today, she had issues with it as well, pretending to "be busy."

Sure, staff can spend happy times together without me. They've been doing it all along. It's natural and good for them to meet outside of work, and without prompting from me. What concerns me is that Cindy has been selling advertising like crazy, and that reminds me of one of Mother's maxims. Whenever something or someone got too good, she'd say "Time to prune or transplant." When a big advertiser spent a ton of money and started to dictate terms, she'd work night and day to get a similar amount of business from their competitor, and then tell them where to go. If a reporter began writing a lot of great stories, she'd assign some to someone else. She didn't want anyone to own her, that's what she'd say. I don't think that worked out well in the end. We lost a lot of good staff and advertisers because of it.

He wrote Prune & Transplant on his list and thought about it.

Not my style. Cindy has done wonders for us, but that's because of the downtown renewal program, which I invented in the spring for the 'Gem District'. She might quit, but there's no other newspaper in the area for her to go to. She might go back to Toronto, but I don't think she's cleared away her debts enough to be able to afford that yet. It's not cheap to live there, though they pay more, I suppose. I need to check what she's earning with us. I'd rather fertilize than prune or transplant.

He added Fertilize, and drew a thin line through ~~Prune & Transplant~~; some degree of his mother's strategy might turn out to be useful.

"That'd be more likely in the case of malfeasance or slackery, not for being successful, for heaven's sake."

While I'm at it, I might as well look at remuneration for the rest of the staff. I was going to do that last year before I went on leave, but I just couldn't handle one more thing then. The thought of doing it now doesn't fill me with butterflies, so I guess I've accomplished something in the interim. But I don't want staff to be underpaid; that would not be fair.

He wrote Salary Review.

Maybe not a formal review, not yet. That'd need a discussion, and expectations, and evaluations and all that. We should get Mademoiselle to do that for us. I just want to look at our payroll first, to get a sense of who's getting what. That'll be a good start.

Both he and Elaine had confirmed that the touchy-feely realm of "human resources" was not either's strength, but he didn't want to make a mistake about it by neglect or accident.

He changed the item to ~~Salary~~ Review Payroll, and sighed at how long it always seemed to take to settle on what he needed to know.

~

Robert returned at lunchtime, happy to announce that he had found the organ loft just as he had left it, no damage, no disarray, no gnarly conundrums to sort out amongst stops and pistons. The summer organist had left a small box of truffles and a thank you card on the bench for him.

Then it was Tim's turn to share his progress, such as it was.

"But don't you have high-priced trustees overseeing all that stuff for you this year?" Robert asked.

"They're overseeing the money for me; presumably they'd notice if there were problems like theft or unusual expenses, but I didn't ask them to give me an opinion on salary levels that were in place before I went on sabbatical. Maybe everyone likes to avoid the topic until somebody asks for a raise or bonus. I'll just check on it, myself. I don't want anyone harbouring ill-will over something I wasn't even aware of. I think I'll treat this as my 'delving' project for this month, since I have nothing else on the go. It'll be good practice. What'll I call it?"

"How about 'Getting My Money's Worth'?"

"N-no, that's not quite it. It's not 'Human Resources' either. If I see anomalies, I'll call it something else then. 'Payroll review' is good enough. By the way, don't mention this topic to Elaine this afternoon. Knowing her, she'll feel she should ask Harold to get the figures or do it herself. I don't want this to be anything official yet."

~

Tim took one bottle of red and one of white to Elaine's, not knowing which was appropriate for the menu. Robert re-gifted the box of truffles and wished her a Happy Labour Day.

Her apartment, minimally furnished befitting her short-term tenancy, was comfortable and light-filled, even though the skies opened just after they arrived.

She placed bowls of crinkle-cut potato chips beside each chair, and poured white wine for each.

"Supper's reheating in the oven," she said, "so we have some time for —what do they call it—chatting? Conversation? I have people in so rarely I hardly know how to entertain."

"You do all right when you're our guest," Tim said. "Our conversations are always smooth, informative, and elucidating."

"That's reassuring. I like to visit you. When I'm in charge of hosting, though, I get jittery. Silly, I know. Anyway, I've likely made you nervous now."

Robert sniffed the air. "I'm not nervous. Whatever's in the oven smells delicious. Cabbage rolls is my guess. Tim says you rarely cook, if that's not telling tales, so how did you come to prepare this dish, whatever it is?"

"It *is* cabbage rolls. The recipe made so much, it could have been halved. I had help, that's how come."

Tim tried to hide his smile. Elaine raised her eyebrows inquisitively at him.

"Something amusing you, Tim?"

"Nope, nothing at all, not me. Not my business how you came to have food in the house or who made it. I appreciate that I'm one of your table guests today, that's why I'm smiling."

"Hm. Well, if you must know, I had a…a guest, and we made this together. He was very patient with me."

"Do tell."

"Not much to tell. We met at your Aunt Stella's condo that time she invited me—pretty much ordered me—to go in, last spring. She was holding a swanky cocktail gathering, and networking seemed to be the main purpose, so I networked. He was there. That is all."

"That's never all," Robert said. "I work on a university campus. I hear everything, and I see all the innocent encounters and the heartbreaks and everything in between. And that's just the faculty, ha-ha. But we're not here to pry, are we, Tim? We respect Elaine's privacy, don't we?"

"Oh, it's not—" Elaine began, and then said, "Well, we met a few times since then, just for a drink or coffee somewhere. I haven't had much opportunity, really. You know how it is."

"Yes, oh yes, I do," Tim said with exaggerated empathy. "I wish you all the best with this, um, friendship. Does your friend have a name?"

"Nope," she said, smiling. "But he's a gentle man, thoughtful, and kind, like yourselves."

She stood. "Excuse me. I think I'm supposed to insert a thermometer in the pan somewhere. And check the salad."

"That's a job for Thermometer Man," Robert said, jumping up. "Please direct me to the heating box."

"Salad Man is on the way, too," Tim said, and all three of them re-prepared the dinner in the tiny kitchen.

~

"That was pleasant," Robert said after lights out. "I like Elaine."

"I do too, very much. I'm not sure whether I should be happy or concerned for her *vis à vis* her new man, though."

"She seemed quite giddy about him, didn't she? She was trying to keep the secret and bursting to tell us at the same time."

"I noticed. Elaine is a most solid and sober person until she gets a beau, and then she's all in."

"That's charming."

"Uh-huh, but when she and that lawyer broke up—when we were over in PEI, remember?—she took it hard. It didn't affect her work; she's too good for that. I'm not sure I could be that strong. But she was hurting for a long time."

"Do you know why they broke up?"

"She wouldn't talk to me about it, but my guess is that it was over her peripatetic career. She'll be gone soon after the end of the year, and it's likely he wasn't willing or able to go with her."

"Well..."

"I know. I don't know if she'll ever find anyone who's okay with his partner moving somewhere new every year or so. I just hope she holds it together until she leaves here. Lord knows I'll need a lot of support then, and before then. And after then."

September 7: P-Review

Tuesday

Soon after Robert left for the city in the early morning, Tim drove down-town to begin work on his thin thread of a delving project, 'Review Payroll'.

In former times, he would have gone to his office, unlocked the cabinet where he kept confidential records, and pulled out the payroll file. He could always find the answer to any question he raised about any aspect of the business.

It's Elaine's office now, and the files won't be in there anyway. I bet Harold's got them in his computer, meaning someone has to get them out for me. I'll have to learn how to operate a computer myself when I get back to work, oh happy day. Now, who would I rather ask for these figures, Elaine, or Harold who produces them?

He considered this question while still in his car in the parking lot.

If I go in and ask her for a printout, she'll just go to Harold and ask him to print it for her, and she'll give it to me, and then the whole office will know that we're looking into payroll.

He wasn't wrong. In an open office like this, staff kept their eyes on their own work while keeping their ears attuned to everything around them. If they wanted to look around unobtrusively, the dropped pencil was always a useful tool. Some even kept pencils on their desk for this purpose.

Elaine drove into the parking lot. Tim hit her number on his phone's speed-dial, and simultaneously drove out of the lot.

"Good morn—oh, is this you, Tim? I see you. Where are you going?"

"Just around the corner. Hang on while I pull over—okay. I just wanted to ask you for a document, but I don't want Harold to know it's for me."

"What is it?"

"A printout of our last payroll. Showing who gets how much."

"Bi-weekly?"

"If that's still how it's doled out, yes. Sorry for acting crazy, but I just don't want to attract attention from the hive, and any time I ever ask about payroll, all antennae start waggling. Can you do it casually-like?"

"I guess. When do you want it? Is this a rush? We have to produce your newspaper in the next eleven hours, so—"

"I don't need it today. Why not tuck it in your purse and bring it to my place tomorrow for supper and singing? Thanks for dinner yesterday, it was really good."

"Welcome. I have to run now or you'll fire me."

"Never. Bye."

I'm acting like a fool. I just want to keep my interests contained for now.

He started the car again, and drove out to the edge of town to join the cars and service trucks lined up at the drive-thru window of the franchise coffee vendor, something he hadn't done in a while.

Eventually it was his turn. "Two large black and two crullers, please" he told the speaker, and drove around the tight corner to pay for and receive his order. He returned to the downtown parking lot and went inside the office, now busy with staff, delayed by the Labour Day holiday, dedicated to finishing in one day what they usually did in several.

He placed one coffee and cruller on Elaine's desk, and took his up the narrow stairs and into the locked room he had designated as PRIVATE, his thinking room.

At the beginning of this year, he had found it difficult to work on his projects at home. He had missed the office hubbub. His house was very quiet, except for Thursdays when Mrs A came to clean it. She left her vacuum cleaner plugged in the whole time, windows wide open even in winter, which distressed him, but she had her routine and was not open to changing it.

He had started going to the Daisy Café for breakfast on Thursday mornings, therefore, and had done some good thinking in this room all the days. If he was stuck, he would wander around downstairs, sometimes to have a short chat with a staffer, which might spark a new thought, and would at least keep him from feeling alone.

The room was furnished only with a table, a rolling chair, and an old cabinet in which he stored the manila sheets on which he had worked out his previous challenges and mysteries. The walls were bare except for a couple of sheets on which he had written motivational phrases from the two men he admired with the surname Holmes: Oliver Wendell and Sherlock. Of course, Sherlock was fictional, though he seemed the more real to Tim, so much so that he had named another room at the end of the hall "Baker Street." He received his few visitors there so they wouldn't see his work-in-progress on the wall in "Private."

It feels like back-to-school. I've hardly been here all summer. Not sure how much time I'll put in here this month, but if I'm digging into work things, it might help to be close to the scene. I'll put up a sheet or two and be ready to work when Elaine gets the payroll printout for me.

He taped up the sheet, and wrote P - REVIEW at the top. Even though he always took care to lock the door, he wouldn't risk writing out the p-word. He knew what he meant.

He sat in the chair and looked out the window to consider how he would conduct this review. Usually the Five Ws plus H led him to a successful conclusion. Would they this time? Did he need them all? Would this apply to everyone?

He moved his head slightly from side to side as he stared at nothing outside. The old glass in the window had whorls in it, making objects outside wobble as he moved his head. It was mesmerizing, and soothing, and...

He woke up when a heavy truck drove past outside.

What happened? I haven't dropped off like that since...since I was here last. Must be something about this room, and thinking...

He shook his head, stood up, and went downstairs to use the washroom. Everyone was busy at work now, and he didn't pause to engage in idle chit-chat.

As he came out of the washroom, which opened directly into the lunch room, he was reminded that the whole staff room layout needed redesigning.

A couple of the clerical staff were at the lunch table.

"Hi, Mister Brown. We missed you yesterday."

"You did? Weren't we closed?"

"Yes, but you know, at the Labour Day picnic."

Tim stopped and turned to face them.

"Picnic? Where? Wasn't it raining?"

They giggled.

"It sure was," said one. "But we went into Cindy's big ol' barn, and we had a great time! It was pretty leaky, but we played a lot of fun games. We were looking for you. She said you were coming."

"Yeah," said the other. "But somebody else said you didn't want to."

"This is the first I'm hearing of it, sorry. Who said—?"

"I dunno, we just thought you'd come. It's okay."

"Well, I would've been there if I had known, you know that. Next time."

What the heck? The only person I spoke with about a picnic on Monday was Cindy Martin. Did they misunderstand her?

He walked around the desks toward the back stairs again. Elaine was walking toward him with a sheaf of papers in her hand.

As she approached, he muttered, "We were AWOL."

"From the barn," she said without expression, and was gone.

He went back upstairs and closed his door.

He didn't fall asleep this time. He took out another sheet of manila paper and taped it alongside the P - REVIEW. With a permanent marker from the drawer in the table, he wrote WHO in the upper left-hand corner on the first sheet. He drew a line under it and all the way across the two sheets. Then he wrote the remaining familiar questions, WHAT WHERE WHEN WHY HOW, on that same line, leaving maximum space between each. He drew vertical lines in those spaces, then enough horizontal lines to make a space for each staff member.

This was a different grid than he had used before. Usually, when attempting to solve a problem, he'd begin with WHO or WHAT, and the other questions would eventually lead to the conclusion, directly or indirectly

This time, it seemed he was preparing to examine every member of his staff on all points, but without any particular thing in mind. What would be the point of that?

His question rang a bell. He turned around and looked at the sheets on the wall behind the door. There, among other *bons mots*, he had written:

I consider everything in order to find something—*Mister Seek.*

He had adopted the moniker "Mister Seek", from the story about Dr Jekyll and Mr Hyde, months ago, jokingly referring to himself as that from time to time since.

The wise dictum was his own invention. He had learned that it was folly not to consider every hunch, suspicion, guess, rumour, and even wild stab at the outset of a quest, because the truth might well be inside one of them, hidden behind a joke or politeness or other go-nowhere convention.

Now, looking back at the large grid he had drawn across two sheets, it seemed like he was preparing to investigate more than just who was receiving what pay.

"Why am I thinking about this, though? I don't suspect the staff of anything. Sure, I'd like to know who told them that Elaine and I said we'd go to the picnic when Cindy had told us to stay away...but that's not the first time wires have gotten crossed in this place. It always got fixed before without a complicated thought-grid like this. This is a payroll review.

That is all."

He put the cap back on the marker and picked up his keys and empty coffee cup. He'd begin filling in the blanks after Elaine gave him the payroll papers tomorrow.

~

At home, he searched for the business card for Conquerall Services, where the multi-talented Corey worked. He called the number.

"Conquerall, this is Amanda."

"Hello, Amanda, this is your favourite customer, Tim Brown."

"Hi, Tim, we've missed you! Got something broke for us to fix for ya?"

"I do, Amanda, and it's a biggie this time. I need the whole upstairs at my office building renovated or reconfigured, a stairway moved out of the ladies' washroom, and washroom doors moved out of the lunchroom. And, the most urgent thing, the second floor emergency exit is barricaded because the fire escape is rotten."

"Woo-hoo, I love the sound of that, Tim! We can take care of all that. What do you want first?"

"The fire escape, I guess, before the Fire Marshall comes and locks us out. It's long overdue. Will Corey be my main guy? I really like how he works."

"He's our main guy, so, yeah. Listen, are you at the building now?"

"No, I just came from there. Why?"

"Well, he's got to see it, of course, and he might have to get an architect to draw it up if it's structural, so the building inspector will approve it. But I know Corey treats fire safety like the place is on fire already. How about first thing tomorrow morning for starters?"

"I can do that. What time?"

"Hang on, I'll call him." Amanda shouted into the microphone of a two-way radio, and Tim heard Corey's familiar "Yuh?"

"What time can you meet Mister Tim Brown at his newspaper office in downtown South River tomorrow morning?"

"What about the end of the day instead?"

"It's about a fire escape, Corey. Fire Marshall has a warning on it."

"Okay. Seven?"

"You hear that, Tim? Seven tomorrow morning?"

"Yes, I heard. Seven o'clock on Main Street. I'll meet him at the front door. Thanks so much!"

Tim marked that in his pocket calendar, though there was no way he would forget. After years of ignoring the building's deficiencies, including the Fire Marshall's warning about not allowing more than two people to occupy the second floor at any time, after all the meetings they'd conducted up there in May and June, he was relieved to finally be getting this work underway. He couldn't handle it last year, but now it was just another construction job.

He was on a roll, and felt motivated to tackle one other task which he had also dreaded earlier: he would call the Human Resources expert he and Elaine had met with in June. He couldn't recall her name, and didn't have her contact information. Elaine would have it. He'd get that tomorrow morning after Corey left, and that ball would be rolling as well.

Tim felt very good about these steps. True, he was still on sabbatical and supposed to be free of work cares. But these two topics could be shoved aside for many more years by the pressures, real or imagined, of his community weekly. He didn't want the building going up in flames or the business going down in failure due to neglect—his neglect.

I see now that getting these things addressed will be therapy, same as rest is. Burdens will be lifted, clear sailing ahead! I'm excited!

Supper was his share of the gently-reheated "roast beast," as his mother had always called it, with all incredible flavours still present. None of the fine wine from Sunday remained, but he couldn't insult the food by drinking a bottom-shelf plonk with it.

His search of the cabinet was rewarded: he found a bottle of a goodish *Hombre Trabajador* at the back, and opened it to let it breathe while he went outside to weed the gardens.

He lingered over the food and wine. This new month was turning away from summer and steering toward work, and he wanted to think positive thoughts about that. In his study, formerly his mother and grandfather's, was a plaque, which he took off the wall and propped up in front of his plate. It read:

> We must sail sometimes with the wind and sometimes against it
> —but we must sail, and not drift, nor lie at anchor.
> - Oliver Wendell Holmes

"I've been drifting around all summer, Oliver. All year, really, and it's been better than therapy. Drifting's not always easy, but I didn't expect it would be. But now, I need to get moving, to sail in whatever direction is needed, to get up on the ol' workhorse again, or whatever. Robert's going to sail bigtime next year, and I think I will, too."

He cleared his plate and finished the glass of wine.
Gotta cast off.

September 8: Safety first

Wednesday

Tim arrived at the office building at about ten to seven. Corey's truck was already in the alleyway, and he was up a ladder, rattling the defunct emergency stairway which stopped about ten feet above the ground.

"Good morning, Corey," Tim said, reaching out to shake Corey's meaty hand once he was safely back on the ground. "It gives me great comfort to have you taking care of me again."

"Yuh," Corey said. "Mighta called me sooner 'bout this. Can we see inside?"

Tim unlocked the front door, and locked it behind them. He knew Elaine and an essential crew would have worked fervently and late last evening, so nobody was expected in until Mrs Rafuse, the receptionist, arrived at eight-thirty. Just in case, he quickly scribbled a note and left it on the counter: *T Brown is upstairs.*

He had learned to place his size-thirteens sideways on the narrow stairs, so he had no problem ascending, but Corey's thick-soled workboots posed a challenge.

"Scary," he said, climbing up slowly.

At the opposite end of the hall, the Emergency Exit sign over the door had been altered to read NO Exit. Corey pulled off the board which John, the caretaker, had nailed across the doorway, and carefully opened the door.

"Don't step out there, Corey," Tim said. "It's not safe."

"You got that right." Corey knelt on the threshold and leaned out to tug at the structure again. Loose bits rattled down on his truck below. "I better move my truck or this'll be on top of it."

"Is it that bad?" Tim was standing a few steps back in the hallway, trying not to be embarrassed at his obvious negligence, hoping it was a simple fix.

Corey brought himself back into the hallway and closed the door. "You better hope a big bird don't land on that out there," he said.

With obvious distaste, he returned the board to its position across the doorway, pounded in the nails and secured it with screws, using the drill hanging from his tool belt. He stepped back. "Who's up here?"

"Nobody...usually. Just me, a little. But we'd like to be able to come up here. We need the space."

"What's in there?"

Tim opened the BAKER STREET door. Corey strode in and measured the dimensions of the window. He did the same in the rooms called WAR ROOM and GIVE PEACE A CHANCE, both of which had been used a lot during preparations for the big news story in the spring.

"Lotta furniture here for nobody usin' it," Corey said. "And this one?" He was standing outside PRIVATE.

"That's my room. I'm off work this year and my Editor uses my office downstairs, so I just come up here sometimes—"

Corey nodded. "Window?"

"Yes, same as the others."

"Okay."

Corey navigated the steep stairs again, turning to face the steps as though going down a ladder. He shook his head.

Pointing to the big steel door at the back of the building, he asked, "Where's that go?"

"That's the back alleyway," He unlocked it and Corey stepped outside.

"Meet me at the front door," he said, and disappeared around the corner.

Maybe he'll condemn the whole building. Maybe I should've paid more attention to Eric MacIntosh's offer to buy it instead of fighting him. Maybe I wasted money painting this rickety old place. Too late for that now.

He unlocked the front door and waited outside. Corey came around the side of the building next to the church parking lot and stepped into the street to look at the second-level windows.

He beckoned Tim to his truck in the alley, and began writing in a notebook, leaning on the hood.

"Here's what you can do right now. Go to this company, tell them I sent ya, and get two of these delivered for the upstairs rooms, one front and one back. They're ladders that hang on the windowsills. If there's a fire, you open the window, hook these on the windowsill, toss the rest out over the edge, and climb down. Do that today."

"That's it? What about the fire exit and the Fire Marshall?"

"Don't worry 'bout the Fire Marshall. If he comes 'round, show him those emergency ladders, and tell him to call me if he ain't happy. You already took the required steps to remediate, tell him. I'll confirm that. But man, ya gotta do something with them stairs inside. I'd rather come down a greased pole than them."

"Hard to go up the pole, though. Will changing them require a lot of demolition?"

"Dunno. Ain't got time to look at it this mornin'. Might have to get an engineer in, much as I hate to see them fellas chargin' for my drawings. "Manda'll call you."

"Okay, I'll get those ladders right now. Thanks so much for coming so quickly."

"Yuh."

A few staffers who weren't part of yesterday's overtime contingent had arrived, so Tim took his note off the front counter and left to look for the safety equipment supplier in the industrial park.

~

It took all of the morning and one phone call to Corey via Amanda, but Tim sourced two suitable second-storey emergency egress ladders from two different suppliers. He was expecting them to be heavy, awkward things that even burly delivery men would have difficulty carrying up those stairs, but they were not.

Tim placed the packaged ladders inside the office door, then parked, then carried each ladder—one at a time because they were bulky—up to the second floor. He left one in his own room, and one in the "War Room" down the hall, as the window in the other room on that side was above an old dumpster. He got a pair of scissors to cut the cable ties holding the ladders together, and placed them in position beneath the windows, ready to use in case of fire.

Both came with reflective EMERGENCY EXIT stickers that would glow in the dark, and he applied the stickers to the doors to both rooms. He straightened up and unabashedly admired his accomplishments.

So much protection for so little money! A ghastly crisis averted! Why did I procrastinate so long? Because I didn't know how simple a solution was available. Corey's on our case now. I hope I can afford to fix things up to modern standards. Can't have the stairs running through the women's lavatory, even though nobody can see in. And those stairs don't seem safe to use.

He brushed the dust from his knees, locked up, and went down those unsafe stairs with ease to look for Elaine.

"I'm going home now," he told her.

"Good. You're too noisy. We grew accustomed to not hearing you up there." She was smiling.

"But first, do you have the material that Mademoiselle La Belle Province left with us in June? I want to look it over."

"You do? My, you must be desperate, or feeling brave. Be my guest."

"But you have the package?"

"I'm pretty sure you took it, Tim. You said you were going to read it, but I suspect your trip to PEI distracted you."

"As it should. I might as well read it now, and decide either to pursue it or forget it. I have it, you say? Must be somewhere in my neat and tidy house, then. I'll go look for it now." He lowered his voice. "See you after supper, with other papers?"

"Mm-hm."

He picked up a wrap from the Daisy and took it home for lunch. Then he spent an hour looking in all the wrong places for the blue and grey folder with the complex, dull brochures in it.

"I must be getting closer, but where?"

He suspected the sunroom, a small, narrow room. He might have been reading it out there. The sofa fit across the end of the room, and it took some wrestling to pull it away from the wall and look down behind it— where the folder was lying. Fortunately, it was rigid, which had prevented it from slipping underneath or into the mattress mechanism, to be lost forever.

Having worked hard to find it, he was more motivated now to read the material. As he did so, the practical applications seemed less grey. He began to think his staff might appreciate the opportunity to comment on their workplace and working conditions. They might have some good suggestions for improvement, as well.

Heck, if I'm going to spend thousands to get the stairs out of the ladies' loo, and keep everyone from burning up in a conflagration, I can spend money on making their work more rewarding. I bet I'm the first in the Johnson-Brown dynasty to think such thoughts. If I don't pursue this, perhaps I'll be the last. I've heard the expression "shirtsleeves to shirtsleeves in three generations". I'd prefer to take that as a warning, not a prophecy.

~

He was at the piano when Elaine knocked on the open front door.

"Come in!" he called. When she came to the parlour, he said, "You know, I believe you're overdue for a promotion."

"Me? To what?"

"To come in the back door. That's where friends and family enter, and you crossed into that elite category some time ago. You have to leave to-night through the same door you came in to prevent bad luck. But next time, please come in the back door—without knocking."

"Why, thank you, I will. If my apartment had a back door, I'd offer you the same."

They turned to the music scores, and rewarded themselves with some good music-making, though they didn't keep at it very long. Elaine had been up late the night before, and Tim had been up early this morning, though not unusually so for either. Perhaps it was darkness falling earlier that set them both to yawning.

Before she left, Elaine took an envelope from her bag and placed it on the piano.

"Your report," she said.

"Any comments or funny looks?"

"Not really. Harold seemed a little hesitant or reluctant for some reason. He asked if there was something in particular he could look up for me, but I said this was all I needed for now."

"Thanks, Elaine. You did it right. By the way, aren't we supposed to meet with Harold about world wide computer failures?"

"Yes, I think so. If you're around tomorrow, perhaps you will ask him about that? I find him a bit...I don't know...just off. He's not hopping to it, since the weekend. See what you think when you ask him."

"I'd be delighted! Or maybe not, but I'm in an improvements mood right now, so if Harold needs improving, I'll see to it."

"Thanks for the music tonight, Tim."

"You're most welcome. Choir starts up tomorrow evening at seven, and Robert would *love* to have you in the alto section. You can afford to take Thursday evenings and Sunday mornings off, can't you? I've always done that."

"It's tempting. If you see me, I'll be there."

September 9: Adjusting

Thursday

Tim most enjoyed his morning coffee when he had something engrossing to read or study or think about along with it. A payroll printout satisfied all criteria.

He made notes, person by person, on a sheet of foolscap, not searching for anything in particular, just dividing one thing by another to produce a third number, and watching the results accumulate down the right-hand side of the page. In the first decades of his career, he would do this exercise after all the accounts were up to date, all bills paid and invoices prepared, just multiplying and dividing and looking for oddities and anomalies.

This didn't automatically indicate something was wrong. Some staff worked irregular hours. One, Ed Garamond, moonlighted with permission, sometimes even during office hours. His earnings were paid to the paper and paid out again with a small deduction for materials. Tim had made that deal with him years ago and was pleased that it kept a graphic designer of Ed's skills working in his small enterprise. He didn't monitor it; he trusted Ed completely to report his earnings and prioritize his work for *The Times.* No edition of the paper had ever been held up because Ed wasn't ready.

Cindy Martin was another whose remuneration often changed, as she was paid a base salary plus commission on ad sales.

He had just arrived at her name on the printout when he heard a noise at the back door.

"Oh, right, today's Thursday! Good morning, Mrs A. I'm mixed up in the days! I guess it's because Monday was a holiday. How are you today? Here, let me help you."

It was difficult to help her carry her cleaning tools, which she did all in one trip from her car. The best Tim could do was hold the door for her, when he was at home. He couldn't imagine how she did it in his absence.

"I weeded the gardens this week," he said to her back as she carried on up the stairs. "Help yourself to whatever you want. Looks like there's lots there to pick."

A bit reluctantly, he moved the payroll papers to the desk in his study. He couldn't work on them at the Daisy Café, not knowing who might suddenly pass by the table. He'd come home later to continue this task.

~

Full of Evelyn's breakfast, Tim walked into the office, pleased to see work proceeding normally. He had always liked Thursdays. Everyone was looking for stories, and for advertisements to pay for them, and subscribers to read them. Thursdays were full of optimism.

"Good morning, Harold. Are you ready to talk to Miss Fong and me about our computer situation?"

"No, I'm not ready. Wasn't Miss Fong going to give me a list of questions she wanted me to address? I've been waiting for those before I begin to set up the report."

"Oh? That's news to me. Can't you tell us what you were going to tell us anyway, and then work on her questions? I was expecting something like an inventory of all our computers and computer-things that we use and rely on, and your analysis of how this Year 2000 changeover might affect them. I'd expect a lot of question marks to start with, but at least I'd like to know how big the problem might be."

"I suppose I—"

"And—excuse me—and please add a column—two columns—to show present depreciated value and replacement cost. That should be in the financial statements for the fiscal year ending last March, so you'll have to add only items purchased since then, which won't have been depreciated yet. All right. Shall we say tomorrow afternoon, if Miss Fong is available? Even if she's not, you can print copies for both of us, as I do want to deal with this issue on paper. Thank you."

Tim didn't wait for Harold's confirmation. He hadn't raised his voice or implied anything other than that Harold should put together a simple report, lickety-split.

Wonder what Elaine wanted to add. She didn't mention anything about that last night. She was expecting a report, same as me. Something new must've come up.

Elaine wasn't in the office, and her button in the IN/OUT board indicated she wouldn't be IN until mid-afternoon.

Maybe she's at lunch. I won't call her. She might be with Mister Mysterious, and I would be loath to interrupt that. All will be explained tomorrow.

Despite Mrs A's vigorous cleaning activity, Tim went home. He closed the door to his study and continued playing with payroll numbers until he heard her at the back door, heading out.

"Did you get your veggies?" he asked.

Her cheeks dimpled deeply as she pointed to a wicker basket she had filled with beets and greens, carrots and tops, and herbs. It was beautiful.

"Nex' year, we have peas and beans," she said, lifting her arms in the air to indicate how high they would grow. "You get poles and dig more, over there." She pointed toward the side of the yard where the landscapers had uncovered so much trouble for Tim at the beginning of summer.

"Maybe not right there, but sure, I can dig a new garden plot, if you'll supervise. Maybe I'll get it started this fall, when Robert's here to help. Enjoy your harvest. Bye-bye."

He turned to go back to the study when he remembered, for the second time, that today was Thursday, and that Robert would be pulling in the driveway any minute now, expecting a light supper before they headed out to the first choir practice of the new season.

"Oh, boy, I hope I get back in the groove soon. Rob should've called to remind me. I should've remembered. Harold's not the only one who isn't clicking today."

A quick review of frozen packages in the freezer yielded two chicken breasts that didn't appear freezer-burnt. He set them out to thaw, got water and whole-grain rice ready, and set the timer for another half-hour in the study.

~

The rehearsal was a happy reunion, and they sang remarkably well. Robert warmed them up with Sunday's hymns first, so they could lead the congregation on Sunday morning. They were strong, singable hymns, and he let the choir sing as though they were at a bar at first, before reining them in so they wouldn't strain their vocal cords, unused all summer.

For their anthem, they rehearsed a favourite from the library. They also read through a new piece Robert had purchased, and were happy with their first go. Then, to finish, he turned off all the lights in the loft except the lamp at the organ, and invited the choir to choose a familiar evening hymn in unaccompanied four-part harmony. They sang "The Day

Thou Gavest, Lord, Has Ended," one of their top three favourites. They ended this successful evening with a collective sigh.

This week had had an elastic feeling, as if it had begun so long ago and also just yesterday. Over their post-practice treat of olives and a glass of port, Robert and Tim exchanged bits of news about their doings as though they had been apart for weeks instead of barely three days.

September 10: Changes

Friday

Robert reported to Tim that he had typed, printed, and mailed his response letter to Les Frères d'Orgue. He was feeling very good about the whole venture: excited, a bit nervous, like a diver's first time jumping off the high board. But nervous excitement was familiar fuel, and he didn't hope to lose that.

More concerning were his Saturday private lessons on campus, which might be shifted to Friday. This would mean that his Friday schedule would be a killer. But he could come to South River early Saturday mornings instead of mid-afternoon, as had been the case last year.

"Or even late on Fridays, if the weather's good and I'm not knackered."

"I like the sound of that, Rob, don't you?"

"Sure, if it happens. I like being here, you know that. It feels like home when I come in the door. Now, please remember I said that when I also say this: I wonder if I might teach a little bit of organ here sometimes, at the church, maybe some Saturday mornings? Not every Saturday, but sometimes? Maybe some students can make the drive? I'm getting so many inquiries. Just a thought."

"I'm not against that, in principle. I might have to work on Saturday mornings, too, once I get back in harness. Meanwhile, my concern on *your* behalf is that you don't use up every hour teaching, even though you love it. It's important to look after your work-life balance."

"Work-life balance? I can guess what that means, but did you mean something specific?"

"I don't know yet. It's in some human resources material I'm reading for work, and it seems like a worthy thing to examine. If there's a questionnaire about it, I'll bring one home. We can fill it out to see what our score is. Well, you'd better get going. See you Saturday afternoon. Be safe on the roads."

~

"Good morning, Miss Fong, how are you today?" He had phoned her office.

"Good, thanks. What's this about the computer report?"

"That's what I was going to ask you. Harold said you said to wait for some reason."

"No, Harold said that *you* said to wait, because you wanted more information?"

Tim made a *tsk* sound and sighed. "I'm coming to the office this afternoon, and he'd better have *something* for us to start discussing. Around three?"

"Make it four?"

"Done."

Is Harold losing it? He's mixing things up and I don't like that. On the payroll list, his earnings are allocated to Archives, Bookkeeping, and IT. T is for Technology, and I is for Information, and he'd better not forget either word. Maybe he's over-worked. We'd better get that HR questionnaire going.

Tim dialed the number for the Everses in Blue Rocks, knowing they would be packing up their belongings today to vacate the rental cottage. Martha would have given away all her food by now, and cleaned out the freezer. He offered to bring them some wraps from the Daisy for lunch.

"You're so thoughtful, Tim. I can still make tea. The parish helpers are coming tomorrow morning to clear us out of here, so we're pretty much down to crackers." She laughed.

He loved the drive to Blue Rocks, especially the first glimpses of the blue ocean, sometimes grey, sometimes hidden in fog, but always a beautiful presence. Then there were the sharp turns in the road, the outcroppings of blue slate, the tiny coves. He used to think how nice it would be to live out there, but after seeing the road covered with baseball-sized rocks tossed up by a modest winter storm, he thought that living at the Top of Town in South River was good, too.

Evelyn had bagged a half-dozen wraps and sandwiches for the price of three, and tucked in a few raisin bran muffins as well. They were delicious with Martha's tea.

"Can you spare the time to go for a little walk, the three of us?" Tim asked.

Martha was delighted to be invited along, so out they went, a tall, thin man on either side of the less-tall, less-thin woman between them. They held hands and walked slowly in the fresh, salt air. When a car approached them on the narrow road, Martha wouldn't let go of either man's hand, so the vehicles had to creep past carefully.

"When did we meet?" Tim asked. "Was it in May? I forget. Seems a long time ago."

"It couldn't have been May," Martha replied, ever the fact-checker. "We had just arrived the last week of May, and then Mort went to that prayer breakfast the next week and met you there. I remember because he mentioned you when he came home, and he rarely mentions anyone he meets at those things, right, dear?"

"I don't pick faces out of crowds the way I used to do," Mort said. "I'm afraid I wouldn't be a Good Shepherd to my flock now. When Our Lord looked at his flock of ninety-nine, He knew one was missing, and went out to find it. I wouldn't have noticed that, not now, anyway."

"You baptized, married, and buried many flocks, Mort. How's your memoir-writing coming along?"

"Done, thanks to you. Once you suggested how I should sort my topics, I was off to the races, with the knowledgeable support of my editor-wife."

"I enjoyed doing it," Martha said. "It was my life, too. We found a publisher that specializes in books about this province, and they said to send it over, so we're hopeful. All our former congregations could make it a bestseller. We had to be careful with naming names, though, wanting to protect the innocent. Innocence is rare when we're telling stories."

The topic of the Everses' city home hadn't come up before, so Tim was surprised to learn that they rented a flat in the south end of Halifax, quite near Robert's bachelor apartment.

"Lovely! I could drop in to see you when I'm at Robert's, sometimes. Would that be all right?"

"You'd better," Martha said. "You're like a son to us, Tim, and we love you very much."

They hugged and said good-bye and hugged again, even though they'd be a mere hour's drive apart, but a change like this one is always freighted with uncertainty.

Tim backed his car out of their driveway for the last time and drove away. Around the corner, he pulled over to wipe his eyes, then drove to the office.

~

Elaine was in. She beckoned to Tim. "Close the door. Have a seat."

"Hello to you, too. How's it going?"

"We don't have Harold, that's how it's going. Said something came up. Said he'd come in on the weekend and make up the time."

"Doctor?"

"Dentist, maybe. Not sure"

"Hmm. He must have some bad teeth. I think he was off in the summer for a similar reason. Did he leave anything for us?"

"This."

Grimly, Elaine passed him a copy of the company's financial statement for the year ending March 1999. Nothing had been done to it, no computer items extracted or highlighted or listed in any way. "What do you think of this as a report we can use?"

"I think we're in trouble. Either Harold is doing this on purpose or he can't help himself, but this failure-to-perform game has to stop right away. I want what I want from him, for starters. Worse, I was nearly annoyed with you when he said you'd asked him to wait because you had other ideas."

"You know I wouldn't do that."

"You could've had a reason, but you would've let me know first. Never mind. Let's stay on this and make sure he doesn't trip us up." Tim sighed. "I was so hoping to have a pile of paperwork to occupy me this sunny weekend. Oh well, I do have payroll to finish analyzing, plus I found that HR folder. It's got some good suggestions, surprise, surprise."

"Good for you," Elaine said without enthusiasm.

"Oh, Miss Fong, you know I will insist that you listen to me talking about what I have discovered, when I discover it. It will stand you in good stead in your next placement, wherever it might be. You can spread the gospel of employment equality and fairness to the good farming folk of Cattle Crossing on the shores of some Great Lake and they will be in awe of you."

"Now I'm motivated."

"I knew you would be. Let's keep in touch. See you Monday."

He went to the takeout spot that he had patronized every Friday afternoon for years. He wondered if he should try something different for a change.

What, though? Hamburger and fries? That doesn't seem right for Friday. Chinese? No. Pizza? That's Saturday. Clams? Not so much. Cook it myself? Why? I just want fish and chips, over and over. What does that make me?

At home, he put the fish and fries on a baking sheet. Then he went for a long, head-clearing walk in the fresh air.

It was a lovely late-summer day as he walked along tree-lined streets, breathing deeply, humming last evening's hymns from time to time. He thought about Martha and Mort a little, and felt joy, not sadness.

He refused to allow any thoughts about work, trying to achieve his own work-life balance. Work would always be right there when he was ready to go back to it. He had not had this particular thought in this particular way before, and he hoped that it signalled progress of some kind in this sabbatical year.

I told everyone last winter that I was taking time off to delve. I hadn't a clue what I meant back then. I didn't think it was me *I should be delving into, but I guess I've been learning a lot about a lot of things, including me. I know I used to avoid confrontations with staff because I didn't want to be nasty, like Mother was. I know now that being assertive doesn't have to be nasty, so I don't have to avoid it. Maybe I'm turning out to be like me.*

Back in the house, he looked in the cabinet for a white wine to compliment the crisp fish. He selected a bottle of *Nezměňujte,* a Hungarian white wine he hadn't tried before. He had picked it up in a bargain bin some time ago and was dubious of it, as wines from that country smelled a bit like turpentine to his nose. Surprisingly, paired with the overheated food in the oven, it was delicious.

"What does this make me?" he asked himself again.

"It makes me happy. So there."

September 11: One fine day

Saturday

Tim was surprised at how quickly the impulse to go to the beach had left him. He and Robert had discovered they were beach fans over the summer, even getting up really early to drive almost an hour just to see the sun rise over sand and water.

That was a special moment. I felt like we were standing on the edge of time, and then Robert recited that beautiful Salutation to the Dawn.

He flipped back the bedsheets and sat up.

Well, that's not the only place for special moments. It's nice here, too, and I like shuffling around my own home and gardens.

As if in response to his thoughts, he heard the sudden roar of a mowing machine in his backyard.

"Just in time for me to wander barefoot in my own oasis. I'll have a nice day right here!"

But first—or second, after a small espresso—he checked the cupboards and fridge to see what he needed for groceries. Then he phoned the salon to ask if his stylist had any time for him, just a trim. She did, at ten-thirty, which was perfect timing. He bounded up the stairs, showered and dressed, and set out on his rounds, waving at the lawn man, not one he knew.

He made the usual Saturday stops, first to the bakery downriver, past his aunt Stella's home. She didn't appear to be home, though there was never any outward sign of habitation anyway; her double-car garage doors were always closed and her car was never left in the driveway.

He took the time to have a quick egg-and-bacon on croissant at the bakery, and bought a few loaves of bread, including an orange and raisin loaf to try.

The cable ferry crossing the South River was docked on his side when he was driving back to town, so he turned down the ramp and lined up with the few other vehicles on board. He paid the fare, exchanged greetings with the deckhand, and returned his wave when it was his turn to drive off.

His stylist had been keeping his beard at "summer-length", so he just needed a trim around the edges. He could have done it himself, but preferred her ministrations and pomades and praise. He had been growing facial hair only for a few months, and still liked the look, even with the grey hairs that were emerging.

At the grocery store, he selected a large chicken to roast for Sunday dinner. It was easy to do, and would provide leftovers, requiring no cooking for at least two days afterward for him or Robert.

But today was homemade pizza day, and, once home, Tim would be on stage for it. It was a performance. He got a kick out of his *amazing* dough-stretching tosses and toppings of whatever had appealed to him in the store.

When Robert arrived, the dough was resting, toppings were chopped and set aside, *Madama Butterfly* was on the radio, and two tin tables were set up in the backyard underneath the trees, with two glasses and a bottle of an Italian red.

"My, this looks so luxurious, Timo. You spoil me and I love it!"

"I spoil *me*, too. I like the freedom I have to follow my own nutty pursuits when you're away, and sometimes when you're here, but there are times when I just want to sit in the shade of these leafy trees and have a glass of good wine and a conversation with a great guy."

"I hope I'm the guy. Mm, what wine is this? It's tasty."

"*Un bel di.* I'll get more, for sure. Now, this is—what did your student call it last month?—'Talk Time'? So, let's talk. What interested your great mind since I saw you last?"

"You saw me just yesterday morning. Nothing challenged me this week except thinking about those wonderful people in Quebec. Otherwise, I was teaching the rudiments of music theory to first-year composition students. My, how they disdain that class. They're way beyond the basics, they claim—until we move out of the key of C. Then they discover they don't know their E-sharp from their F-natural. How about you?"

"I bade farewell to Mort and Martha. Hey, guess what? Their apartment is about a block away from yours, isn't that good news? Of less interest, I expected to dig into a work project, mostly looking at numbers, you know, my favourite toys to play with. But somehow, in a series of confusing misunderstandings, the reports didn't materialize, nor did the employee who was supposed to present them. But it's only a delay, and there's no immediate deadline, so that's good."

"Frustrating, though. I'll take my students over your employees. I teach them, but it's up to them to pay attention. Could you fire your recalcitrant employee?"

"It's not so easy. There's a process, and it's long and arduous. Anyway, dismissal is the last resort, to my mind. I'm hoping the human resources expert will show us how to avoid situations like this. Let's go watch me toss pizza dough, something I'm good at."

September 12: Fellowship

Sunday

Tim woke to the unmistakable sound of a whisk beating something in a mixing bowl, and the aroma of espresso coffee when Robert brought two tiny cups upstairs.

"What's the emergency?"

"I felt like making breakfast for you, since you make so many for me. It's baking in the oven now, so you have thirty minutes to get yourself presentable before I dish it out. Nothing fancy, just an egg bake thing."

The "thing" was eggy, creamy, and cheesy, and served with rashers of bacon. It ticked all the breakfast flavour boxes.

They were both in good cheer as they drove downhill to the church, resplendent in the morning sun. Its new coat of white paint and rainbow steeple were courtesy of *The Times'* "Gem District" campaign to pretty-up Main Street.

Robert proceeded directly to the organ bench in the sanctuary to play preludes, while Tim headed for the church hall to put on his choir gown. Some of the gowns, which were dry cleaned over the summer, had been returned with name tags missing. Chaos reigned while gowns were tried on, taken off, others tried, and then the first ones tried again, which fit now.

By the time Robert pressed the buzzer to signal the choir's entry, everyone was gowned and in processional order, so they would arrive at their seats in order and their music would be in the tray underneath. The minister gave the Invocation and Robert played the chord to begin the Doxology. Not all knew what the word meant, but they knew the music by heart, and sang the hymn of praise earnestly:

Holy, holy, holy, Lord God Almighty,
Early in the morning our song shall rise to Thee.
Holy, holy, holy, merciful and mighty,

God in three persons, blessed Trinity.

Three more hymns would follow in the hour if they were lucky, sometimes only two if there were additional events in the service, plus the choir's anthem. The rest of the hour was taken up with scripture readings, prayers, and the sermon. It was a busy hour, but even so, it had the potential to drag. That was not in the choir's hands.

Several choristers were there mostly—or only—for the music. Tim always noted the sermon topic as printed in the weekly bulletin, and he usually tried to listen at the beginning. If the minister kept on topic, and was working toward an interesting conclusion, he would stay with it. Those Sundays were rare, and did not include today.

He wondered what it would have been like to hear Mort Evers preaching every Sunday. From his conversations with Mort, he thought he might have paid attention. Mort had always landed his point in their conversations and didn't stretch credulity although, as he had recently told Tim, he sometimes did change his mind. He'd been delivering sermons for over half a century and Tim was impressed that he was still willing to explore the great concepts.

Thinking about the Everses caused Tim to sigh. His sigh came during a pause in the minister's oration, which earned Tim "The Look" from Robert. For Tim, that was the highlight of today's sermon. Robert required quiet decorum from his choir, and occasionally warned them about yawning, communicating with anyone in the choir or congregation, smiling, nodding off, fanning themselves, chewing something, or doing anything else that might distract the congregation. This wasn't about worship; it was simply good behaviour for anyone facing an audience.

In quite a large departure from the norm, the minister announced this morning that some members of the congregation were planning to gather after the service at the Daisy Café next door for a light lunch and moment of fellowship, now that the café was open on the Sabbath. He and his wife would be there, he said, and they were looking forward to greeting all who could spare the time. Cost of coffee and tea would be covered by Fellowship Committee funds.

Robert stared directly at Tim and almost imperceptibly turned his head from side to side to say, *We're not going.* Tim raised his eyebrows and nodded slightly to reply, *Yes we are.*

Tim wasn't much of a "fellowship" fellow. But to him, this announcement conveyed great news about Evelyn.

She's done it! Ev's finally got that new cook operating the weekend shifts! She has Saturdays as well as Sundays off now. She didn't tell me, that sneaky vixen. We'll have to stop in for a minute to check it out.

It was one of the more successful congregational social events the church had put on in recent memory. Half of the diner was roped off for a PRIVATE PARTY, and those booths were occupied by the time Tim and Robert got there. Several hands were waving to them, but rather than squeeze in or appear to choose favourites, they simply asked for mugs of coffee and joined others who were also strolling around, to visit, not to eat.

After they had asked or answered "How was your summer?" multiple times, they felt comfortable escaping.

Once in the car, Robert said in mock annoyance, "I clearly told you, 'No!'"

"Did you?" Tim laughed. "I'm sorry, I must've missed your signal. Did you see mine? It didn't hurt you to go, did it? The congregation loves you, you know, even more since you've graced the pages of *The Times* twice this summer. You're what passes for famous in these parts. It makes people proud to say they know you. Don't just take my word for it. I saw how the choir members kept introducing you around. That's what they call fellowship, pilgrim."

"All right, so I enjoyed it. I thought it was going to be some stuffy church supper kind of thing where we'd be trapped eating marshmallows in lime jelly."

"Horrors! Next time, we'll rush over so we can get a booth, and then you *will* be trapped. We taste-tested that food for Ev last month, remember?"

"When you were laid up with your twisted ankle. Speaking of Evelyn, what do you suppose she's doing with her weekend off?"

"Want to ask her over?"

"Sure. Dinner's roast chicken, right? That practically cooks itself. We can maybe even go for a drive before she comes."

~

Robert often dozed off in the car if there wasn't a salt water view, so Tim challenged himself to find a road that led to the ocean. He drove a short distance down Highway 103, and turned onto an unremarkable road that became scenic as it entered the hamlet of Petite Riviere. Soon they arrived at Green Bay, on their left. On the right were tiny rental cabins perched helter-skelter on the rocks, overlooking the wide bay and the ocean.

Robert was inspired to stay awake. "I don't understand it," he murmured at the window. "All that water."

Tim didn't think this was a question, so he didn't try to answer. He didn't understand all that water, either, but he was glad they saw it today.

~

There is no more homey aroma than a chicken roasting in the oven. Evelyn commented on it as she burst in the back door.

"I could smell the bird soon's I got out of my car! Good thing you don't have near neighbours or they'd all be over here, but I'm the lucky one. Here, gimme a hug, you gorgeous fellas. One at a time, that's what I always tell 'em."

She was wound up, but nobody minded. Evelyn radiated energy most times; today was just more. They soon sensed what was fuelling her: her absence from the diner.

"I can hardly stand it, staying away from the shop, but I didn't want to distract them. What I wouldn't give to be a fly on the wall today, but we have that machine that kills flies, so that wouldn't work."

"What worries you about it, Ev?" Robert asked.

"Not worried, not much, just bustin' to see. I want it to work so bad. If the renter's makin' money, then Kenny and I will do well, 'cause they're paying us a base rent plus a percentage of sales. I'll find out soon enough. That place has never been open and serving customers without me, not in decades, anyway."

"What if there was a good crowd in there today, after church, say?"

"That's what I'm—oh, were you guys there? *Were* you?"

"We just dropped in for a moment," Robert said. "It was standing room only on the church side and a lot on the regular side, too. Looked like a success to me."

She threw her arms around Robert's neck. "Oh, you dear! Thank you for telling me that! Oh, whew! Now I can relax. I *was* worried."

"Welcome to my world," Tim said. "I feel like there's a vein that runs real blood between me and my business. I don't like it much. I've got it under control a lot, mostly, but it was great when I was able to get Elaine to take over for me. I was lucky that she turned out to be someone I trust implicitly. Neither you or Kenny can get fully away like I'm doing, but getting your weekends free is a great step, Ev. Here's to you!"

They toasted her success with *Cari Amici*, an interesting pinot grigio.

It went with the *de rigueur* potato chips, but didn't overwhelm the gravy nor clash with the roasted Brussels sprouts.

Best of all, it didn't impair Evelyn's ability to drive herself and a plate of leftovers home later.

September 13: Mister Solve

Monday

Robert left to begin a long day of a full work week. Tim left after a second round of orange and raisin toast and coffee, though not with a clear vision of what his week would entail.

I hope Harold was in the office on Saturday and got his work done. I'm keen to address problems and work on solutions; I just don't want him to be what the problems are about.

Staff were at their desks, except for James Olsen, the photo-reporter, who mostly only came in to file a story or to receive directions for one. Harold was not at his desk.

Tim went to the receptionist. "Any word from Harold, Mrs Rafuse? Shouldn't he be in by now?"

Tim looked at the clock next to the IN/OUT board, and noticed Harold's white dot was in the IN box.

"I just assumed he was in the building somewhere, Mister Brown, but I haven't seen him. Maybe he forgot to mark himself out on Friday?" She checked her notepad. "No message from him. Shall I call him?"

"No, I'll wait. Maybe he left himself IN from the weekend, just for fun."

Ed Garamond was at his drafting board, working on a *Sale!* advertisement for *Ladies Lingerie!*

"Hi Ed. Inquiring minds want to know, have you ever had to design an advert for men's lingerie?"

Tim thought it was a good-enough joke, not at all risqué or offensive. Ed didn't seem to share that opinion.

"Something I can help you with?" His voice didn't sound like it was a sincere offer. "I'm under the gun with these."

"Say what? Sorry, pal, I meant no offence." He was talking to the back of Ed's head, bent over his work with what Tim felt was exaggerated concentration. "I see you're busy, but I do have a question: were you in on the weekend, by any chance?"

"Why?"

"Wh—because I want to know. Specifically, *if* you were in, I wondered if you noticed any other staff in here. Specifically Harold. That's all."

Tim began to feel just a little light-headed, like he'd been enveloped in a bubble of helium gas. His stomach was flipping, and he felt like laughing, oddly, if he could breathe.

"Yes, I was in for a while, as usual," Ed said to his desk.

Tim walked away without saying another word. Unfamiliar as it was, he thought the rising emotion he was feeling might be anger. Or grief. He would avoid either at all costs, especially in the office, especially with an employee he really liked.

He walked toward the stairs to take refuge in his room, then quickly turned around and went to Harold's unoccupied desk. The surface wasn't totally bare, but Tim could tell at a glance that no company secrets, such as payroll or financial statements, were lying there. The file drawer in the desk was locked. The lock button was pushed in on the tall file cabinet beside the desk, and Tim knew that meant all the drawers were locked.

He got up from Harold's chair and went casually—he hoped—to Elaine's office. He went in, closed the door, and plunked down in the guest chair.

"Yes?"

"Do you know if Harold will be in today?"

"I haven't heard that he would *not* be."

"Do you have the keys to Harold's desk and file cabinet?"

"All those keys should be in the safe. Mind telling me what's up?"

"Let's get the keys and go see."

Elaine had memorized the combination to the safe, as Tim had instructed her when she first took over his job. He remembered joking that he didn't know how to change the combination, so he'd have to lock her inside when her sojourn was up. She opened it easily now.

They were looking for keys with tags corresponding to the master list when there was a knock on Elaine's door. Through the glass panel, they could see Harold standing outside.

Elaine put the list back in and locked the safe while Tim went to the door.

"Someone said you're looking for me?" Harold said.

"Of course I am. Come in, Harold, and close the door."

Elaine returned to her chair, and she and Harold looked inquisitively at Tim.

"We were expecting to meet with you Friday afternoon, Harold, with a report about any of our computers that might be at risk. You skipped out and left us a copy of last year's financial report."

"I thought that would be better than nothing."

"You knew it wasn't. It was a risky move on your part. If you were suggesting that we can look up things ourselves, then…that thought doesn't end well for you, does it? Anyway, I came in this morning to pick up the thread, and there you are—missing again. No call. What's up, Harold?"

"I told Mrs Rafuse I'd have to be late."

"She said she didn't hear from you this morning. Did she lie, Harold?"

"I left her a note when I was here on the weekend. Just a sec, I'll go ask her."

"Do that later. First, where's our report? Not started? Half started? The only answer I will accept is the complete listing we had requested, identifying what computers might be in jeopardy of failing on January 1, 2000, and their replacement cost, should they need replacing. Now, precisely *when* will you have that report ready for us to review, with you present?"

Harold grimaced as though considering his answer was mentally—or even physically—difficult. "Um…next week?"

"Next *week*? I'm sorry, but what am I missing here? We asked you about it *last* week. We even talked about it last *month*. Today's only Monday and you're telling me you can't get it done until *next* week? How many computers do we have, Harold? Not hundreds. Are you overworked? It can't be that the report is so complex. Are your duties too much for you? Is that it? If so, tell us, man. Don't get yourself into a corner like this. This is not making any of us happy. Is it?"

Harold's face twitched again. He shrugged and said, "Have to do payroll for Friday. I'll try to get it done before then. Wednesday, I guess. Wednesday afternoon."

"Is that good for you, Miss Fong? Wednesday afternoon at one o'clock?"

She nodded and marked it in her calendar. Tim did the same.

"All right then, Harold," he continued. "We have a firm date. Also, please keep this in mind: we're going to review everybody's job descriptions in the coming weeks. It sounds like your tasks might have grown too onerous. I know we've added a lot of things to your position once we discovered that you could do more than payroll and bookkeeping. You agreed to take them on, but if we need to shift some of your workload to someone else, or to a new hire, we'll do it. Meanwhile, speak up. Don't leave me not knowing what to expect, okay? And come to work during work hours, please."

Harold said, "Okay. Thanks," and left the office.

Tim watched him walk over to the reception desk, hands in his pockets. He said something to Mrs Rafuse, stepped back, looked around and bent down. When he straightened up, he was holding a piece of paper, which he handed to her.

He came back to the office door on the way to his desk to say, "My note must've fallen on the floor. She has it now." Then he left again.

From where he was standing, Tim hadn't been able to see whether Harold had found the note on the floor or had taken it from his pocket.

"What just happened?" he asked Elaine.

She shook her head, perplexed. "Harold seems to be troubled, somehow?"

"I don't know whether it's *his* trouble or something's wrong with his ability to work, but either way, it better not become *our* trouble. Harold's not the only member of our staff with a bad attitude this morning. Ed Garamond would hardly speak to me, I cannot imagine why, but since I hadn't any prior encounter with him today, I can only assume that there's some kind of poison gas going around. Keep your powder dry, Miss Fong. I'm going for a walk, and then I will see what trouble lies in that payroll report Harold gave you."

~

Tim walked with vigour and determination, hoping to outwalk the bubble of confusion. He completed one lap over both bridges, then retraced his steps in the other direction. When he was halfway across the newer bridge, the one farthest from his office building, he stopped.

Slow down, Tim. Don't get in a state. Don't blame. Harold has been a good employee, and if you want him to continue to serve you well, don't dig a hole for him, because you'll end up being the one with the personality problems.

Thinking of personality problems reminded him of "work-life balance".

Do the HR people have words and phrases like that for everything? Maybe we've just been lucky all these years, resolving disagreements naturally? Maybe once in a blue moon something comes up that needs a new approach. Nothing wrong with that. I loathed the way Mother dealt with disagreements, belittling the staff into submission. Including me. That's not going to happen on my watch...but I don't know what will happen.

He resumed his walk at a more leisurely pace.

I'll call Mademoiselle right now. She'll have the right words and plans to keep us from stepping into doo-doo.

The HR brochures were in his car. He took them and went to his upstairs room to call Stephanie Duplessis-Lachance and explain his concerns.

"Is it urgent, Mister Brown?"

"Maybe not urgent, but pretty important, I think. Two of my best employees suddenly seem unhappy around me, and I haven't a clue why, since I am rarely in the office to do or say anything wrong to them. I don't want this to get worse. I don't know if that is something you look at or—"

"I can ask you some questions. What we can do will depend on your answers."

"Yes, of course. When—?"

"I will be in your area this week."

"Wednesday? Wednesday morning, by any chance? Tuesdays we're usually flat-out with the newspaper deadline, but Wednesdays are pretty relaxed."

Tim crossed his fingers, hoping against hope. If she said Wednesday afternoon, he might have to change the meeting with Harold and Elaine, and he didn't want to have to climb down so soon after chasing Harold up that tree.

"I am presenting at a conference in South River on Wednesday, later in the morning. If you 'ave time Wednesday morning at eight o'clock, we could talk for an hour?"

"Oh, Miss Dulassie-Enhance, you have no idea how grateful I am for this." That he scrambled her name in his haste to respond might have given her some indication of his need. "My editor, Miss Fong—you met her last time—she will join us. Wednesday morning at eight. Thank you! *Bonjour!*"

Is 'Bonjour' correct? I'd better stick to English. She probably thinks I'm an idiot. An idiote. *Un eejit.*

On a scrap of paper, he wrote:

RE HR: Miss D-L
WEDNESDAY 8:00 AM
YOUR OFFICE
<u>MUST MAKE</u>!!

He descended the stairs nimbly, as only he could do, and walked nonchalantly to Elaine's office. He handed her the note. She raised her eyebrows.

"You're fast."

"I'm lucky. She'll be in town anyway. We've got her for an hour. I'm going to make a list of questions for her. I'll give them to you tomorrow afternoon so you can read them over and add anything you think I've missed."

"Tomorrow afternoon. You know that's our deadline, right? Or have you forgotten by now?"

"I haven't forgotten. Don't let this interfere with your deadline. You can read my questions at home afterwards, ha-ha."

"You're not that funny. I probably will, because I'll be so *very* curious, ha-ha. I'll follow your lead at the meeting, by which I mean that I'll be in the room. Can't guarantee much contribution beyond that. I'll take notes. I might learn something. Now, if that's all..."

"I'm going! Thank you!" Elaine closed her door behind him.

He went upstairs and checked his watch: eleven o'clock.

So that's how Monday morning passes in the offices of The Times. *How did I ever produce a newspaper before? Were these shenanigans going on? I don't recall. Maybe I just ignored them, but wouldn't they have worsened if they weren't addressed? Did they? Or did they just resolve?*

"Well, I'm here to solve things now, to be proactive, as the brochure says. So, Mister Solve, let's see what we can proactively solve with our pals down at Conquerall Services."

"Hello, Amanda, it's Tim Brown."

"I was just going to call you, Tim. Corey says you have some tricky stairs there. He's hoping it won't involve engineers, because they'll cost double what we have to charge you, but he'll have to pull off a few boards to be sure, maybe poke a few holes, you know?"

"I guess there's no way around it, Amanda. Fix it or continue to have no legal access to the whole second floor, which doesn't make sense. When can he take a stab at it?"

"How about Wednesday morning, early? Just to look, he said, and take some measurements."

"Oh, no, I just booked a meeting for eight o'clock Wednesday morning. It's a popular time. Any chance he could make it Thursday morning?"

"Hang on, Tim."

Amanda paged Corey, and waited, but no response came.

"Sorry, he's likely got his head stuck in a sewer, Tim. Can I call you back?"

"Sure. Call my cell and just leave a message if I don't answer. Try any morning, as early as he likes, just not this Wednesday."

He hadn't liked the discomfort of the morning, not one bit, but he found himself feeling better than he expected to, especially about his refusal to get drawn into frustration or worse.

Positive action, that's what does that. I don't know what the right action is but if I avoid saying things I'll regret, I think we'll work it out. Ed has always been a steady guy, and Harold, mostly.

He slipped the payroll printout from the envelope.

I kind of like being back here, too, messing around with the newspaper business. I don't like that something's wrong, but I do like trying to resolve it. Now, what was I going to resolve with this payroll report?

He studied the printout for an hour, checking, comparing randomly, looking for oddities and anomalies. He did find a few irregularities in rates of pay, for which there might be good reasons of which he was not aware. He wanted to check on that, but Harold didn't know he had the report yet, and, given the earlier dust-up, he'd wait.

Once he had become as familiar as possible with work classifications, pay rates, and other details, he copied them to the double chart he had taped to the wall last week, grouping them by payday amount, low to high, rather than by name. He printed neatly. If something was going to jump out at him, it shouldn't be his handwriting.

Amanda hadn't called back.

"Well, Mister Solve doesn't wait for things to happen. He makes things happen." He called Amanda's office.

"Any word from Corey?"

"Oh, gosh, Tim, I'm so sorry, I got busy and then forgot to call you back. Yes, Thursday morning he can do, if it's at seven."

"I'll take it! Thanks!"

He decided that he'd had enough good luck today, so he carefully locked his door and left the building. A few heads lifted as he walked past, and nodded or smiled at him, as usual. Some did not.

Some of them still like me. They don't have to, but they do. It's the change in demeanour of a few others that I'm sensing. If Mademoiselle Stephanie has some tricks for me, I'll be all ears.

~

Tim filled a pie plate with leftovers, covered it with aluminum foil, and put it in the oven to warm. Searching in the cupboard for remainders of last week's wines, he found some of a Spanish red. This wasn't recommended to pair with roast chicken, but it would do nicely for a pre-dinner perambulation around his front and back gardens.

He enjoyed strolling the flagstone path in the back, and he admired the criss-cross pattern in the grass the mowers used when cutting out front.

One thing for sure, the foggy and rainy days do keep the lawn looking fresh. And we still have a good crop of vegetables to come. This is a whole lot more rewarding than staying in the office until dark, like I used to do. I don't care how early I have to go to work, but I won't be staying late next year. Except maybe on Tuesdays.

He carefully set the wineglass down in soft ground to free both hands to pull a weed that had grown tall inside the branches of a shrub. Weeding felt meditative.

I did put in a good day's work today. I don't know what I'm looking for, but it won't hurt to examine everything, as I have told myself many times, in case something shows up. Meanwhile, the HR person will come the day after tomorrow, and then Corey. Quite different helpers, those two, but both could make a big difference to everyone's comfort at work, mine included.

He had put the kitchen timer in his pocket so he wouldn't ruin supper. It rang now, so he went inside to enjoy it.

September 14: Leftovers

Tuesday

Tim was going to stay out of everyone's way today, newspaper deadline day. He planned to work on his own; on what, he wasn't sure, but he sensed that a lot of work was waiting for him.

He entered the office building, and was confronted with chaos. Huge rags of tarps were hanging from the ceiling, obscuring whatever was making the ear-splitting noise behind them. Mrs Rafuse, the receptionist, was speaking with the stylish human resources woman. Both seemed oblivious to the racket and to Tim.

He headed toward the source of the noise when—whoosh!—he heard water pouring down, a lot of water, followed by shouts of dismay. Lifting the tarp, he saw his drenched staff salvaging soaked papers. Some had thrown themselves bodily across their desks, trying to protect their work. Ed Garamond's advertisement sketches had turned to ink smears.

Corey the carpenter's head appeared upside-down through a hole in the ceiling.

"No worries about a fire up here," he shouted. "I found the water pipes. That's some good!"

Elaine Fong stood calmly in the midst of this chaos, attention focused inward. She drifted toward Tim. "Did you bring your assignment?" she asked. "I have a paper to run."

~

"So," Tim said to the man in his bathroom mirror, "you thought you could handle a stressful day at work? You thought that pulling a couple weeds would calm your nerves after finding Harold and Ed in hissy moods? Having a bad dream about it isn't exactly handling it."

He showered and dressed.

"But dream-Elaine handled the dream crisis quite well, didn't she—by shifting the burden to me. Gotta admire her for that."

He shook his head to dispel the scene, and pulled a double-espresso from Gloria. *I hope this doesn't mean that I'm best suited for sitting on a beach. It'll be too cold for that pretty soon. I wonder if I'd like one of those Caribbean island beaches? Didn't that landscaper fellow say he worked hard all summer so he could be a beach bum down south in the winter? It sure sounds appealing this morning.*

He wondered if the dream was a message in disguise, not from any deity, not from mythology, but from the part of his heart or brain that was disturbed yesterday when Ed wouldn't make eye contact with him, and when Harold was behaving oddly. Other staff had also seemed to avoid him.

It makes sense that my subconscious is dealing with those things. The dream was just notifying me that they're both unresolved.

"Well, thanks, Mister Obvious. I'm dealing with issues as fast as I can. I don't know what the carpenter was doing in that dream, though. If any-one can find a problem and fix it in the same moment, Corey can. I won-der how he'd handle those guys on staff?"

He chuckled. *He'd just tell them to keep it out of the office, I bet. "Just do your job," that's what he'd say. I wonder if he gets bothered by stuff like this?*

Tim put on his shoes to go downtown, then hesitated.

Why am I even going there today? I should let sleeping dogs lie. My dream wasn't a real disaster, far as I know, and I don't want to show up and cause one.

He kicked off his shoes.

Tomorrow and Thursday will be busy days. That's enough. I'll just hang around here today, maybe learn more of that careful human resources lan-guage...and turn the chicken rack to soup.

While he put the bones in a pot to simmer, he thought of the fading dream again.

That Elaine. She sure isn't part of the problem. She's a rock in a stream. Whatever was going on in the dream, she stayed focused on the job at hand which, for her, was to make deadline with a full newspaper—she even expected me to submit columns. That's hilarious!

~

He had a wonderful day. He went out to the garden he shared with Mrs Mother Princess Aquino and picked some fresh vegetables and herbs for the casserole, and a handful for the soup as well. Picking, scrubbing, and dicing things fresh out of the ground was even more enjoyable than weeding.

Mrs A was right: we should plant a bigger garden next year. Maybe I'll dig the sod this afternoon to get it started. No, I should spread corrugated cardboard on the ground first, to kill the grass and weeds over winter. Then it'll be easy to turn over and till next spring.

He shivered. *Is this the first time I've thought of winter? Speaking of such, I'd better get my firewood delivered. Good idea! Now I have a pleasant errand.*

After lunch, he put the pot of chicken to cool while he went to visit Buck, the woodsman.

Buck was working in his yard amongst rows and piles of firewood cut to length for furnaces and fireplaces all over his corner of the county. Shreds of bark were strewn on the ground, and the air was filled with the aroma of softwood sap.

Tim shook Buck's meaty hand, and retained some spruce gum.

"Sorry," Buck said. "Got a hole in my glove, I guess. That stuff's hard to get off. Your newspapers'll stick to ya."

"It's okay," Tim said, laughing. "I'm making chicken soup today." He picked at the sticky patch. "It'll melt off in the soup. Should add a little spicy flavour."

They engaged in the traditional Scuffing of Gravel while running through a few rounds of important topics such as the weather ("pretty good") and business ("pretty good").

"Didja get to PEI like you said?" Buck asked. "Have a good feed of lobsters over there?"

"No, darn it," Tim replied. "We did go to the Island, and we got lost a lot, and it poured rain, so we came home early, no lobsters. Not PEI's fault. But we lucked into a cabin on the beach down in Queen's County, which really was life-changing. So my summer was great. You?"

"We took the ferry over to Rose Blanche to visit the wife's family. Lovely people. We had a great time."

"Where's Rose Blanche? Is that near Rose Bay?"

"No, no. It's on the Rock. Newfoundland. Port aux Basques area. Gorgeous. All rock there. Nice to get away from trees for a break."

"Sounds lovely. Speaking of trees—"

"Your wood's over here." Buck indicated one of the rows of cut and stacked wood. "Been drying out all summer. It'll burn perfect. You ready for it now?"

"Anytime. The woodshed's still there, moved ahead a bit and reinforced, so you should be able to dump the load right next to it. Much as I'd like these warm days to continue, that wood makes me almost eager to sit in front of the fire. What do I owe you?"

He paid Buck for this future pleasure, shook hands with him again, then shooed a flock of chickens away from his car.

Back at home, Tim scrubbed his hands with detergent and a nail brush before straining the chicken bones and skin from the broth. He added vegetables and soup mix and returned the pot to simmer on the stove while he considered what additional resources might be valued by the humans who worked for his enterprise.

Later, after it had cooled, he portioned the soup into containers to freeze, and made a small chicken casserole with a quick pastry topping. He put it in the oven to bake for suppers now and future.

He felt quite virtuous. The chicken had fed him, Robert, and Evelyn on Sunday, plus leftovers for them yesterday, and he was looking at many more meals, all from the same bird.

Maybe not all at once. I'll have half the casserole tonight, and freeze the rest. I'll appreciate it some dark and stormy night, in front of my blazing fire.

To accompany the meal, and to reward himself for managing a peaceful and productive day, he chose a bottom-shelf *Bois de Chauffage.* It wasn't remarkable, but was acceptable for a Tuesday.

He opened the HR brochure to read with supper, and began to jot down questions on a sheet of foolscap.

The questions!

He slapped his forehead, looked at the clock, and made an executive decision. He called Elaine's number and was glad when she didn't answer.

"Miss Fong, this is Mister Stumblebum. I am just getting to the aforementioned HR brochure now, and will not have a list of anything for you to peruse tonight nor tomorrow morning, you'll be happy to know. Miss You-Know-Who will be at the office tomorrow at oh-eight-hundred hours. I will arrive an hour before that, should you wish to confer with me at all. I wouldn't blame you if you didn't. Good night."

All in all, Tim's day had been more comfortable than the morning's dream had indicated it might.

The aromatic tree gum residue was still sticky at bedtime.

September 15: Ready?

Wednesday

Tim debated. *Should I take a thermos of coffee to the office for us? What if our guest prefers* café au lait*? I'd be very happy to do that at home, but I don't know what they scoop into the coffee pot in the lunchroom, nor who's in charge of the* lait*. And our mugs there are...eclectic.*

I better not chance it. I'll go to the Daisy at seven-thirty for three take-away coffees, with the usual packets and sticks on the side. They might still be warm enough when our guest arrives. It's not a reception, anyway; we're there to work.

Elaine arrived at the office with three coffees as Tim returned from the same errand next door.

"At least we're hospitable," she said, prying the lid off one of her drinks.

"Everything go okay last evening?"

"Yes, very smoothly. I was able to leave the print shop a little earlier than usual to run a few errands, so I'm glad you didn't rush to bring me homework."

"I got caught up buying firewood and making chicken soup. A nice homesteading day. I know I have the year off, but it still feels a little like hooky, or dereliction of duty."

"Never you. Stay here and enjoy your coffee. I'll keep watch at the front door."

Stephanie Duplessis-Lachance arrived not long after, also carrying three coffees. They all laughed when she and Elaine entered the office, now with nine cups of coffee on the desk.

"*Alors*, let us make best use of our time together, shall we?" their guest began. "You have an 'important but not urgent' situation here in your office, and you feel that the services of my firm might be of value to you, is that correct?"

"*Oui*," Tim said, as Elaine nodded.

"Are you able to describe this situation briefly?"

"I'm on leave this year," Tim began, "so I'm not around the office much, not for newspaper work, anyway. I do have a room upstairs in which I carry on my own activities. I like to keep in touch with the staff, too. I've known most of them for a long time. We don't socialize outside of work as a rule, though sometimes we do. A garden party, a funeral, things like that."

"*Un enterrement*...a funeral is not socializing, surely?"

"One was," Elaine spoke up. "A beloved employee had died, and Tim let it be known that he was going to scatter his ashes very early on a Saturday morning. Almost everyone showed up, and many brought family members. Then the café opened early for us and gave us coffee and muffins and it became quite a...a jovial time, really."

"I see. Go on."

"So," Tim continued, "Miss Fong and I had been discussing whether we should ask the staff if they'd like to do something to observe Labour Day, like a family picnic. We asked an employee what she thought. She thought it was a great idea. Praised us for being so thoughtful. And then she suggested that we—Miss Fong and I—should not be involved."

"Why?"

"Maybe it just evolved?" Elaine said. "As I recall, she began by telling us not to bother, that they would organize it themselves, and she'd give us the bill if there were any expenses. Then it seemed to us that she felt we shouldn't go. So we didn't."

"Is that why you called me in?"

"No," Tim said. "That's just for background. As it happened, it rained on Labour Day, but we heard they went to Cindy's barn anyway and had a great time. We think somebody told them we *would* be there, so they wondered why we hadn't showed up. I'm sorry: does this make sense?"

"I believe so. Proceed."

"Since then, two of our staff who hold senior positions have been acting strangely. The newer one has been missing deadlines, handing in material late that's obviously not what we asked for, and leaving work early and coming in late. And a longtime employee, who has always been friendly, gave me the cold shoulder. That may seem trivial, but it's a disturbing change. Do you have anything to add, Elaine?"

"I agree with Tim; there've been changes in behaviour lately, though not consistently. Work went smoothly yesterday."

"Did you find it so, Monsieur Brown? Smooth?"

"I wasn't here yesterday."

"How do you think things would go if you were away from here during the workdays?"

"I *have* been away. A lot. Elaine can answer better."

"I don't notice any change. Whenever Tim comes in, staff say hello, or wave at him. They are really fond of him. And loyal. It's lovely to see it."

"One other thing," Tim said. "I obtained a copy of our payroll report because I wondered if our employees were being paid fairly, in particular, our ad sales executive who organized that party. We'd been thinking there might be growing interest in a union, you see, and I wanted to be proactive, to ensure everyone is being paid fairly before we got into it."

Their consultant glanced at her tiny watch, and reached in her voluminous designer handbag for some documents.

"I don't 'ave much time left this morning. I suggest you do these two things: invite all of your employees—every one of them—to short private interviews with you in the coming days. Do not single out some and omit others or there may be real trouble. There are guidelines in this envelope. You will explain to everyone that you are hoping to ensure that all staff are treated fairly according to the latest standards and—if you are sincere in saying so—you may say that an across-the-board salary review will follow."

"Should both of us attend those interviews?" Elaine asked. "I'm here temporarily, so maybe I don't need to participate?"

"You are here for how much longer?"

"January, sometime, likely."

"You should be there, otherwise for the next four months you will be implying to staff that you are a lame duck, eh? Keep each interview to no more than twenty minutes, and follow the guidelines. Enjoy them. Get to know your people."

"Is there a charge for this?"

"*Oui, monsieur.* You may keep the materials in this envelope at no cost, and use them if you wish. If you want me to return and assist you with establishing good staff relations that will withstand most work disruptions, then you will sign the enclosed contract for my retainer, which will include today."

"If we—goodness, that's an unusual approach, isn't it? Today is free on its own, but if you come back, we'll pay for this hour?"

"Exactly. I meet many employers who don't want to help themselves, in which case I don't want to bother with them, either. You 'ave the tools you need for now."

She stood, her designer heels putting her almost on a level with Tim, who also stood. She extended her manicured hand.

"I wish you *bonne chance. À bientôt.*"

Elaine accompanied her back to the front door, while Tim ferried the eleven untouched coffees to the lunch room.

When he returned, Elaine pointed to the big envelope on her desk. "You'll study this first? I have some newspaper things to do."

"Sure. I'm curious to see what she's got in there. Big brown envelopes are intriguing. Thanks for coming in early, Elaine. I'll be back for our next appointment at one o'clock, remember?"

"How could I possibly forget? The employee who can't count how many computers we have is going to advise us about what will happen if they all fail to boot up on January first. Yippee."

"Want to know what was the best thing I heard this morning?"

"What?"

"That you're planning to stay into January."

"Ha! That's *if* I don't get contracted by someone who begs me to start on New Year's Day, which I will do everything I can to avoid. If it's a maternity leave situation, the maternal person should be starting to make plans right about now for getting her replacement in by February or so. I haven't been looking yet. I'm in no rush."

~

Tim needed some comfort after the meeting, and Elaine's mention of her inevitable departure sharpened the need. Picking up the HR envelope, he drove home.

"Gloria, I know I can count on you to soothe my anxieties with a jolt of your elixir."

After the dark liquid dribbled into a mug, he made it a latté, and toasted a thick slice of whole-grain bread. He inhaled the nutty aroma of the bread, slathered it with butter and jam, and carried everything to the dining room table. He sat down to examine the contents of the envelope.

A folder with the familiar corporate logo was on top, containing the same materials he had been trying to read recently. He set that aside. Next were several photocopies of an INTERVIEW RECORD, held together with a paperclip. A sticky note advised him to copy one for each employee. It was a single page with five questions, and space to write the responses.

At first glance, the questions appeared to be quite innocuous. The fifth question was, "Anything you'd like to add?"

This is what a human resources specialist gives us? I could have written these myself, no charge.

A page entitled INTERVIEWER'S GUIDE was printed on pale blue paper. The subtitle was: READ THIS CAREFULLY BEFORE CONDUCTING INTERVIEWS.

It listed DOs and DON'Ts, such as DO stick to the time limit. DO schedule another interview if any issues arise that require more extensive discussion. DO read the questions *exactly* as written for each interview; DON'T shorten or lengthen them in any way. DON'T discuss the employee's responses in the interview, except to clarify if necessary.

That's interesting. A little robotic. I prefer casual conversation, not this rigid, formal approach. But I'm here to learn.

At the bottom of the pile, or top, if he had taken the contents out that way, was the retainer contract for Mademoiselle. Having recently scrutinized Robert's touring contract, he was familiar with contract format and standard clauses.

This one could be terminated by either party with no notice, requiring only that the current month's retainer be paid in full in advance. He—the Contractor—would be entitled to the services of Mademoiselle—hereinafter referred to as the Consultant—for X number of hours per month, including by telephone, or in person, including travel time. He was surprised to learn that she would be travelling from Chester, just a few exits up the highway toward the city.

I just assumed that someone who did such hifalutin work in such red-carpet couture *must come from Halifax, if not Montreal. I wonder what my attire says about me? Probably that I'm a South River boy, born and bred, struggling to work on my little community weekly paper.*

"Well, I yam what I yam," he said as he rinsed his dishes. "And I yam not so anxious now. I'll sign her contract and give her simple interviews a try. Can't hurt. Might help."

He put a few eggs in a saucepan to boil, set the timer, and went back to the questionnaires to see if there was a special technique he could try in this afternoon's meeting with Harold.

~

"Hi, Harold. After you."

Tim approached Elaine's door at the same time as Harold, and held the door open for him. Elaine was on the phone when they went in, but quickly ended the call.

Her chair faced the closed door. Tim pulled a chair to the end of her desk, and Harold sat facing them, his back to the door. Elaine's desktop, as usual, was clear.

Tim drew a breath to begin, but Harold beat him to it.

"May I begin?" he asked, pleasantly.

"Sure," Tim said.

"Please," Elaine said.

"Here's my assessment of the situation *vis à vis* the computers, and things containing computers, in *The Times'* inventory," Harold said, passing copies of a two-page spreadsheet to Tim and Elaine. "I'll give you a moment to peruse it, and then I'll lead you through the categories."

He paused, and Tim and Elaine bowed their heads over the document as if giving thanks for blessings received, which, in a way, Tim was.

I wish we had mental telepathy right now. "Hey, Elaine, look at the new Harold! Fastest turnaround ever!"

Elaine spoke first. "This is interesting, Harold. According to this, we have more computers than I would have guessed. Are you sure it's up to date? I mean, of course it is, but there are more machines here than we have staff. If I'm not reading it wrong."

"I felt surprised, too, Miss Fong, and understand that you feel the same. But here's what I found."

Calmly, almost soothingly, Harold explained that some computers were no longer in inventory as they had been depreciated long ago, but were still around and occasionally used for some purpose.

"And of course, the new portable laptops are somewhat redundant, as employees who want to be able to carry them out of the office for work still use their desktop models, too."

"You can explain the sense of that to me sometime, but not right now," Tim said. "I'm concerned about the incredible possibility that all these computers will shut down at midnight on New Year's Eve, do I have that right? And they will stay off, unless and until some digit gadget is discovered and installed. And the cost of that installation may exceed the value of the machines, if I can call them that. And we'll be in a service-call lineup so long that the stone age will have time to return. Am I close?"

Harold smiled indulgently. "I know it is stressful, Mister Brown. Uncertainty is never a comfort zone for a business owner. Now, let me answer some of your original questions. One, which ones are most susceptible to this Y2K Bug, as it's called; and two, what would be your company's financial exposure? Correct?"

Tim nodded. Elaine was watching both men very closely.

Harold calmly led them through the report, and they marked each device with an X, indicating it might be in trouble, or a question mark, meaning that Harold would further assess whether its contents and capability made it even usable now, given swiftly changing computer programs. Most received an X.

"Okay, those Xs are the vulnerable ones," Elaine said. "Is there nothing you can do to repair the glitch in advance? Whether I'm here after the New Year or somewhere else, the answer is relevant to me: this threat will affect my work wherever I go. I wouldn't like to show up in a new job on January first to find smoke drifting up from all the computers. Nobody produces a newspaper without computers now."

"I can," Tim said brightly.

"Unlikely the printers could print it if you could, though," Harold said, "not to burst your bubble. But there is some hope. In small, self-contained businesses as we are, there may be an easy fix before the end of the year. If they do turn on after midnight, then we'll try connecting them to the network one by one—if the network survives. I guess a lot of computer experts will be sipping their New Year's Eve champagne at their offices. Happy times if the lights stay on, but just darkness if not...but I'm in touch with the best experts available around here, so let's not panic yet."

"What's the government saying? This sounds like it could be an economic disaster. Isn't that a government concern?"

"It's on the news every day. They don't know much, but they're looking into it."

"Oh, swell," Tim said. "'I'm from the government, I'm here to fix your computer.' That's troubling."

"I just had a thought," Elaine said. "Given that this bug was inadvertently built into computers since they were invented, are there new computers being manufactured that don't have it? Or a replacement component?"

"We're hoping," Harold said. "I've got a standing order at all our main suppliers. So does everyone else. However, I do have good news: there was one related bug that might have taken us down last Thursday, but didn't."

"*Last* Thursday? Why didn't you—?" Tim stopped when Elaine gave him a warning glance.

"Please explain, Harold," she said.

"September the ninth of this particular year, in some programming shortcuts, is written as nine slash nine slash nine nine. Some shut-down codes may also be nine nine nine nine. Here, we passed."

"Shouldn't you have warned us about this, Harold?"

"It wasn't…I was aware of it, of course, nine nine ninety-nine, but I wasn't advised about the total risk until the tenth. We were all clear. We wouldn't have been able to do anything about it anyway. Folks, I know these are uncertain times, and I want to limit the stress for both of you. I have already shared my frustrations with the so-called experts for missing that one. Rest assured, I will continue to monitor all warnings and innovations on your behalf."

"Paper and pencil, Harold, paper and pencil" Tim said. "Letterpress printing. Horse and carriage. Why did we ever abandon those for these devices we don't understand?"

"Well, sir, I understand how you feel, but I ask you: did you ever really understand how that horse worked any more than you understand your car?"

They all laughed. It was a relief to have Harold being congenial again.

"All right," Elaine said, "we now have the report we asked for, and a little more knowledge about the company's exposure. Can we meet for updates? I suggest the first and middle of each month until it's the new year or resolved, whichever comes first."

"Yes, of course. If I learn something important in the meanwhile, either bad or good, I'll alert you both."

"That sounds good," Tim said. "Alert me in person, please. I'm not hooked up to one of these computers, and now I have a great excuse to put off that happy day until after 'Y2K'."

"Got it. Have I answered your questions for now?"

They nodded.

"Good. Then I'd better go. Staff won't be happy if payday's late. Have a good day."

Tim closed the door behind Harold. "Who was that?" he asked quietly. "That wasn't the shape-shifting Harold who was in here Monday."

"I prefer this one, though that story about September ninth doesn't fill me with confidence."

"What part?"

"The way I understand it," Elaine said, "the computers would have shut down just after midnight on the eighth, right? He should have warned us weeks ago—when we began asking him about it, in fact. It was nine-nine-nine-nine all day last Thursday, but no mention of it."

"Come to think of it, he was acting weird last Thursday, too, remember? That's the day he said you told him not to give us this report because you had something else in mind. Which you didn't. It's all very strange."

"It is. Even so, he says he didn't know about it until Friday, long after the exposure for failure had passed. That doesn't sound like he's up on tech issues at all. He didn't tell us anything, he just acted weird. Perhaps he didn't know, or discovered too late and just kept it from us, hoping it would work out, which it did. Now he tells us about it like he's a know-it-all, or a gambler. If he's in touch with the best experts around here, last Thursday's exposure was a test, and I think they all failed in the communication department."

"My takeaway is that everyone in town—in the world—is in the same boat as we are," Tim said. "If a nuclear bomb were aimed at us, I mightn't be so sanguine, but I'm willing to keep learning as the day approaches. I'll make some inquiries. Given my aversion to computers, I haven't cultivated any techy friends, but perhaps I have some, inadvertently."

"Go ahead. I'll try to locate all these computers soon. We seem to have an awful lot of them."

~

Tim looked at the kitchen wall calendar, saw the red dot reminding him to check the humidifiers in the piano, and that reminded him that today was "singing with Elaine" day. He dialed her mobile number, which went to voice-mail.

"Me again. Thanks for your great support today. Twice! I left without reminding you to come up tonight. If you're looking for excellent chicken soup, let me know and I'll heat some for you."

Elaine called back while he was outside for a moment. "Can't come tonight, sorry, but thanks so much. I forgot to mention that I traded this evening for this morning's early meeting. Soup sounds delish. If it's frozen, save me some for next time."

She "traded" the time? With her mystery man? I'm happy for her. I hope he treats her like the rare gem she is.

He called her phone again and said, "Message received. Enjoy yourself. In other news, I'm meeting a carpenter at the office tomorrow morning at seven, to see if he can salvage the second floor. The work might not be finished by nine. I'd come in late if I were you. If I were me, I wouldn't miss it."

For the rest of the time before supper, he rotated between the HR interview guidelines and Harold's computer listings. He started another document on foolscap, deliberately using a mechanical pencil to ward off unknown technical glitches. On this paper he recorded Notes and Obser-vations from his two encounters with Harold this week. If he was going to have only twenty minutes during the HR interview with him, he wanted some background for comparison afterward, to see which Harold he was interviewing.

After supper, since Elaine was not there to witness the carnage, he pulled a Liszt sonata from the music cabinet and attacked it with enthu-siasm. It was far beyond his capability. He was thoroughly defeated after four lines, but that didn't stop him from persisting.

September 16: Set?

Thursday

The six o'clock alarm woke Tim, and he laughed at himself. He was usually awake well before the alarm. *Early work appointments two days in a row and I'm struggling, is that it?*

"No," he decided as he quickly made an essential coffee. "I'm not struggling. I'm sleeping well. How's that for progress? Given all the potential for stress yesterday, I think I did quite well. Corey's a different scene altogether. If he doesn't bring the house down as he did in that dream, I'll consider today a win as well."

He placed Mrs Aquino's cheque on the kitchen island and left to meet his carpenter.

Corey and Tim pulled into the parking lot at the same time. Corey introduced his young assistant, Tyler. Tyler's unlaced work boots seemed very large for such a small fellow, but that wasn't Tim's concern. He unlocked the door and held it while the two men carried a stepladder, a telescoping ladder, some tarps, and a very large toolbox into the building.

He locked the door behind them and followed at a safe distance. From his previous experience of Corey's work, he knew that the best way for him to help was to stay out of the way.

Corey and Tyler concluded that the ladder-like stairway had intruded into the ceiling of the ladies' washroom because a washroom for women had been an afterthought, likely added when the gentler sex had joined the workforce during World War II. The corridor leading to the big loading door at the back of the building had had to be kept clear for large shipments that no longer came here. Rather than build them somewhere else that made sense, the steps were squeezed in, narrow and steep.

In the newspaper's early days, Tim explained, the loading door was used to receive blank paper and take out printed papers. Printing was done off-site now, so this door was used only for the occasional large delivery, such as furniture Tim had scavenged for use upstairs last spring.

Plus, it was a second exit. There was no getting rid of it.

"Nobody would approve a setup like this nowadays," Corey said. "I wouldn't build it. Not sure what I can do about it. Let's have a look."

They thumped back out to the main office, noting the load-bearing pillars and the location of Elaine's office, the only fully-enclosed room other than the washrooms and storage closets.

Slung over young Tyler's shoulder was what Tim had thought was a large messenger bag, but when Tyler set it on the table in the lunchroom and opened it up, he saw it was a portable computer. After taking a few moments to set up, Tyler called to Corey that he was ready, and Corey began to call measurements to him. Tyler entered those in his program, confirmed or asked for correction, and they carried on to the next area.

Tim tiptoed to the table.

"Can I see?" he asked, and Tyler showed him the sketch that was forming on the screen, a bird's eye view of the office layout.

Corey came in to look at the screen, and they pointed out this and that to each other.

"Okay, now, watch this," Tyler said, and touched a key. Elaine's office, which had been against an outer wall, jumped to the centre of the office space.

"Oh, that's interesting," Tim said.

"What's the clearance in front there?" Corey asked, and Tyler named a figure.

Corey took his tape measure out to the reception desk and took more measurements. He returned to the table, pointed to the screen, and dictated the numbers to Tyler, who keyed them in. On the screen the office jumped a little bit sideways and forward.

"What we're lookin' for," Corey explained to Tim, "is where we could put a proper stairway up, on this side of the buildin'. We can't fix it where it is, but the washroom doors can open onto that hallway. You'd prob'ly have to lose a little space over here, but once you have a proper stairway, you'll gain the whole upstairs. Nobody sleeps up there, so the code doesn't stipulate a fire escape. You got those emergency ladders, right?"

"They're up there. One in front and one in back."

"Good. The Fire Marshall will state a maximum number of occupants for the second floor, but it'll be somethin' like a dozen, so if you don't hold a big meetin' up there, you'll be fine. Down here, see, you can move the wash basins aside, and put the washroom doors over there and keep them toilets away from the food area. We can tear out that old stairs once the new one's in. You'll have a lot more room. And the ladies will be happier."

"So will the gents, believe me. Gosh, Corey, it sounds like you'll have to tear the place apart. I agree the changes sound great, but we'll still have to operate a business while you work."

Tim had a flashback to his nightmare. *Maybe it was a premonition, not a dream.*

"I don't see many walls to tear down," Corey said, "just the boss's office. I don't think it's all load-bearing walls, just the one that's against the outside wall. The rest is them pillars."

"I'd suggest you go with glass panels and open tops for the downstairs offices," Tyler said. "They'd look nice, and the air could circulate. Don't close it in with a bunch of boxy offices with doors on them. It's too stuffy and the space will seem small."

"It still sounds like a lot of demolition and construction, lots of disruption. We painted the place in one weekend about six months ago."

"Can you do without going up them old stairs at all for a couple weeks?"

"I suppose…I don't really need to be up there. But I wouldn't want to miss any of the action."

"Yeah. Once that corridor and stairway space is free, then we can shift everything thataway to make space for a nice, easy stairway leading down to the front door. Down here you'll have nice offices, meetin' rooms, lunch room, and the boss' office, and other offices upstairs. You just tell us how you want it."

"Can you print off these drawings, Tyler?"

"Sure can. And more than just flat sketches, too. You'll practically be able to walk around in the new space on this screen. You tell us what you want and we'll show you what it looks like in three dimensions, right, Corey?"

"Yup," Corey said.

"That sounds very sci-fi. I didn't know Conquerall Services had that capability."

"Tyler's just new," Corey said. "Before him, we woulda been going by guess and by golly. He saves us a lot of time and mess, and that saves you a lot of money."

"I sure will appreciate that. Show me a good plan I can afford, then. I'd love to share these drawings with the staff, and invite them to comment, too. They live here all day, after all. When will your presentation be ready?"

"Tomorrow? Monday? You're lucky that you're our first," Tyler said.

"We want to get this service going. Maybe you'll give us a good reference."

"I will, if you do what you say you can. Let me think…tomorrow afternoon would be good, I think, right after lunch. I'll check with the boss and call you by noon today. Okay, fellas," Tim said with a shrug, "carry on. Who knew the construction business would get into computers? Oh, speaking of coomputers, Tyler: how did you make out with the nine-nine-nine-nine scare last week?"

"Piece of cake. That bug wasn't in this baby, but I checked that out months ago. You?"

"Same. Sailed right through."

~

He was only slightly late for breakfast at the Daisy. When Evelyn served him, she leaned down and whispered, "Best weekend ever!"

"We always enjoy having you over."

"I meant *here*! Our new weekend crew did really well, so *we* did really well, just layin' around at home. I could get used to that. Dinner with you guys was great, too, hon. Now, you be sure to lead your worshippers over here after church every Sunday, so my retirement plan will work out."

"We aren't in charge of those arrangements. I think those 'fellowship' gatherings will be once a month, first Sundays?"

"Yeah, but they're serving brunch *every* Saturday and Sunday to the public. You know it's good food. You guys should go."

Tim nodded and smiled.

Ev's really into sales now, imagine that! She'll probably retire sooner than I will, and with more money, especially if I keep dumpng all of mine into this old building. But, no, that's wrong: this renovation won't be paid for with my money. The Times can pay for its own expenses. Milton at the bank will fall all over himself to get me a loan or a line of credit. Easy-peasy.

After breakfast, Tim walked back to the newspaper office, taking the long way across both bridges. He wanted a few minutes to check in with himself following this morning's meeting, and the two yesterday. Each one meant a little or a lot to the smooth operation of his business, depending.

Yeah, depending on things beyond my control. Interviews with each employee won't just be simple twenty-minute chats, oh no. The support material says that every employee is an individual, and I should not assume they agree or disagree with any statement, so I should just ask the questions, clarify if necessary, and follow up in Phase Two, whatever that will entail.

He stopped momentarily to let a car turn into a driveway, narrowly missing him.

Then there's the computers situation: not much anyone can do, I guess, except to keep an eye on Harold. Something about his September nine story does sound fishy. He was cooperative enough yesterday, though. What about Ed Garamond? I won't bring it up; I'll just see how it goes. Everyone's allowed a mis-fire once in a while. I hope the staff like the idea of upgrading the office layout. They won't like the construction while it's going on but there's no way to avoid that noise and dust. Except they have those little computers in shoulder-bags to use at home, or at the Daisy. Ev might see an increase in sales of coffee and muffins.

He arrived at his building, looking great in its still-new exterior paint following the Main Street improvements campaign in the spring. That had met with opposition at first, too.

Oh well. You can't make an omelette without breaking eggs. Avoidance doesn't lead to peace, either, so here goes.

The first eggs to get broken belonged to Elaine.

"Friday afternoon? Why not Wednesday morning after everyone has straggled in?"

"I don't want to put it off, Elaine, and besides, I didn't want to get involved in another time-off situation. We always let staff decide when to show up on Wednesdays, don't we, and the less we mess with that, the better. We can 'advise' them that there will be a short presentation tomorrow at one o'clock in the lunchroom, and everyone's encouraged to attend. I can try to schedule a second presentation for those who are unable to attend, if they ask for it. There'll be print copies to look at anyway."

"What's your rush?"

"I want them to see what's being planned so they can make suggestions."

"Will you use their suggestions, though?"

"That's the point of it, Elaine. With this computer-aided thingy, they can show us what any change would look like with the click of a couple keys. So it doesn't require days and money to draw it all. Pretty spiffy. If somebody suggests we do *this* to get *that*, and it works, well, hey."

"Hey, then."

"You say hey, but I don't believe you're convinced. What do *you* think I should do?"

"No, no, go ahead. Nothing ventured, nothing gained. You want me to sit in, I fear?"

"Yes, please. It'll be a half-hour, forty-five minutes tops. I'll get Ed to post a notice, will I?"

"Let me do that. I need to see him anyway. Will that be all, or...?"

Now something's off with Elaine. Maybe it's just my imagination. I'm getting jumpy around humans these days. Let's see if I can make the bank manager happy.

He walked the dozen steps to the bank.

"May I see Milton Barkhouse, please? It's Tim Brown, and no, I don't have an appointment. I see him standing right over there, so perhaps he can squeeze me in."

It rankled Tim a little that the tellers always asked his name whenever he asked to see the manager. Maybe Milton had them do that so he wouldn't have to remember names of customers, even long-standing ones.

"Tim! What brings you here? Let's go inside my office of possibilities!"

"You're cheery today, Milton. Did somebody qualify for a big loan?"

"Perhaps they did, Tim, perhaps they did. You know the bank business, up one day and higher the next, ha-ha."

"Good for you. Perhaps I can help keep you happy. I'm considering some renovations to my building, so I'll need a construction line of credit. Secured by the asset itself, of course."

"In what amount?"

Tim pulled a figure out of the air. "If it's more than that, I'll revise. It should be quite a bit less."

"But—all that money going into that old building, Tim? I know you painted the exterior—"

"And the interior, earlier this year. Looks great."

"Well, meaning no offence, Tim, but all this seems to me to be putting lipstick on a pig, ha-ha. Remember I suggested that you could build a completely new building for your business in the business park, and we would finance it for you? That old building should be torn down and re-placed, by a developer, for retail. Your lot is still worth something."

"Are you still tooting that horn, Milton? Wasn't Eric MacIntosh behind that scheme? Have you forgotten how he got caught with his hand in the cookie jar, charges laid, court case pending? *The Times* proudly led the charge on that story. Why would you even mention his name to me?"

"Those charges won't stick, Tim. He has an iron-clad defence."

"Does he, now? I think his iron cladding will be in the form of bars on his cell. You should keep your nose clean, Milton."

"The bank manager in a small town like this has to support all sorts of development, otherwise the town would crumble. Anyway, Tim, let's not argue. I'm ready to support you all the way. When do you expect to need this line of credit?"

"You'd consider a line of credit after what you just said?"

"Sure, Tim, sure. For you. It might not be for as much as you're thinking, given the condition of the asset, but we'd never turn you down outright. Maybe we'll match you, dollar for dollar. Do you have the plans yet?"

"Uh, no, not yet. We're just at the talking phase. It probably won't happen for some time. Months, maybe next year. I was just checking."

"All right, well come right over when you have the details and I'll do my best for you, whatever way you choose to go."

Tim got into his car and drove the short distance up the hill to the shopping plaza where another bank had opened its doors a few years ago. He went into the small lobby, asked to see the manager, and was invited to go right in.

The manager stood, extended her hand to Tim, and said, "Hello, I'm Valerie Coolen."

"Tim Brown. Thanks for seeing me without an appointment."

"My pleasure, Mister Brown. How can I help?"

Tim made his story short and to the point: he currently did his banking business elsewhere, but he was becoming concerned about having all his eggs in one basket, and he had plenty of eggs, both personal and business. Today, he was shopping for a construction line of credit to finance some remedial work in his business office.

"Interesting. May I ask what is the nature of your business?"

Tim had noticed a copy of this week's edition of *The Times* on a side table in the waiting area.

"I'll show you. Excuse me." He stepped out and brought in the paper. "This is my business. I own this newspaper."

"You're *that* Timothy Brown? I thought your name rang a bell. I've been trying to call on all the businesses in town, but I haven't made it down to your section of Main Street, or the Gem District, as people call it now. I guess I felt that enterprises so close to the other bank would be harder to woo. Perhaps I was wrong?"

"For daily deposits, maybe so, but can we explore a line of credit?" He floated the same figure he had mentioned to Milton.

"I can't see why not. Will you have a quote from the contractor?"

"Yes, and something more. My contractor has engaged a young wizard who is mapping out the whole project on his portable computer, in 3D, I hear. He's presenting it to us tomorrow at one o'clock. Would you like to come down to our office and see it for yourself? It's pretty interesting to watch internal offices and stairways slide around without causing one fleck of dust."

"I'd really like an opportunity to see that. One o'clock in the newspaper office?"

"Correct. Just a half hour. We'll ask staff for their input, too, but not tomorrow. We just want them to see what's possible first, and to think about it. Just to be clear, I don't want to use my own money for these renovations."

"That's fine, Mister Brown. I hope you'll be able to use ours. Thank you for giving us this opportunity. I'll see you tomorrow." Valerie Coolen shook his hand again, and he departed, returning his newspaper to the lobby as he went.

From his car in the parking lot, he phoned Amanda at Conquerall Services. Yes, she knew all about Tyler and his fancy computer. He was standing right in front of her now, having just come to ask if she'd heard from Tim. Yes, Tyler said he would be there about a quarter to one tomorrow, and he'd show how the whole building would turn out.

It was late lunchtime. Tim wasn't very hungry but he was close to home. Mrs A would still be at work, but her vacuum cleaner artillery would be winding down soon, so he decided to chance it.

He found the rumbles and swishes of the washer and dryer and dishwasher soothing, like white noise. With some cookies and a mug of tea, he sat again at the dining table and made notes, not just about Harold this time.

~

Almost wordlessly, Robert ate the light supper Tim had prepared. For his part, Tim, who often curated his week's exploits for Robert's entertainment, didn't have any stories ready to share. There wasn't any trouble between them; they just needed to be quiet.

Choir practice had a vigour of its own, as usual, since twenty-some adults were in attendance. Robert woke up and put them through their paces with his usual vigour. Tim wondered how low Robert would have to be before music failed to bring out the best in him.

He also noted that Elaine wasn't at choir practice, nor had she been last week. *I wonder if this is an indication of her intentions for the future? That she doesn't want to join because she knows she'll be leaving us in the bleak midwinter?*

He shuddered at that chilling thought, and tried to focus on supporting his breath with his diaphragm.

At home afterward, Tim poured two glasses of port and opened a can of smoked almonds for their usual post-practice de-briefing.

"All right, Rob, let's exchange some words and call it conversation," he said. "Is anything bothering you? Please tell me, if so."

"Gosh no, nothing, certainly not with you. It's just…it's the first week of term, and I've been meeting students, which I am sorting into the Good, the Bad, and the Ugly. I'm amazed that some of them manage to find their way to the classroom. It's tiring. So I'm tired, that's all. Not discouraged."

"Good to know."

"I can hardly wait for Saturday. Pretty please, can we just hang out in the sunroom and let our minds go blank, maybe pretend we're at the beach? Not answer the phone or the door? I think I can survive until then."

"We'll have to make one phone call, and answer the door just once. This week's supper is takeout, so our supper will be delivered, thank goodness."

"Excellent. Sounds like you could use the break too? What's on your mind?"

"If I only knew. I've had a number of meetings, or encounters, some of them very early, including this morning. Long days, in other words. But it's not about the hours or the topics, it's the people. No two are alike, and sometimes, they're not even like themselves! Is it a full moon?"

"Exactly! Everyone's gone looney. But I know it's not a full moon, though, or the choir would've been off, and they sure weren't tonight. What a nice sound. We're going to have a good year, I think."

"Cheers to that. Everything else will get sorted, won't it?"

"It always does, Timo. How about we let sleep knit up the raveled sleeve of care now?"

They went to bed, but Tim didn't fall asleep right away. Too many thoughts were whirling in his head.

Elaine seemed put off today. I wasn't expecting that. She was spot-on yesterday. Maybe I'm involving her in too many non-newspaper things? I suppose I shouldn't, but I'm not even supposed to be at work, and she is.

The nerve of Milton Barkhouse telling me, of all people, that Eric will get off after all the work we did to get the evidence the Mounties needed to lay charges. Milton had better watch his step around me...I like Mrs Coolen. It'll be interesting to see what she says about the presentation tomorrow. It's all up to Tyler in his Seven-League Boots, and that tiny computer. I really hope our construction will be finished before the year two thousand. Maybe they'll find a cure for that bug, anyway...

September 17: Go!

Friday

Robert was moving around the house, preparing for the commute and workday ahead as though going to his execution.

"Buck up, my brave one," Tim said. "If you're going to be martyred, go like the nuns in the *Dialogues of the Carmelites,* each one in line, bravely singing as she goes to her beheading, until—*awk!*" He dropped his arm like a guillotine blade.

"Ouch! I wonder how many commuters on the highway this morning feel as though they are heading to the guillotine?" Robert sighed. "Ah, well, you've put Poulenc's music in my head, so I thank you for that. Fare thee well. I'll try to keep my head high *and* on my shoulders while bravely singing *Salve Regina.*"

Poor Rob has taken on too much work, I can tell. Probably trying to get as much teaching done as he can before he starts touring next year. We'll talk about that this weekend. I've taken on a lot, too, but I feel like doing it, and it feels good to feel good.

Tim heard the rumble of a truck motor in his driveway and, looking out the den window, saw a woodpile moving past as Buck delivered his winter comfort.

Buck and another man got out of the truck cab to survey the area. Of course, Tim went out the back door to watch the show. Men and trucks in his driveway almost always signalled the arrival of goods or services he wanted.

"Your yard got all prettied up since last year," Buck said. "Seems a shame to dump this load on that nice lawn. I think we'll stop at the top of the driveway."

"That'll add a lot of steps, won't it, from the pile to the woodshed? Will it harm the grass that much? I can try to take care of it this week."

"Not you. You'll hurt your back or have to go to work. Then the snow will fall before you get back to it and the woodpile will stay right where we dump it."

"Oh, now, I don't know if I'm as bad as all that."

"You're the guy that stacked the firewood in that porch there because it was closer to the house, ain't it?"

"You're right, Buck, I did."

"Norm's here to stack it. It was in the price you paid. Just show him where you want it. I have to go find someone to look at the differential on the truck. She's got a clunk. I'll help finish up when I come back. We'll be gone before noon. Come up and see us sometime."

Tim showed Norm the woodshed, asked him not to block the cabinet holding the hibachis and barbecuing supplies, then got out of his way. There was a loud clatter as Buck dumped the wood, lowered the box, and drove away. Tim couldn't tell if the differential had clunked.

Norm was already at work stacking the wood.

Buck sure can read me. I would've been staring at the woodpile with a very gloomy outlook after three armloads. And he's right, I wouldn't have finished it. I'm no operatic martyr. Look at wiry Norm out there, fairly fly-ing. He'd be too fast for any guillotine.

Tim took toast and coffee to the sunroom, and thoroughly enjoyed watching the woodpile diminish and the neat rows rise while the week's questions drifted through his mind.

I'd better get specific pretty soon. I have a bunch of files open, questions raised, projects in the chute. I should tie up some loose ends soon or I'll for-get what I was looking for. I see three prongs: making sure we pay the staff fairly; ensuring they feel appreciated; and providing a safe and comfort-able workplace.

He was pleased with this summation, and was encouraged that he had come to this.

Still musing about those prongs on his way downtown to see the renovation presentation, he said aloud, "I hope the staff agree."

~

Employees hanging around outside the lunchroom seemed to have a slight party atmosphere as Tim entered the building. Every now and then, one would separate from the group and go look in the room, and then come out and report to the others, gesturing to show the dimen-sions of something that was just out of sight.

"Good day, everyone, what's going on?" Tim teased. "Somebody show-ing a movie?"

"Movies on Friday afternoons! Hey, can we bring a TV in here?"

"For news purposes, maybe. I think this will be more interesting than a movie, though I do like cowboy movies. Excuse me."

He squeezed through the door and into the room, where Tyler was clicking keys on his laptop. He wasn't watching the little screen on the device, though. A pull-up projector screen was at the end of the room, in front of the washroom doors, and on the table was a large, boxy device from which a bright light shone onto the screen.

Tyler was accompanied by a woman Tim didn't recognize at first, until she said, "Hey, Tim, nice to see you," and he recognized her as Amanda from Conquerall Services. Part of her disguise was the tailored pants suit she wore, not the denim coveralls she was wearing when he met her months ago. Her hair, pulled into a tidy updo, completed her transformation.

Tim smiled and said, "Welcome to my world, Amanda. Nice to see you, too. Are you ready for us?"

"I hope so. It's Tyler's show; I'm just here to start and stop him. Why don't you bring your people in now and we'll make sure everyone can see the screen."

As Tim beckoned the staff to enter, he saw Valerie Coolen, the uptown bank manager, just entering the building.

"Thank you very much for coming, Mrs Coolen. Go right in. It looks like they're putting on a big production in there. I hope you enjoy it."

Elaine was the last to enter the room, and the receptionist, Mrs Rafuse, stayed at the door to keep an eye on the entrance. She could answer the main switchboard from anyone's phone.

Tim looked around, counting heads. He turned to Elaine, who also stood in the doorway.

"Is John not coming?" John was the building's caretaker, after a fashion. He could usually be found in the basement, in an old recliner chair next to the ancient boiler, snoozing.

"I gave him the notice. He said he didn't expect it would involve him."

Tim sighed. "As much as anyone, maybe more. James, would you find John and tell him his presence is requested *aysap*, please?"

Everyone could hear as James Olsen, the reporter, trudged to the top of the basement stairs and called down, "John! Mister Brown requests that you appear up here, on the double. Hear me?"

James returned to the room. "He heard me."

"All right, then: let's begin. Most of you know I'm Tim Brown, publisher of this great newspaper. This is Elaine Fong, our crack editor, and

I've invited Valerie Coolen, a business acquaintance, to join us. I'm contemplating some much-needed renovations to this old building, which was designed by my grandfather. He designed my house, too, so I can state from both experiences that architecture was not his strength. Fortunately, we have two presenters here, Amanda and Tyler from Conquerall Construction Services, who have gone high-tech. These folks have some ideas about how we can fix up the place to make it more workable and livable for everyone."

"About time," someone muttered, but Tim didn't try to identify the female speaker.

"Now, just one last thing from me. I wanted each and every one of you to see what Tyler is going to show us now, because I want your opinion and your comments—but not today. Today is for observing, for thinking about it, and talking informally amongst yourselves. Starting next week, I'll set up meetings with each of you to discuss this and anything else that's on your mind about your work here. Now, please welcome Conquerall Services. Enjoy the show!"

Tim leaned against the back wall and congratulated himself on his quick thinking. *That was a brilliant idea to mention those HR interviews. We'll cover both topics at the same time without anyone getting nervous about having a formal interview.*

Amanda, a cheerful and effective speaker, briefly introduced her company and their purpose for being there today, which was to show construction drawings of the present interior and options for improvements. She stepped aside and Tyler turned on his projector. Amanda asked for someone to turn off the overhead lights. All eyes were on the screen.

Using a mouse, Tyler drew red circles around problem areas on the drawing, well-known to most of the audience. Then, with a click, the drawing changed and he marked green circles around the changes.

There were murmurs of approval, though Tim thought he heard someone give a quiet snort.

"You can't put the stairs there," someone said. "Instead of running over our heads in the ladies', you'll be running through the boss's office."

"You're right," Tyler said, "unless we do this." He clicked on a tab that moved the editor's office to the middle of the space.

"Wow!" came from several viewers.

"Wish we could do that with our whole cube farm," one of the staff said. Tyler clicked again, and larger offices appeared in 3D, with glass panels on top of the walls and each with its own door. There were murmurs of approval, until someone said, "Hey, how come there's only four or five offices? Who's getting laid off?"

Tyler turned off his projector, which was heating up the room, and the overhead lights came back on.

"Over to you, Mister Brown," Amanda said.

"Thanks very much, Amanda and Tyler. This looks great. Now listen to me, folks, and listen carefully: no layoffs are indicated by, nor will result from, these renovations, you hear me? None. Zero. I want to put the kibosh on any such rumours. Now: Tyler and I met here only yesterday. Putting together this presentation in such a short time demonstrates the kind of customer service I have come to expect from Conquerall, though this flashy computer thingy is new. However, he didn't have time to con-figure the upstairs, and I didn't want him to spend time on that part until we've heard from all of you. You know what it's like up there now. But imagine if you held his green clicker-thing and could draw walls where you like. I'm not going to give you three choices or anything like that, not at this stage. I want *you* to sketch whatever you're interested in seeing in the space, upstairs or downstairs. There are only so many ways you can do it, so I expect some overlapping. In my dreams, we'll end up with a place that is efficient for work-flow, comfortable for workers, and just plain nice. Any questions?"

"I've got some suggestions already," said one. "Will I give them to you?"

"You're fast. Just draw them out on a letter-size sheet of paper as best you can, or on graph paper, so we can compare them easily. I'll be meet-ing with each of you at a convenient time next week. Thank you all for your attention. Let's thank Amanda and Tyler for this excellent presenta-tion."

Staff applauded quickly and cleared out of the lunchroom. Tyler and Amanda packed up their bulky apparatus and Tim helped them carry the things to their truck.

"That was great, folks, really great. Do you have prints of those sketches for me?"

"Not with me," Tyler said. "I didn't have time. The shop printer can't handle this program, but I can get copies made over at the community college. My teacher does stuff like that to help us get going."

"You're a student there?"

"I was. I graduated from carpentry and then went back for computer courses, so now I'm a kind of a hybrid experiment, I guess."

"And you snatched him up, Amanda? Well done! You're a great presenter, by the way."

"Thanks. It's a nice change. Cleaner work, for sure. Can you come down to our office later this afternoon to pick up your copies? I'll have a ton of things to catch up on as soon as I get back. Corey'll be hollering."

"Tell him I said hi. I'll come down around four."

The uptown bank manager was waiting for Tim on the sidewalk.

"Excellent presentation, Mister Brown. It helped me to visualize what goes into construction costs. I'll be recommending their service to my clients. Everyone wants to save time and money, especially if you're paying interest charges on borrowed money, right?"

"I like what you say, Miz Coolen."

"Valerie, please."

"Valerie. I'm Tim. Gotta run now. I'll be in touch very soon."

Inside, the staff was back at work. Elaine's door was closed. Ed and Harold and James were on the phone. Cindy Martin hadn't arrived. John, the caretaker, had stood outside the room during the presentation, and shifted away as soon as the projector was turned off.

Tim felt a little deflated that nobody seemed interested in talking about the proposed construction, but they did have work to do, as Elaine had reminded him, and they had never been water-cooler chatterers.

He was hungry. He went to the Daisy to pick up two sandwiches from the deli cooler, plus a cup of tea and an apple, and came back to his building and his upstairs retreat.

It is a retreat, isn't it? I bet this room'll be the first to go, once they start tearing out that crazy stairway. No, maybe they'll have to move Elaine's office first, then put in the new stairs, then work their way down the hall, demolishing as they go. Oh, joy.

Tim didn't feel a tingle of joy now, the way he had while Tyler was clicking red spaces to green. He was a little deflated by the slightly contrary noises from some of the staff, and the complete absence of post-presentation praise.

To dispel this cloud of thought, he decided to call Blue Rocks to see if his good friend Mort was available for a Friday afternoon stroll along what they had called the "Camino de Blue Rocks". His phone was in his hand when he remembered that the Everses didn't live there now.

"Oh—!"

He hadn't called or dropped in to visit with Mort or Martha *every* Friday, but often enough that he had come to feel like they had been there forever. He had basked in the warmth from Martha's always-on oven, and her soup of the week. He had walked with Mort, slowly at first while the older man was recovering from surgery, and slowly again when Martha had joined them. He really missed them right now.

Well, I can call them anyway, can't I?

He ran through a few standard excuses first: they'd be busy, maybe they're out, maybe Mort's having a nap. Then he recognized this for what it was: his seemingly-inescapable disposition to hesitate, to second-guess himself, to distrust his own decisions.

Nothing's inescapable, though, is it? If you can see the dragon, you can slay the dragon.

"Begone, dull care, I prithee be gone from me," he sang as he found the Everses' city number in his phone, pressed Send, and waited.

"Hello?" It was Martha, sounding as though she was close to laughter.

"Martha! It's m—!"

"I *knew* it was you! Mort! It's Tim! Oh, Tim, we were just talking about you, and how nice it would be if you would call to say you were coming over to see us. But you're not. Or are you? Are you over at Robert's?"

"No, no, sorry, I wish I was, or that you were here. I just finished a staff meeting, and I have to pick up some documents in an hour or two, so I can't come in to see you today. Can we visit on the phone a little? Do you have time? Tell me how your move went. Are you happy back in your apartment? Can you put me on speakerphone so Mort can hear?"

They had a great visit, talking and sharing stories of little things that had happened since they had last seen each other, one whole week ago. They talked for quite a long time, and nobody seemed in a hurry to end the call. Then Tim heard a beep-beep-beep repeating in his ear.

"Uh-oh, folks, my battery is about to give out. We'd better hang up now, but I'm so glad we had a chance to connect today. I feel so much better than I did. Thanks for reminding me that everyone has their personal issues, Mort, not just me. I'll carry that into my negotiations next week. Hugs and kisses, both. Bye-bye."

He poked his head around Elaine's open door as he was leaving.

"Everything okay here?"

"Yup. Good presentation, Tim. You'll really like the changes."

"Thanks. You say that as though you won't see them. You'll surely be here for the dust and noise phase. The longer you stay, the nicer it will be."

"You better work on that sales pitch. I'm not buying it yet."

Elaine was smiling, Tim was relieved to see.

"Thanks for the advice. I'm leaving now. I have to go down to Conquerall Bank to get the printouts from Tyler."

"They're a bank, too?"

"What? Gosh, no, that's the name of the community, Conquerall Bank. I think it's named for a shoal offshore that's named for a ship that was wrecked on the shoal. I have no idea what I'm talking about. Conquerall Construction Services is downriver, anyway. Would you like me to bring you a copy of the sketches this weekend?"

"Awfully thoughtful of you, but no, thanks. I'm going to stay here today until I catch up on yesterday's work, and that will leave the weekend free to catch up on today. The construction project is outside my contracted duties, except for the inconvenience. Have a nice weekend, Tim."

~

Tim put a cork in the bottle of *La pêche aux compliments* he'd opened to go with his fish and fries. He had bought it because of the label, thinking it meant it would pair well with, or "complement," fish, but it did not. Perhaps the off-taste was a result of his having salted the fries too much, or having taken a bite of fish when it was scorching hot.

He poured a tumbler of ice water to soothe his burnt tongue, and took it to the piano to revisit the English folk song he had been singing earlier today. He and Elaine had tackled it on one of her visits. The tune hadn't appealed to them, but it seemed more meaningful to Tim today, so he sang it between soothing sips.

> Begone dull care, I prithee be gone from me!
> Begone dull care, you and I shall never agree.
> Long time hast thou been tarrying here and feign thou wouldst
>   me kill.
> But in faith, dull care, thou never shalt have thy will.

He was suddenly aware that the work week was over and he was tired. As he put the house to bed, and then himself, he recited aloud how many ways he was tired.

"I'm tired out, played out, burnt out, weary. It's all from doing work-work things, too. Am I ready for this? Wonder what I'll do when Elaine is well and truly gone. I won't have time to get involved in these side projects. Did you hear her, 'working today to catch up with yesterday'? I used to do that, but she's smarter than I am, and Harold has been doing the bookkeeping on the computer, so I wonder what's keeping her so busy."

He thought of Robert, arriving tomorrow. "He said he'd be worn out, all in, knackered, whacked, pooped. We'll make a great pair."

As he drifted off to sleep, he thought, *Today went well, though. Funny how it hit me about the Everses not being here. I'm glad I phoned. It was so good to talk with them. I just feel good around them.*

September 18: Manifold

Saturday

The Atlantic coast of Nova Scotia was enjoying a stretch of warm and sunny end-of-summer weather. Leaves were hinting at their autumn colours, temperatures were cooling, days were noticeably shorter.

"Gorgeous weather!" was a frequent greeting, followed by the frequent response, "We'll pay for this!"

September is smack in the middle of hurricane season, and one tropical depression in the ocean far to the south had just been assigned a name by the hurricane centre. It was days away, and might veer in any direction but, as deer in the woods know instinctively, only the foolish ignore a far-off coyote's howl.

Tim wasn't a close follower of weather forecasts, but he had heard this one. When grocery shopping this morning, he noticed a number of carts piled high with jugs of drinking water and shelves bare of batteries. Those were unreliable predictors of a storm, but good indicators of worry about one.

I guess I'd better do the same, though the Town usually keeps the water running.

He picked up a few extra boxes of crackers, tuna and other canned items, and some juices. If the power was knocked out, his options were limited. He had the hibachis in the woodshed, where he could cook meat as it thawed in the freezer, if the power stayed off long enough to need that. He added two bags of briquettes to the cart.

He decided that he would not do today what Elaine was undoubtedly doing right now: working to catch up.

Work can be caught up, deadlines will be met, but there's no way to catch up on time. I'm going to just put one foot in front of the other today. I won't let myself get down, and I won't try to be "up." When Rob arrives, I'll just be Quiet, Steady Tim. If he's exhausted, he'll appreciate that. If he's buoyant, I'll rise to the occasion without faking it.

After lunch, he carried the bags of charcoal to the cabinet in the wood-shed. He was amazed that there was little sign, other than the neat rows of firewood, that one and a half cords of it had been dumped in his drive-way and neatly stacked. It seemed that Norm had even varied his trips to and from the shed to the pile so as not to imprint a path in the still-green grass.

Why is it that I get this great service from labourers like Buck and Norm, like Corey, like Jake who cuts the grass? They seem to take such pride in their work. Do my staff do that? Do they do their best? Do I hold them back or inspire them? Maybe both or neither, this year. I pop in, stir things up, and then disappear until the dust settles. I do, don't I? I think Mademoiselle was wondering about that when she asked if things would be different with staff if I stayed away. I bet I aggravate Elaine sometimes, thinking up extra projects and dragging her into them.

He sat on the edge of the woodshed to think about this, then said to himself, "Good topic, Tim, but not for today. Empty your head. Go for a walk. Rake the leaves."

He checked the old rake in the tiny tool closet at the end of the wood-shed. Its handle was splintered and a few tines were bent or missing. That inspired a trip to the hardware store, where hurricane-prepared-ness was doing a brisk business.

Tim examined the array of pricey gas-powered generators. He couldn't see himself hauling an apparatus the size of a mini-car into posi-tion, or refilling the tank from a heavy and slippery portable gas tank, or yanking on the starter cord while a storm raged around him—all to pre-serve a few hundred dollars of food in the freezer. He bought a couple battery lanterns, a box of matches, and a new rake.

Back at home, he heard a vehicle roar into the driveway. He hoped it wasn't Robert, given the racket.

Robert shut off his car, ending the noise, got out, took out his bags, and slammed the door.

"What the heck?" Tim said. "What happened? When did that start? Did you hit something?"

"All I know about cars is where to put the gas. That roaring started just as I turned off the highway, thank goodness, or I would've freaked out. As it was, I had to drive all the way through town sounding like a ce-ment truck, with everyone staring at me. Sounds like the muffler fell off, maybe?"

They stood and looked at the car, then at each other, and laughed.

"Look at us, looking at it like we know what we're looking at," Tim giggled. "I haven't a clue, but you cannot drive this noisy thing back to the city." He glanced at his watch. "Here, quick, put your bags in the house and come with me. Let's see if we can find some luck."

In Tim's quiet sedan, they drove to Greene Auto Sales & Service, not far from his house, and pulled up in front of the showroom windows.

"I knew Gar'd be here," he said, and got out. "Come on, Rob, this should be fun."

Garland Greene, the large and loud owner of the auto dealership and mayor of South River, was holding forth inside with a potential customer. To Garland, everyone was a potential customer.

When Tim and Robert appeared, Garland excused himself and strode over. He was holding his huge hand out for a handshake, but when he was within reach, he bear-hugged both men.

"Tim! Rob! What a pleasure to see you guys! Have you finally come in to purchase a fine new car, Rob? Tim got a great deal on his lease in June, didn't you, Tim? You betcha. My goodness, his old car had died years before, he just wouldn't admit it. We couldn't even sell it for rust. What're you lookin' for, Rob? I've got a lot to choose from and it's gettin' near the end of the month, so you know we'll give you the best deal. What colour do you like?"

"We're not shopping, Gar," Tim said when the barrage ended. "Rob just arrived from the city and his car started making an awful roar. I know it's late on a Saturday, and I don't expect you to do anything about it today, but he can't drive it back to the city on Monday. Can you get it towed over here and look at it next week?"

"Hey, nice talking to you folks," Gar called to the other people.

"Be right back," he said to his receptionist as he passed the counter. She glanced at the clock.

"Don't worry," he said, "I won't be ten minutes. C'mon, fellas. Let's go to your house."

Garland Greene got into the back seat of Tim's car and jumped out as soon as they turned into the driveway. He put out his hand for Robert's keys, but changed his mind before getting in.

"You get in, Rob. I'm too old to squeeze myself into that little thing. Pop the hood and then turn it on."

The noise was impressive. Gar shouted for Rob to shut off the engine. He lowered the hood and latched it.

"Your manifold's rusted out. Good thing you didn't drive it far with poison gases leaking into the vehicle. Roll down all your windows and follow us back to the shop."

"Now?"

"You betcha. I wanna make sure you don't try to drive this thing until it's safe. Come on."

Tim led the noisy parade the short distance. Robert pulled in and jumped out of his car as soon as he parked it.

"Clean out whatever you need, and bring me the keys," Garland ordered.

Robert and Tim moved boxes of music scores and other items to Tim's large trunk. When they finished, Gar escorted them to the used-car lot.

"Just look at them, that's all I got time for today. Stick your head inside this one, isn't it pretty? Like new, low mileage, and all-wheel drive, which you absolutely have to have on the highway. I'll put new snow tires on it for you, too. These little SUVs are very popular."

Robert got in and sat behind the wheel. Gar reached in and turned the key, so all the dials on the dashboard flashed to life. He tooted the horn, then shut the car off again.

Robert got out, grinning sheepishly.

"You like it, don'tcha? When're you leaving?" Garland asked.

"Monday morning. Early."

"Hmm. Okay. Rob'll have to take your car, Tim. I'll send a loaner over for you Monday. Okay? Maybe Sunday. Gotta run or my receptionist will quit. That's family for ya. See ya, boys. No worries."

~

That crisis might have derailed both of them. But Gar's ebullience and apparent belief that any dragon could be slain or tamed made him their knight in size large armour, and they were relieved to be rescued.

When the time came, pizza was delivered hot and just the way they liked it. Through the evening, whenever any topic arose with the slightest tint of a complaint, they would imitate Garland Greene by inventing an improbable "solution for that." They found themselves hilarious.

When he read the label on the bottle of Chianti, Robert laughed again.

"Listen to this, Tim: 'The straw basket enclosing this signature shaped bottle is called a flask—that's fiasco in Italian.' What an appropriate wine for today! We're soothing a virtual fiasco with a real one!"

Perhaps it was just their need to laugh, or maybe it was the wine, but the day couldn't have ended much better.

September 19: Positive

Sunday

Even though they'd entered the weekend feeling whipped following yesterday's near-calamity and eleventh-hour rescue, their emotional sun shone brightly this morning. All was well, and all manner of things would be well.

Gloria, their coffee queen, bestowed satisfying beverages upon them, made from a fresh bag of beans Tim had picked up yesterday. He was even motivated to cook Toad in a Hole—buttered slices of bread with the centres cut out, into which he dropped an egg and fried it with breakfast sausages.

"If you quit the newspaper, I bet Evelyn would hire you to make this," Robert said.

"I can't seem to quit. I took the year off and I'm working anyway. I'll be working from the grave. I was sure my mother was still lurking there for years after she died. I could've used her help sometimes."

"Would she be a help to you now?"

"Oh, my goodness, no. Things would've turned out so differently if she were still with us, and not for the better, I think, not meaning to speak ill of the dead. She'd still only be sixty or so now, like Aunt Stella, so she'd be quite capable of doing battle with anyone, most of all me. You know, I think sometimes it's better to miss a person than to actually have them around."

"That's a good outlook, actually."

Tim insisted that Robert drive the sedan to church for practice, as it was arguably twice the size of the damaged vehicle and he would need to get used to it. Robert adjusted the driver's seat, the steering-wheel, the rear-view mirror, the side mirrors, and the driver's seat again. He navigated around corners as though towing a long load, but there was little traffic in the way. They arrived safely at the church without any yelps from Tim, though he had to hold them in.

Aside from singing his part, Tim didn't find the service held his attention this morning. To ward off his penchant for drifting to thoughts about work or whatever was his current quest, he turned to the back of his hymnary and read the Listing of First Lines, trying to recall the tunes of each. This was the mental equivalent of lightly tossing a ball and catching it; when it stops, nothing is gained. Time wasn't wasted, but had passed, a kind of meditation.

After church, they didn't go to the Daisy Café, though the concept of brunch appealed to them as they got close to home.

"Does someone else serve brunch around here?" Robert asked. "There are dozens of brunch places in the city."

"More hipsters there. Let's try the Oak Island Inn."

Robert twirled the wheel expertly now, and drove them to Western Shore for brunch in the inn's spectacular dining room overlooking the waters of Mahone Bay. Robert's mimosa and Tim's Bloody Mary made the meal seem festive, too.

As he paid the bill, Tim suggested they drive out along the Mahone Bay side of the Aspotogan Peninsula, and back on the St. Margaret's Bay side. Robert said he'd go, but Tim would have to drive. Tim said to never mind, because Robert would just doze off, mimosa or no.

So they returned home, and took their sleepy selves to the sun room sofa (Robert) and the den recliner (Tim) for blissful snoozes. As well-fed people like to say, they didn't expect to be hungry ever again.

Later, Tim went out to retrieve a few papers from his car while Robert rearranged the boxes of music scores in the trunk so they wouldn't slide around.

A small red SUV turned into the driveway and pulled up next to Tim's car. The driver got out, handed Tim the keys, and said, "Gar Greene says to bring this over to the shop first thing tomorrow morning to sign the papers."

"Sign? We're—I'm not buying this."

"Insurance or something? I don't know anything about it. He just asked me to do him a favour. He said it's not a regular loaner."

Another car pulled across the driveway and the driver gently tooted the horn.

"Just see Gar. Early. Gotta run."

"This is the one you sat in yesterday, isn't it, Rob?" Robert had come out to see what was up. "Looks kinda nifty. Maybe you should buy it?"

"Oh, I hope there's no need for that, is there? I'm working as hard as I can to keep ahead of expenses, not to take on new ones. As it is, I'll have to pay for fixing that manifold."

"Manifold? You remembered the name of a car part? That's a first."

"I noticed the word because—in the old Confession of Sins, remember?—we asked for forgiveness 'for manifold sins which we from time to time have committed' and so on. So when he said it was the manifold gone wrong, it seemed appropriate somehow. The cost of repairs will be a sin, I know that."

"Your memory is magnetic. Do we still confess our sins? I can't recall when that last happened."

"You wouldn't, Timo. You don't sin."

They locked the racy-looking loaner and went back into the house. Amazingly, suppertime was approaching.

"I have ingredients for dinner," Tim said, "but I don't think I have room for a full meal. I can heat up some excellent chicken soup. Would that suffice?"

Robert agreed, and made croutons to float in the bowls. They opened a chilled bottle of an Australian Fumé Blanc called *Mother Julian,* another of Tim's wide-ranging explorations of vineyards.

He read the label: "'This 14th century English nun, having survived a serious illness, devoted her life to an attitude of optimism. She is the patron of solitary women, writers, solitude, and cats.' She sounds like a nice girl."

"I like her," Robert said. "Friday morning, remember, you invoked brave but sad Blanche de la Force resolutely going to the guillotine. After multiple battles, we're ending the weekend inspired by a gentle cat-lady with a positive attitude. I'll have more of whatever she's having, please."

September 20: Inside job

Monday

Robert was happy to commute in Tim's car. He asked for permission to take his coffee and toast in the "dining car", and was gone before the sun was up.

Moments later, Tim drove the loaner over to the dealership. He was aware that being on the receiving end of Garland's favours was to be well looked after, and he made certain he would not miss out on Robert's behalf this morning.

The town's mayor always spent the first hour of his workday at his business, greeting customers as they brought their vehicles in for servicing. Garland Greene had perfected the art of doing small or timely favours for his customers, which is why his dealership was the largest in the area, and also why he had been acclaimed as mayor of South River at each election since being elected the first time. A happy customer was very likely to buy another car from him, or vote for him again, or both. Both opportunities came around every four years or so.

As Tim expected, Garland was already in his showroom, extolling the features of a shiny new truck to someone. His sales staff would come in later, to Gar's annoyance, after this early showroom traffic had diminished.

Gar asked the service clerk to pass some papers to Tim for his signature, then Tim's phone rang. Immediately, he feared Robert might be having trouble on the highway, so he quickly answered without looking to see who was calling.

"Are you all right?"

"Hello, Mister Brown? Something's wrong down here."

"What? Who is this? What's—?"

"It's Jean. We're locked out." Jean Naugler was one of the newspaper's clerical staff.

"What do you mean, locked out? You don't have your key, or—?"

"No, we're forbidden to enter. There's a sign on the door that says 'Entrance Forbidden'. There's a bunch of us here. Should we go in anyway, or —?"

"Is Miss Fong there?"

"Yes, she's here. Her phone's not working. Can you come now, please? We're not sure if we should go in or what."

"I'll be right there." He disconnected abruptly, but she'd understand.

"Where do I sign?" he asked the service clerk, who was checking in another customer. "I'm sorry, but I have an emergency. Can I just sign and run?"

She pointed him to the sticky arrows on the forms. He scribbled his name in or near the spaces, and went quickly to the exit.

"Wait, you need copies," the clerk called.

Tim said, "Back later!" and sped away in the quick little red car.

Calm down, now. Maybe the door lock is just stuck. All I need is a ticket for speeding and a long drawn-out conversation with a policeman about why I don't have papers for this car.

He pulled up in front of the Johnson Building, home of *The Times*. Jean Naugler and Elaine Fong were standing at the door. Ed Garamond had joined them, and John, the caretaker, was slowly coming down the street, apparently not yet aware that anything was amiss.

The small crowd parted to allow Tim to see the sign taped to the door. A bold, red X was printed on it from corner to corner. In the centre was a black border around the red words

ENTRANCE FORBIDDEN BY ORDER THE FIRE MARSHALL

Below that was a scrawled signature and a date that he couldn't make out through the glass.

Tim looked at his employees and they looked back at him.

"Any idea who put this here?" he asked. "Or when?"

No idea.

"Anyone smell smoke?"

No smoke.

Tim took out his key and easily unlocked the door.

"Wait here, please," he said.

He quickly walked through the building, sniffing, looking for any sign of danger. He bounded up the stairs to the previously-declared-unsafe second floor. Everything was in place: no smoke, no sign of burglary.

He went back to the front door and held it open for the staff. More had arrived.

"Come in. There's no danger." He pulled the sign off the door.

"Should you do that?" one asked.

"I'll take responsibility. This is possibly intended for the door to the second floor. I've never seen it before. I don't know why it's here or why now. Nothing has changed."

Staff filed in, chatting excitedly. John wasn't among them. Jean said he was next door at the Daisy. Tim thanked her for phoning him, and went out to move the loaner car to the parking lot. Then he came back in, went into Elaine's office and closed the door.

"Good morning," he said.

"Good morning."

"That was a different way to begin the week."

"It was."

"Your phone's not working?"

"As luck would have it, no, it isn't. I'm glad Jean had hers. I'll run across to the kiosk in the mall today. They should be able to fix it or replace it pretty quickly. I dropped it yesterday. It seemed okay but it wouldn't turn on this morning."

"Who put that sign in the door, I wonder?"

"Not me."

"I know that, Elaine. Is something wrong? You don't seem yourself this morning."

"I suppose you could say that. I'm just...it has nothing to do with work. Just ignore me, please."

"Okay. If there's anything I can do, please ask, all right?"

"Thank you."

Tim left her office and gently closed the door. He picked up the sign, went upstairs to his room, and flopped in his chair.

What the heck was that all about? The sign on the door. Elaine in a funk. Dropping her phone wouldn't do that to her; it must be something else. I hope it's not another breakup. Where did that sign come from? When did it come in, and who brought it? Who stuck it on the door?

He steepled his fingers and looked out the irregular window. These were too many questions for one head: he needed to employ his trusted delving resource: sheets of flip chart paper.

He jumped up, pulled out a sheet from the cupboard, and taped it to the wall next to the ones he had put there several days ago.

He wrote ENTRANCE FORBIDDEN at the top, and WHO WHAT WHERE WHEN WHY HOW quickly down the left side of the new sheet.

He began with HOW.

"It was taped to the inside of the door, that's the HOW. The door was locked, so whoever put it there had a key, *ergo* was an employee. That's the WHO."

I must have improved my delving skills over the months. This is going more smoothly than most.

WHERE was Inside, that was obvious, but he changed it to WHERE FROM? to mean where did the poster come from.

WHEN was puzzling: it had to have been on the weekend, but nobody who was in the office had called him about it. He circled the word.

That left WHY.

He felt a pang of hunger. He hadn't had breakfast. Then he remembered that he was driving Gar's vehicle, still without papers. He locked the door to his room and went downstairs.

"Did you find out who put up the sign, Mister Brown?" Mrs Rafuse asked. "Was it a prank?"

"Haven't a clue. Someone who was in on the weekend might know. I need to run an errand. I'll check later."

He drove back to Greene Auto more slowly than he had left.

I'd like to poll the staff about who was in yesterday, and who left last, though the door is kept locked at all times whenever the receptionist isn't in, so who would know who was last? Will they be offended if I ask? I'm not accusing anyone of anything.

He got out of the loaner car and went inside. Garland had gone to dispense his wisdom at Town Hall. The service clerk found his paperwork under the counter.

"How's the other car doing?" Tim asked, "or should I ask?"

"I doubt if they've even looked at it yet," the clerk said. "Mondays are booked solid. We'll call you after they get to it. Maybe tomorrow? Just drive this one carefully, please. It's not really a loaner. Mister Greene took it off the sales lot, that's why we didn't have the papers done."

The clerk followed him out to the red car and hung a dealer license plate from the back hatch latch. "There: now you're legal. Better check the tank. We don't put much gas in them until they're sold."

~

Tim stopped at a gas station for half a tank of fuel. A burger joint was nearby, so he drove the tidy little SUV around the tight corners to the drive-thru window and received a bag with a meal deal inside.

He wanted to put this fake Fire Marshall issue to rest today, if at all possible.

I'll make my tea in the lunchroom. I might pick up some intelligence while the kettle boils. Staff will be talking about the kerfuffle. I bet the sign is fake, anyway. For sure the Fire Marshall didn't drop in late Sunday afternoon to update his inspection and then stick that sign in the front door without anyone knowing. Someone would've had to let him in, and they'd call me. Dollars to donuts, it was a prank. But why? Should I ask Mrs Rafuse to ask everyone if they came in yesterday and what time they left until we find who left last? Would that prove that was the person who put the sign in the door? No, but...

He parked, took the fragrant bag of food upstairs, then came down to plug in the kettle for tea.

A few employees were eating and talking. Nobody paid attention to him. He didn't want to interrupt them; that would seem like an announcement.

He strolled out to the desks. Ed Garamond was sitting at his easel. Tim took a deep breath and walked over. He didn't want a repeat of their disturbing encounter last Monday, but he felt he shouldn't be afraid to speak to his favourite employee.

"Hey, Ed, before you get settled there, I was wondering if you heard anything about the sign in the door this morning? I'm not accusing you, I hope that goes without saying."

"Hey, boss. Nope, I haven't a clue, sorry. Do you have the sign? I'd like to take a look at it."

That was a relief, Ed being his old friendly self.

"Be right back."

Tim dashed up the stairs, returning quickly with the sign. He handed it to Ed.

Then, in response to cries of "Kettle!", he hurried to the lunchroom.

"Sorry, sorry," he said, quickly unplugging the steaming kettle. He sloshed it around. There wasn't enough water left to make a cup of tea, so he filled and plugged it in again.

"You know the rule, Mister Brown: never leave the kettle unattended."

"I do know that. Tell you what: can someone buy one of those smart kettles that shut off when the water is hot? Please? Just give the receipt to Harold."

That was the ice-breaker he felt was necessary. Now he could ask them his questions. None were in the office yesterday. One had dropped in on Saturday "to use the washroom, sorry."

"Better to use it than not use it. I'm not pointing any fingers, you understand. I just wonder how the sign came to be taped on the door."

Ed Garamond appeared at the lunchroom door, and handed the poster to Tim. "It's real," he said. "We don't have that kind of paper here. The date, as far as I can make out, is six-nine of ninety-seven, which is either the ninth of June or the sixth of September two years ago."

"Was it that long ago when the Marshall did his inspection? That's when he told me we couldn't use the upstairs for meetings or whatever he said, until the fire escape was upgraded. Well, you know we're working on that now. So, this is old, not a new ruling. That's good news. But, who stuck it up? Was somebody pulling a prank?"

No one had any answers. Tim thanked them, made his tea and went upstairs to eat his lunch.

~

On the flip-chart sheet, he wrote Fire Marshall on the WHERE FROM? line.

Another question done.

He was surprised how the time was flying, in spite of the early start. What happened to his plans for today?

My plans weren't planned, that's what happened. I proudly wouldn't allow myself to think about work all weekend, so I was caught flat-footed when this little emergency came up. Boy, it sure did seem urgent for a while. Just shows you what a misunderstanding can do, but how were the staff to know?

He thought about Elaine, how withdrawn she had seemed this morning. He didn't want to be bothering her all the busy workday, but he was concerned, so he locked up and went to her door. She beckoned him in.

"Any clues?" she asked.

"One, thanks to Ed. It's a real sign from the Fire Marshall, issued in September of ninety-seven."

"Was it caught in a time warp since then? Or had he been back to renew it?"

"I hadn't thought of a time warp: good one. But if the Marshall had come back, he wouldn't have wandered in on a Sunday afternoon. I still think it's a prank. Anyway, I have it on good authority that our new window-ladders are adequate protection, so I'm not worried. Are you aware of anyone working late yesterday?"

"No. Wasn't me. If I hear any rumours, I'll call you." She held up her mobile phone. "On my new phone."

"That fast?"

"Yup. The screen was cooked, but they were able to transfer the data and download the—"

"Bow-wow-wow, Miz Tech-Talk. I think what you're saying is that you're up and running again, and for that, I'm happy. I'm going home now. I'm going to restart this week tomorrow, and get some things achieved, do you hear me? *Achieved!*"

He uttered that last word as a sneeze, and Elaine said, "Gesundheit!"

They laughed, and Tim left.

Now Elaine's back to normal. Ed, too. He wasn't bouncy, but at least he wasn't chilly. My goodness, people are challenging creatures.

That evening, while Tim was out tending his supper on the hibachi, he missed Elaine's phone call, but she left an interesting message: "You might ask John if he was in yesterday to sleep in his nest beside the boiler. He did that all day today."

He spent the evening puzzling and devising.

September 21: Schedule

Tuesday

Tim arose with no lack of energy. His eyes were tired from having stayed up late working, but he was energized by the plan he had struck last night, and by how well he expected it to work. A few details were yet to be sorted out because they involved other people, but he would be able to cross them off the To Do list first thing this morning.

He drove his notes and foolscap sheets and his positive attitude downtown. In his room, he happily copied the schedule he had devised onto another manila sheet. He took it downstairs and displayed it on a flip chart board next to the reception counter.

Not unexpectedly, Elaine was first to arrive. She was surprised to see Tim inside already.

"Another false alarm?" she asked. "Or a true alarm? I guess, as a journalist, I should ask *was* there an alarm and, if so, what kind was it, and do you have proof?"

"Good catch, Madam Editor. No alarm today. Remember Mademoiselle gave us that envelope and recommended that we interview every one of our employees? Well, we're doing it this week, by golly. Here's the signup sheet. I'm going to stand right here and capture every delightful employee as she or he arrives this very morning."

"I see. Well, good luck with that. Today's a deadline day for me."

"But of course. We'll start interviews tomorrow, out of deference to your work schedule. We're merely a dozen or so souls anyway, and the interviews will be very, very short, so we'll fit them all into two days, I assure you."

"I am assured. Carry on."

"But *with* you, Miss Fong. You don't want to be a 'lame duck', remember?"

"Maybe I do. Can I have a look at the times you're offering there? See? I can't do it then, or then. Got your marker?"

She crossed out the earliest and latest times on Tim's schedule.

"That's fine," Tim said. "I do prefer to start and end my workday on my own terms, doing my own things. Like right now."

He enjoyed greeting the employees as they arrived for work. He explained the reason for the chart, and invited each to pick a time.

"Is this about those drawings for the renovations?" some asked.

"Are we going to get raises?" more than one asked, and two added, "Am I in trouble?"

All clerical staff had arrived by eight-thirty, and had chosen their times. Ed Garamond listened and wrote his name in a Wednesday space without comment. Harold Awalt waited while Tim explained the project, then said he'd like to check his task list on his computer, and would come to sign up later.

Tim noticed that Harold had one of the new portable laptop computers slung over his shoulder.

Why does Harold need to work at home? Why can't he get his work done during the regular day? I'm going to learn a lot in these interviews.

James Olsen didn't keep regular hours, but since today was deadline day, he was expected in by noon, either to file a story or to run out and get one if Elaine found an empty space that advertising couldn't fill. Cindy Martin, the ad sales rep, would likely come in today. He'd call her if not. John, the caretaker, hadn't materialized.

He made a list of the yet-to-arrives, and asked Mrs Rafuse, the receptionist, to ring his cellphone when any of them came in, and to please not let them leave until they had seen him or filled in a spot.

Where he would conduct these interviews was a question that had come to him several times, but Tim had pushed it away because he didn't have a good answer. In Elaine's office would be ideal, but maybe not so much for her. Not having another room with a door that closed was a problem that renovations would fix, but that wouldn't help right now.

One solution would to be to go offsite, but that would involve travel time. He toyed with asking Evelyn if he could reserve the "private booth" in the Daisy, but it was still a public place, maybe not private enough. It wouldn't be good if a customer ignored the "Reserved" sign and sat in the booth anyway.

Upstairs would definitely be private, though he remembered that staff said they could hear him talking to himself up there last winter. He had found and covered an old pipe hole where sound had leaked through. They wouldn't be talking loudly in these interviews, anyway.

Upstairs, one at a time, plus him and Elaine: would three be in violation of the fire code? If Elaine moved up there solo, though, that would be permitted.

He went down to the main floor. Everything was running smoothly. No voices sounded stressed, nobody was looking for something that couldn't be found. He tiptoed to Elaine's door, which was slightly ajar, and tapped on it.

"Mmm?" she said, without looking up. "I know it's you, Tim. Nobody else acts like they're scared of me. Plus, I heard you coming down the stairs."

"You think I'm scared of you? Sure I am, ha-ha. I know who wields the real power around here. May I ask you just one question about the interviews?"

"Oh, please do. Otherwise, you know, quack-quack."

"Come on, now, that's not...you're not lame, ha-ha. Listen: would you like to move your centre of operation to my room upstairs for the interview days? We are sadly lacking in rooms with doors, other than the washrooms and this office, and I think we should offer as much privacy as we can for everyone's interview."

"Upstairs? No phone, no hookup for my computer?"

"There are plugs."

"Those are electrical outlets, Mister Neanderthal. Computers need access to a—never mind. Upstairs doesn't have a computer port because you declined to have it installed. When your renos are done, you'll have them everywhere. Hold the interviews here. I'll send Olsen on an out-of-town assignment and use his desk if I need to. I'll be in here with you most of the time, anyway."

~

Tim spent the rest of the day working on his revised, handwritten questionnaire. He was very pleased with it. He had made what he considered slight alterations to the strictly HR form he had been instructed to adhere to, but he thought it made sense to tick all the boxes at one time.

He wished he could keep the interview topics confidential until they were all done, just so any discussion wouldn't get swirling around before everyone had their moment. But the very word "confidential" often caused troubles.

If I say, "Be sure to tell the others," they'll forget to do it. If I say, "Please don't say a word," everyone will hear right away.

He made copies of the renovation designs he had picked up late Friday. He had forgotten to do this yesterday, but nobody had asked for them. He put one set on the table in the lunchroom and one on the easel with his interview schedule.

Every name had been crossed off the list and assigned a time except for John, the caretaker; Cindy Martin; and Harold. Tim asked Mrs Rafuse if she would kindly find or phone the first two. Harold was in plain sight, so Tim walked over to his cubicle.

"Did you forget about choosing an interview time, Harold?"

"Huh? Oh, yeah, what's that about, again?"

Tim patiently explained: questions about the renovations, and a few other questions about the workplace and work experience.

"Oh, right. No, thanks, I don't...I don't think I need to do that."

"Don't you? That wasn't the question, Harold. I'm *advising* you that I want to have a brief conversation with you about work, plus your comments and-or advice about the renovations, if any. In your case, for example, you might offer some comments about installing computer cables for work stations."

Tim knew he was hauling words out of thin air, but hoped he was close enough to make sense. Out of respect for Harold, he tried to keep his voice low in the open office.

"It's not really a big deal, but if you ref—decline to attend, it *will* be. I can't make it any plainer than that. The schedule is still over there. Please go now and sign up."

Tim left without saying more, and went back upstairs to tidy his room in case Elaine decided to use it after all. He taped blank sheets over his worksheets.

I hope this works. She can easily see my work, but I'm not going to tape every inch. All my records are right there in the cabinet. She won't look at them, they mean nothing to her, but still...oh, get over yourself, Tim. Elaine knows everything already. All these sheets would do is show how I work out some problems, and I showed her that in May. She can look if she wants. Trust her.

Of anyone he had ever worked with, Elaine was by far the most trustworthy.

She's a real trained professional. I'm just an amateur at this game. Sure, I've been at it since I was twelve, delivering papers, but what does that indicate? That The Times *is being run by an experienced paperboy? I'd better call it quits for the day. I'm starting to pull the tapestry down again, aren't I? Well, stop it, me. I've got two good days of Meet The Staff coming up, and I'm looking forward to it.*

On his way out of the building, he passed Elaine, who had come to rest in the middle of the office, where she was ready in case something came in before the need for it became apparent. He laid an envelope marked FOR WEDNESDAY on her desk, then walked past the flip chart by the door. Harold's and John's names were still not marked on it.

Water finds its own level, he mused on his drive home in the peppy little red car. *That's what Mother used to say. People create their own fortune in life, is what I think she meant. It's what I mean, anyway. I don't want to cause anyone to lose their job by my misunderstanding of the situation, but I sure as heck don't need to pay someone to be unreliable. Harold has been really valuable, and I'd hate to lose him, but it's not out of the question. John has never been reliable. Oddly, that makes it harder to dismiss him, since I've tolerated his shenanigans for so long.*

~

He concocted a beef stir-fry for supper, and selected a bottom-shelf red wine to accompany it. It was a little too bottom-shelf for his taste, so he poured the remainder in ice cube trays and put them to freeze for future recipes.

For the remainder of the evening, he rehearsed tomorrow's interviews using his hybrid HR/Renovations questionnaire:

The Times *Employee Engagement Survey*

with (employee name/date)

---

1. *How do you feel about your day-to-day work?*

   ____

2. *Do you feel pride in your work?*

   ____

3. *Do you find enjoyment in your co-workers?*

   ____

4. *Are your benefits and pay satisfactory?*

   ____

5. *Would you recommend this company to your friends for employment?*

   ____

6. *How do you feel about the upcoming interior renovations?*

   ____

7. *Anything else you'd like to discuss (set another time)?*

   ____

He had struggled with the word "feel" in the question about renovations, but he had deleted an HR question containing that word, so he thought he would bridge the gap by using it three times.

September 22: Feelings

Wednesday

The interviews were to begin at ten-thirty. They would do three back-to-back, take a one-hour break, then do three more. Tim had allowed thirty minutes for each, not the recommended twenty, to give time for coming and going and niceties.

He hoped these would be relaxed conversations. He expected they would be an endorsement of the company and its policies, as he had always sensed. Those endorsements would now be on the record, and he didn't want to rush away from that.

He arrived in the office at ten to unlock the door upstairs just in case Elaine changed her mind about moving up to it. She hadn't arrived yet, which was unusual but not concerning. He unlocked her office door, turned on the lights, and arranged the chairs. He would sit behind the desk, the employee would sit opposite him with his or her back to the door, and Elaine would sit to the side, where, he thought, she could also keep an eye on the office through the window, if she wanted to.

He would record the salient points of each interview. Elaine would observe.

At least, he hoped she would. He was wondering if he should phone her when she arrived, looking like something the proverbial cat had dragged in. She went straight to the washroom, and when she emerged, she went into her office and closed the door.

Tim stood outside, uncertain what to do. He hovered beside the sign-up sheet, trying to look unconcerned.

In a few moments, she opened her door, and attempted a wan smile. "You can come in."

"What's up?" Tim said, closing the door behind him. "Are you ill?"

"Does it show? I'm sorry I'm late. Something didn't agree with me, I guess. Oh my. It's over now, I think. How do I look?"

Her colour was returning.

"It's against company policy to comment on a fellow employee's appearance...but you are looking better. Can I get you something? Water? Coffee? Alka-seltzer?"

"I'll get it. Open the door." She looked at her watch. "I'll be right in as soon as I give instructions to Mrs Rafuse."

They began at ten-thirty sharp. Tim was surprised that he felt nervous as he introduced the questionnaire to his first subject, Sharon, a file clerk. She had been Tim's last hire before Elaine had arrived.

"Good morning, Sharon, and thank you for coming. Please don't be nervous." He saw that her hands were shaking and her cheeks were flushed. "We're asking everybody the same questions today and tomorrow, to get a snapshot of our company, what's good and what's not, and what we can improve. Please relax and just speak freely, okay?"

Sharon nodded, but her eyes were on the questionnaire in front of Tim.

"Here goes, then. Question Number one—"

Poor Sharon's responses were positive, but monosyllabic: Good. Sure. Yes. Yes. Yes. Good. No.

The HR material advised against suggesting responses if an employee had difficulty coming up with any. At this moment, Tim couldn't think of any prompts.

He looked at Elaine. "Anything further, Miss Fong?"

"No, nothing from me. Thank you, Sharon, you've been very helpful. You may go now."

Elaine stood and opened the door for the relieved employee. She closed the door again and sat. "One down," she said to Tim, who was wearing a perplexed look.

"Are they all going to go like this?" he asked. "She's usually quite friendly. What made her so nervous?"

"Probably the closed room syndrome."

"I hadn't heard of that. What is it?"

"I just made it up, but I bet it's a thing. A junior employee sitting alone in a formal setting with not one but two superiors: could be pretty intimidating. Let's keep on; if the rest of them are like that, clerical staff at least, we can revisit. If they were in a group they'd all talk at once."

"And you said you don't know anything about human resources. Can I announce that you are our new Head of HR? Will you sit in this chair and read the questions?"

"No. I'm going to check for messages now. Leave the door open. I'll be back at eleven."

Next was Jean Naugler. She had worked for the paper for years, and didn't appear at all intimidated by the closed room.

"Good morning, Miss Fong and Mister Brown. You know, I always meant to tell you how much I like the way we—most of the time—address each other formally like that. It's respectful, and glory knows there's little enough of that these days. So, how can I help you?"

Her responses to the questions were the same as Sharon's, in essence, but she used more words. When it came to Question Four about benefits and pay, she spoke thoughtfully.

"Are they satisfactory? Is anyone ever really satisfied with their wages? I mean, after taxes and the other deductions we have, there's not a whole lot left, not for us in the 'pool', anyway. The folks who work 'out front' likely make more, and they're able to earn more on top of their base. I know Cindy does. I'm not pointing fingers at all, I think she's sweet, but I'm just using her as a f'rinstance. I work as hard as anyone, and I do my job well. If there's any extra money lying around that you're not using for other things, like renovations, it'd sure be satisfactory to see it in my paycheque. Is that fair?"

She caught Tim off-guard, and he laughed. "It certainly is fair, and I appreciate your candour—and the good work you do for us. We have five minutes left, if you have more observations to share?"

"No, I...well...I would just say...you are very trusting, Mister Brown, and we all really appreciate it."

"Thank you."

"But you should take a good look at everyone, especially those who like to speak on your behalf. I guess these interviews will show you some things, but I don't know if you'll see. Some people bear watching, is all I'm saying."

"Any names?"

"Not at this time, no."

"All right. I'll respect that. Thank you for the heads-up, Mrs Naugler. I'll take your advice. Our time's up now, but you know we're approachable anytime."

They had no time to confer about Jean's oblique warning because Mrs Rafuse, the receptionist, was at the door. She handed her headset to Jean so she could take over the reception desk for the next half-hour.

Rachael Rafuse was born to the role of receptionist. She was welcoming, hospitable, and kept things simple, if a little too simple sometimes. Tim had observed that she could read the room, any room, at a glance.

"Gosh, folks, I don't think I've ever sat down with you like this before. I know you and I haven't, Miss Fong, but did we ever, Mister Brown? Maybe when you hired me. Anyway, how can I help?"

Her responses were thoughtfully expressed, and matched the yeses and nos of the previous two. She reminded Tim that her last pay raise was more than two years previous, and while her rate of pay was steady, considering the current rate of inflation, her buying power had eroded by nearly five percent.

"Has it been that long? That's not intentional, I assure you. I should've —but that's for another discussion. Duly noted, Mrs Rafuse, and I do appreciate that you've done the math for us. We'll be talking."

"No two exactly alike," Tim said after Elaine had closed the door again. "I wonder if we'll be able to bunch them into categories when we're through."

"No matter how varied people are, you can always draw a circle around some according to one criterion or another. It's been interesting. Now, Mister Brown, shall you vamoose my office for the next hour, please? See you at one o'clock."

Tim took the envelope of questionnaires to the café. All booths were full and the place was noisy, so he brought a coffee and muffin back to his upstairs lair to review how the morning had gone.

I can't judge the project yet, but I'm glad we did those three interviews together to begin with. I would have given up if too much time had gone by after poor, frightened Sharon. But Mademoiselle said to do everyone, to leave no one out. I'm beginning to see the wisdom in that now. I suspect we'll have tougher nuts to crack as we proceed.

He finished the bran muffin and slice of cheddar, drained the coffee, and went for a walk around the bridges, one loop. Inside again, he used the washroom, which required him to pass through the lunchroom.

"Is everyone making suggestions about how to renovate this crazy setup?" he said to the staff. They were eating lunch or doing crosswords or knitting.

"We were talking about our interviews," Jean Naugler said. "I hope that's okay; you didn't say we couldn't."

"Talk all you like. I enjoyed them."

"Me, too," Sharon said shyly. "I was some nervous, though."

~

The afternoon sessions got underway at one o'clock sharp, with Helen, one of the "hybrid" employees who did typesetting, now called word processing, and produced copy for advertisements. She was quick at selecting fonts and arrangements of text for Ed Garamond's artwork, and they seemed to work well together.

Helen's job satisfaction was quite high, because of the variety of her work and the challenges. But she wouldn't turn down a raise in pay, she said. She was being paid at the typist rate, not the art designer rate.

"I hadn't thought of that. Thank you very much for pointing that out. We will talk specifics another time."

"Sooner rather than later, I hope. And I hope it's you I'll be talking with…you know."

"Who else would it be?"

"Oh, I just mean…not another employee, unless, oh, never mind. It's fine."

"No one outside of this room will review your salary with you. It's confidential. You can share your information with anyone you like, though we prefer you don't, because people tend to compare without knowing all the circumstances. Well, I think that does it for now. Thanks very much for your candid answers."

In the intervening five minutes, Elaine said, "That was an interesting comment, about hoping she'd be discussing her pay rate with you."

"I don't think she meant to snub you—"

"Not what I was thinking."

"She was just being nice to me, wasn't she?"

"Could be. Or she might have been hinting that someone else *has* been discussing pay with her. Let's keep going. This could be interesting."

James Olsen was next. He was always interesting. He had been a very green rookie reporter with a camera when Tim went on sabbatical but, in his early delving projects, Tim had bumped into situations suitable for James to write up for the paper. James had learned a lot from Tim, and seemed to have grown up a lot in the year.

The allotted time was passing quickly, and the men were happily reviewing past stories, when Elaine reached for the paper in front of Tim.

"If you don't mind, I'll take this interview," she said, not waiting for Tim's response.

"James, we have to ask all our employees these questions in just a few minutes, no long discussion needed. First one: How do you feel about…?"

James zipped through his answers. Sure, everyone was nice, though he wasn't in the office much. Sure, he'd recommend the company to his friends as long as they weren't reporters, because he didn't want the competition, ha-ha.

In response to the question about pay, he said, "Why's everyone talking about pay all of a sudden? What's the big deal?"

Before he could retract or cover that comment, Elaine said, "How does that make you feel?"

"I dunno. A little bit squeezed, I guess. I mean, I'd like a raise, who wouldn't, but I'd rather come to you and ask, or you come to me and offer, you know? I don't think we need a...anyway, yeah, things are great. When Stacy and I buy our house, I'll talk to you then. Oh, yeah, the reno plans look great. I'd like to do a photo-story, tracking our renovations along with that computer-aided design they're using. Pretty smart. I think we're the first to use it in this area."

James left and closed the door. Elaine handed over the sheet with her notes on it.

"You can talk good-buddy talk anytime and with anyone," she said, "but not during these interviews, got it?"

"I'm sorry. Thanks for rescuing me. You did a great job. Care to carry on?"

"No, you can. I'll speak up if I need to. Who's next?"

Tim went out to look at the sign-up board. Nobody's name was in this block. Tim went to the reception desk.

"Any luck reaching Cindy Martin or John?"

"Miss Martin said she'll try to get in tomorrow. I haven't seen John since he came in."

"Is he downstairs?"

"I don't know, sir."

"But you told him about these interviews?"

"I did."

Tim took a few steps toward the basement door and hesitated. He returned to Elaine's office.

"We don't have a third this afternoon. We're done. Evidently John can't be bothered, and Miss Martin said she'd, quote, try to get in tomorrow, end quote."

"I see. Perhaps today was the easy day. Well, I can use the time, and I won't predict tomorrow. Good project, though, Tim—I mean, Mister Brown. I've learned some things today."

"Me, too, though I'm not sure what. It's like pieces of a jigsaw puzzle without a picture as a guide: it doesn't look like a basket of kittens, but it might be an old windmill. Say, are we singing tonight? It's Wednesday."

"Oh, gosh, Tim, I can't, sorry. I really missed it last week, but—"

"I missed you, too. Since you didn't come to sing with me, I tried a piano piece that should come with a health warning on the cover. Nearly wrecked me!"

"Well, be good to yourself. I enjoy our Wednesdays, and I hope to join you next week. I just have a...an errand that I wasn't able to make this morning because—"

"Say no more, Elaine. Have a good evening. We'll climb another hill tomorrow. Choir practice is tomorrow at seven, if you'd prefer the real thing."

~

He took something out of the freezer to thaw for supper, and then dialed Conquerall Services. The call went to the recording.

"Hello Amanda, it's Tim Brown. I should have some design comments for you by the end of the week—no, the beginning of next week. I'm sure Monday morning's as good as Friday afternoon to you. I wonder if you would ask that smart young Tyler to include wiring for electrical heating throughout. We have a big ol' boiler in the dungeon now, and we have to keep it running all summer just to provide hot water for the washrooms and lunchroom sink. The heat has always been spotty in winter, hot in the middle, cold in the corners. Any questions, you know how to reach me. Have a good day."

There, John. Your boiler will be gone, and that means you can take your recliner chair home. With the money I save on oil and salary, I can hire a cleaner to come in a few evenings a week and probably cover the electricity, too. I've been loyal to you, for what? For you to play me like a fool. That game's over.

He needed a jacket for a late afternoon stroll around his little estate. More leaves had fallen on the flagstone walkway, but it was still very therapeutic to stroll and sip from a glass of *Trompe-moi 2 fois.*

As he walked, he thought about today's interviews. *Odd that James and Helen both hinted that they'd been talking about their pay with someone else, as though I would know about it. Maybe it's just talk, but it'll be interesting to see if anyone else brings that up tomorrow. These interviews are good for exposing things like that.*

He weeded the vegetable gardens a little bit; Mrs Aquino would be there tomorrow morning and he didn't want to start his day with her scoldings in his ears.

Mrs A would be a tough HR manager. She'd be good, though. She knows what needs to be done, and I know what she wants. Simple.

He clipped a few herbs.

Elaine's good, too. James barely hinted at talking about salary with someone else, but she didn't ask 'Who?' She knew he wouldn't have told her. Too direct. Instead, she asked him how that made him feel, *and he talked. Maybe we've all learned something today.*

After supper, Tim checked the humidifiers in the piano first, and then played a whole hour of music he knew well, for his own pleasure, and to remind himself that he was good at some things.

September 23: Fall

Thursday

It was raining steadily. At the back door, Tim watched for Mrs A to arrive in the driveway, and went out to help her get her tools inside.

"Wow, it's really coming down! I forgot to check the weather forecast. Is this the hurricane they were talking about?"

"This just rain. Hurricane later."

"Oh, swell. I guess we don't need to go out to the gardens now, but I was wondering...should we have a final harvest soon? What about frost?"

"I come, we do later. After the storm."

"Okay, sure. Pick all you want..." She was already on the stairs.

He left for downtown.

It seemed especially warm and welcoming in the diner as he shook off his umbrella in the entry. "Come in, handsome stranger," Evelyn called from halfway back. "I'll give ya shelter from the storm."

Her slightly ribald greetings had made him feel welcome for years, in spite of the lousy coffee. Now that she had added a very drinkable dark roast, the diner was nearly perfect.

He opened his copy of yesterday's *The Times* and sipped as he browsed.

"You're not in it," Evelyn said, delivering scrambled eggs and toast.

"The two best days in a person's life are when he's in the newspaper, and when he's not. Those can also be the two worst days. How're you, Ev?"

"Run off my size nines, Timmy. My punishment for success."

"But you have two-day weekends now."

"I love it. Storm comin', so I can snuggle in, too. Gotta run, hon. Later."

It's true. Success exacts a price. I was given everything I have. All I have to do is maintain it, so my story is different from Ev's. But still, if I'm AWOL for too long, I risk losing it all. Cheery thought.

Cindy Martin was their first interview of the morning. Tim introduced the reason for the short meeting.

"Oh, gosh, is this what this is? That's not what I heard."

"What was your expectation?" Elaine asked smoothly.

"I thought this was to sign up—no, no I didn't, sorry, I'm confused. I'm thinking of something else, obviously. Silly me. So, you have questions? I'm ready. Shoot."

Tim had to interrupt Cindy's enthusiastic responses in order to get through all the questions in the time allotted. She loved her work, loved her clients—"most of them, anyway ha-ha"—didn't see a lot of most employees because she wasn't in the office much, but they'd all had a great time on Labour Day.

"It was raining then, too, so we had to run for shelter in my leaky old barn. We really had fun. Too bad neither of you could make it," she said. "People were asking about you. I think they were a little disappointed that you weren't there, but that just means you're popular, right?"

Tim and Elaine exchanged glances.

"We didn't go," Elaine said, smiling, "because you advised us not to. Remember?"

"Did I? You sure? That doesn't sound right. We planned it, like I said we would, but we were hoping you'd come. Oh, about remuneration? My contract's okay, thank you very much, but I have an idea about how we could make more sales. I know you sell the paper in Liverpool, but what if you dedicated a two-page spread for Queen's County? Sort of like a separate newspaper within the paper. I could sell a lot more ads for that than I do now."

"That's very interesting." Tim put down his pencil. "We're out of time for now, Miss Martin, but we'll definitely schedule another meeting to discuss your great idea. Thank you for coming."

"Who's next?" he asked Elaine when Cindy was gone. "Do we have a moment?"

Elaine went out to check the flip chart. Ed Garamond was next on the list, and he was walking toward the office now.

"Go right in, Ed," she said, by way of alerting Tim that this was not the moment to debrief after Cindy's interview.

Ed had worked for *The Times* for over fifteen years. He signed on when Tim was still scrambling to take charge of the paper after his mother's demise, so early details were lost to Tim in that fog. But he did remember that Ed was confident and competent right from the get-go, and he had always been grateful to him for that.

Tim hadn't planned to, but Ed extended his hand and Tim took it in a friendly shake. Tim knew what it meant: Ed's grumpy response to Tim's ribbing was water under the bridge.

As they sat down, Elaine reached over to take the questionnaire and pencil from Tim. "My turn, remember?" she said, and he didn't argue.

"Mister Garamond, we're asking all employees the same short list of questions, just to get a snapshot of the company's people at this moment in time. If there are particular issues arising, we'll certainly be willing to schedule another time to address them. So, question number one: would you recommend this company to your friends for employment?"

"Sure. A better pension plan and better benefits would be good, a competitive advantage, but I hear that someone's working on that."

"Who is your designated contact for that?"

"Oh...nobody. Just a rumour. Could be wrong. I try not to listen to office talk. Anyway, as far as work is concerned, nobody gets in my way, and that's not the case everywhere."

"Care to elaborate?"

"No, not right now, unless that's what this meeting is about. I'd want more than twenty minutes, though."

"Fair enough. Next, how about your day-to-day work? Do you feel enjoyment in it?"

"I'm a graphic artist, paid for doing graphic arts, which I enjoy, with a lot of cut and paste, which I don't so much. But I've been permitted to freelance, on my own time, so I get to do bigger, more creative pieces, which I appreciate very much. I haven't been able to squeeze in much of that lately, since Cindy has been pumping out the advertising contracts. Maybe we can talk later about shifting more of my routine stuff to Helen, since rumour has it you're looking at making some changes."

"How do you feel about changes?" Tim jumped in. "Any concerns in particular?"

"I'd rather not say at this point. It's just rumour, as I say, and rumours make me cranky."

"When I'm acting as an investigator," Tim said, "rumours make me happy, as they often contain good nuggets. To be clear, I have not heard any rumours of the kind that you're hinting at. But I'm hearing *about* rumours, which is different. I hope you know, Ed, if major changes were coming down the pipe, or even minor ones, I'd tell you and ask for your input first, as I've always done, right?"

"The renovations presentation came as a bit of a surprise."

"To me, too. I asked the carpenter to come in to give me an idea of what would be involved to get safe access to the upstairs, and he brought the young computer tech with him, which was a surprise. They were eager to show how quickly the computer could show plans and calculate options. I asked them to set it up quickly so all the staff would know what might be done—to get ahead of rumours. Will you be giving us your comments?"

"Next week, sure. Perhaps you didn't know that I was on a career path to architecture back in the day. I found graphic arts a lot glitzier, and switched. I paid my way through art school with it. I had my eye on big city magazines, but I got tangled up with a South Shore gal, and here I am. We like it here, the kids don't want to move away from their friends, but there's precious little glitz. Wouldn't be much architecture for me here either, so it's all right."

"I didn't know about the architecture, Ed. I sincerely hope you can look at our printouts from both of your professional perspectives. I know you'll indicate where the Art Director's studio should be in heavy black marker, right?"

Ed looked around the office they were in. "I think this one would do, ha-ha."

"Everything's on the table, Ed. Get your oar in. I'd appreciate it. We hope to do this only once."

"We need to finish now, gentlemen," Elaine said.

This time, Ed shook her hand, and Tim's again, and left.

"Can you stall whoever's next?" Elaine asked Tim, looking at her watch. "I need to make a call."

Tim went to the schedule: Melody Meisner was next. She was standing by the reception desk, chatting with Mrs Rafuse.

"Am I late? I'm ready when you are. Mister Brown. Will I come in now?"

"We're just getting a breath of fresh air, Mrs Meisner. We'll start as soon as Miss Fong comes back."

Tim was grateful that Melody Meisner had written both her names on the chart. He recognized all his employees, of course, and always remembered at least one of their names, but not always the right one when he needed it. He used to call the receptionist by her first name, but mostly got it wrong, so he switched to her surname. He was pleased that staff liked him using surnames; it seemed to show respect, putting everyone at the same rank.

Elaine returned and nodded to Tim that he could take the lead on this one.

Melody's responses were similar to others', expressed carefully. She wasn't shy or shaking, but she wasn't going to step outside wherever she perceived the line was, either. Tim wondered if he should ask her if she'd heard any rumours, but couldn't think of how to slip it in, so he let it pass. They thanked her for her help, and the session ended.

Tim had brought a muffin and cheese from the Daisy for lunch. He went to the lunchroom to make tea. The employees were watching him, and grinning.

"Is my shirt on backwards?" he asked, and then realized: he was using the brand-new kettle.

"Hey, thanks, whoever went to get this. It's the same as mine at home, that's why I didn't notice at first." The old kettle was on the countertop. "Does anyone know anyone who needs or wants that?"

"I do," Jean Naugler said.

"Good. Please give it to them with our best wishes, Mrs Naugler."

Upstairs, Tim stared out the window and thought about the first two interviews. *Cindy and Ed both hinted about rumours. As Mister Seek, I learned that rumours are investigation gold, and so are hints. What lies beneath these mumblings? Maybe Harold will spill the beans. He's been erratic lately. I hope the Harold that shows up is prepared to make sense.*

He really wanted some fresh air before they were sequestered again. It was drizzling, so he put on his jacket, took the umbrella and walked across the bridge to the nearby shopping mall, where he strode past the brightly-lit stores a few times. It felt good to get his pulse rate up from exercise rather than from being nervous or startled.

The final three interviews began with two women who begged permission to be interviewed together.

"Well, we—" Tim began, but Elaine interrupted him.

"Let's give it a try. Come in, please."

She gave the usual intro, and then asked them why they wanted to be interviewed together.

"We're sisters, I don't know if you knew that, Mister Brown? We have different last names, because I married, but my sister didn't. I was her reference when you were considering hiring her; maybe you remember that. We always talk about everything, anyway, so we'd know what the other one said to you before supper was on the table, right?"

The sisters nodded to each other and smiled.

Elaine proceeded with the questions, this time in the order Tim had written them. It was clear that the married one was her sister's spokesperson, but she looked for her sister's confirming nod after she had given each response. They were quite charming, and neither of the interrogators minded this departure from the rules.

Perhaps the real reason the single sister wanted her married sister in the room with her was that it seemed she didn't have a very well-described job. She had been hired to help old GB in his final years, and had kept on working with his system until Harold took over and began digitizing the records. She quickly learned how to operate the scanner, and said she had done "a pretty big bunch" for Harold. She had not learned how to operate a computer.

"Really? Neither have I. The way things are going, we'll both have to learn. Maybe we'll go to classes together this winter, ha-ha."

Both women "didn't mind" where they worked. They didn't have any opinions about the renovations. They were relieved when the questions were over.

The married sister asked, "So, does this replace the other meeting, Miss?"

"Yes, it does," Elaine said firmly. "It's cancelled. If there's anything you were going to say there, you can say it to us and we'll take care of it."

"Well...we just don't want to take sides, you know?" Her sister nodded. "You treat us really well, and we don't see why we should put up a wall between us, that's all. Maybe I shouldn't have said anything."

"It won't leave this room, I assure you," Tim said. "And I agree with you. There won't be any wall between us, unless the carpenters build one, so don't worry about that."

After the sisters were gone, Tim said, "I bet the younger sister didn't finish school, and that's why her big sister is looking out for her. If so, we should see if we can get her on the high school equivalency path. She's quick to catch on to things. By the way, what was that about a meeting?"

"I haven't the foggiest," Elaine replied. "But I thought it was a good opportunity to shut it down, whatever it is. Something's behind those hints."

They finished early, thanks to the two-fer combination. Neither John nor Harold had signed in for an interview, but Harold was in the office, peering into his desktop computer's screen.

"Let's forget interviewing John," Tim said.

He explained to Elaine what he planned: to give John notice of layoff sometime in November, once they had a reliable construction schedule. He would give him several months' pay in consideration of the number of years he had been employed with *The Times*. His unemployment benefits would kick in after that. He'd be paid to sleep for a year, but he would have to do it at home.

"We can live without hot water for hand-washing for a few weeks. We even have a new electric kettle now that can fill the sink for washing coffee mugs. I'm not going into another winter with that old boiler and John's shenanigans. Whatever I asked him to do was never in his job description, according to him, but it was hard to pin down what *was* in it. We can hire an office cleaner to clean, and for certain we can call Conquerall anytime we need light or heavy carpentry. No boiler, no need to pay him to sleep in the cellar."

"Your call. Speaking of which, let me make a call. I'm trying to make an appointment. Come back in fifteen."

When two o'clock rolled around, Harold walked smartly to the office and said, brightly, "Is it me, now?"

"Yes, Mister Awalt," Elaine said, "though you didn't sign the sign-up sheet like everyone else. Come in, please. Mister Brown will be conducting your interview."

"Okay. What's with the formalities?"

"Several people observed that they enjoy being addressed by their surnames, but we haven't been doing that across the board, so I'm making an effort to do it now."

Tim began at the top of the questionnaire. He didn't know if Harold was going to be evasive. He wanted to be sure not to say anything that could later be construed to have caused unfair advantages or disadvantages.

However, Harold asked if they could come back to the first "feelings" question after he had heard the others, "just for context".

"That's fair. Number two, then: do you feel pride in your work?"

"Isn't that the same as the first one? If you don't mind, can I see your question-sheet so I know the context?"

Tim looked at Elaine, who raised her eyebrows slightly and nodded slightly. Tim turned the page toward Harold, who leaned forward to scan the list.

"Okay, I see where you're going with these. You want us to respond in the affirmative to each one, so you can say you have proof that we're all happy with our positions."

Elaine spoke quickly as Tim was opening his mouth to refute this allegation. "Is that how you feel about these questions, Mister Awalt? That we're building a case of some kind? Can you share more about that?"

"Sure. It's obvious. If I said I *don't* like my day-to-day work, you wouldn't like that. You'd want to give me the boot, right? If I say I don't feel pride, same. Same for getting along with co-workers. I understand them very well, that's what they tell me. Our pay—that needs to be negotiated bigtime. Benefits—what benefits? This company is the same as all the others where there's no union: all the power is in the hands of management, and the workers can like it or lump it."

He pushed the sheet back to Tim. "As for interior design, I need twice as much space as I occupy now, for my IT and payroll work. The Archives are still shrinking, but slowly. I do that work when I have time."

"Is anyone assisting you with archiving, Mister Awalt?"

"Nope. I have to come in on weekends to sort out where we are and what's next, and review what little the clerk got done during the week. She's slow."

"And the payroll? It's all automated now, isn't it? I suppose that's at risk in the computers this New Year's, too?"

"Sure is. But I'm looking out for that, like I told you."

Tim nodded. "It'll sure be interesting. I suppose I don't have to remind *you*, though I will, to print off a complete and up-to-date payroll statement on December thirtieth. We can always write the cheques by hand if need be."

"Sure, but the banks mightn't be able to process them if they're hit by the bug, too."

"Good point. Then remind me to issue the final pay of 1999 in plenty of time for staff to deposit or cash cheques or whatever they want to do with them."

"Sure. Is that all for now?"

"Just one more question, Harold," Elaine said. "When is your next meeting?"

"What meeting? For this, you mean?"

"No, not for this, and not with us. With staff."

"I don't know what you mean. If there's been staff meetings, you haven't included me. That's not right."

Tim leaned forward. "Is someone trying to organize a union here, Harold?"

"It's not a crime."

"If anyone wants to investigate a union, you are correct: that is not a crime. If someone on staff is agitating other staff, in secret, that is of concern to me. I'm not suggesting that *you* are doing that, but I believe somebody is, and I *will* find out who. If our staff want to join a union, after they understand all costs and benefits, I'd be happy to support them, for the record, in principle. If someone is making my staff feel insecure, or is trying to insert himself or herself *between* them and management, I will deal swiftly with them, as labour law permits. If you know who it is, I will be grateful if you let us know asap."

Harold did not respond.

"Thank you, Mister Awalt," Elaine said. She stood and opened the door. "That'll be all for now."

"That went sideways quickly," she said, after gently closing the door behind Harold. "Are you convinced that he is behind these random rumours?"

"Convinced enough to risk putting my own rumour out there. Let me ask you: would you have hired Harold if he had presented himself at the interview with the attitude he brought in here today?"

"Unlikely. Or I might have done, hoping he was just trying to show me his competence. People change all the time."

"You haven't, Elaine, except to become even more excellent. You relaxed and warmed up as you became familiar with this place. I know it's tough, accepting responsibilities for a new enterprise every year or so."

"Hmm. I didn't see my name on the sign-up-sheet, so I'll decline to participate in this discussion at this time. You might trap me into saying I like it here."

"But you *do*, ha-ha. I must say, Harold's got nerve, though. This has been a slice, Miss Fong. I am *trés* grateful for your participation. We're good at 'good cop, bad cop', aren't we?"

"Yes, we *were*, but I'm glad it's done. I assume you will write up your notes and follow up with Mademoiselle?"

"That's my plan, starting tomorrow. Tonight, I shall sing in the angelic choir. Robert started us on a lovely Christmas piece last week. There's still time to join..."

"Have a good evening, Tim."

~

On the way home, Tim remembered that there was a car repair still outstanding on his To Do list. He continued past his house to Greene Motors.

"Mister Greene called you this morning," the service clerk said. "He was standing right here when he did it. You weren't there so he left a message."

"What'd he say?"

"He said the repair estimate was here. Would you like to see it?"

Poor Gar. Maybe this guy's temporary. If he isn't, he should be.

Tim took the multi-page work order and drove home. He listened to the message, in which Garland Greene basically said that Robert's car was toast.

"Burnt toast, Tim. We can't let him drive it with just a patch, and the cost of fixing all the things that are wrong with it would exceed the value of the vehicle. There's a bunch of outstanding recalls on it, too. I guess he hasn't taken it in for proper servicing anywhere in a very long time. Are you guys twins? Your old car was rotten, too. Let me know what you want to do. Have a good day."

Tim peeked at the total on the final page of the estimate. He didn't know how much money Robert might earn from his concerts next year, but he thought it would be a shame if he had to use it all to pay for these repairs.

Supper was warming in the oven when Robert arrived.

"Mm. What's for supper? It smells good."

"We're having things that smell good. Pickings were slim, but I found two kinds of leftovers in the freezer, so it's pot luck. Your choice."

Robert wanted to go to the church early for a short rehearsal with the four section leads. The choir would pick up their lines much more quickly if the person with the strong voice singing near them had it right.

Tim went with him. If he stayed home for that hour, he feared he might get distracted and forget where he was supposed to be until choir was half over.

It was a busy rehearsal. They sang through Sunday's hymns, rehearsed a familiar anthem from last season, and read through new anthems they'd sing this season. And Robert distributed a new Christmas carol.

"Our concert," he said, "should your concert committee agree to present one, will be a mere ten weeks from now. We will not be singing old chestnuts."

Some choristers said, "Aww."

"Well, maybe a few. But," he continued, "we will tell the Christmas story through a series of carols from countries around the world, and I mean 'around', not just from Europe."

Some choristers said, "Ohh."

"And," Robert finished, raising his eyes to the heavens, "we will sing them in their original languages. Yes, in only ten weeks. Take out your copies of 'Riu, Riu, Chiu' and let's air out your Spanish."

Robert's rehearsals never dragged. They pulled the choir along, especially if they liked the piece from the get-go. He played the new Spanish piece through at concert speed, then they read it through with clapping, as the sheet music slipped off several laps.

Of course, hands went up to ask for help with pronunciation, but the most delightful surprise for the basses was that the piece began with them singing in unison, and that the first three words were imitation birdsong.

"Birdsong counts as a foreign language, doesn't it?" asked an alto.

"Indeed it does," Robert said. "That's why we can't let it slow down. Birds don't drawl."

It wasn't Christmas in the parking lot outside. Several choristers had been greeting each other with "Happy Fall" or "Happy Autumnal Equinox", as that celestial line had been reached today. The air was unusually warm and the humidity was as high as it had been in mid-summer.

Something powerful was pushing tropical air north towards Nova Scotia. It was still a hurricane, predicted to make landfall somewhere along the coast Saturday night.

"What if, Rob?" Tim asked as they relaxed with their usual tipple. "It seems like we'll have a goodish storm, no matter what. I hope you can get here before it hits on Saturday, or maybe don't come at all. We'll manage without you in church, if they don't cancel. Now, to take your mind off that, I have news for you."

Tim showed Robert the estimate from Greene Auto, and played Gar's phone message. Robert was glum.

"I hate to spend that much money on it."

"I agree. I don't think Gar wants you to. Shall I ask him to prepare a quote on that little roadster I've been driving, with a generous trade-in allowance for your old car, har-har?"

"I guess so. Do you like it?"

"It's fun. I never drove a red car before. I'll see what Gar can do. But I'm glad you've got my car at least until this storm has passed. I feel better knowing you're in a heavy vehicle on the highway."

September 24: Personnel

Friday

The early-morning television weather forecast was equal parts ominous and uncertain. Hurricane Felix had already scrubbed and flooded its way through the Caribbean and was roaming up the Atlantic seaboard of the United States. Forecast models on television looked like coloured spaghetti, as there was considerable uncertainty about which way this giant predator would go.

One strand of spaghetti ran all along the coast of Nova Scotia, and right through South River.

The best news was that Felix had already begun losing strength as it roared into the cooler water of the North Atlantic, but "losing" was a relative term. Communities along the coast knew well what destruction heavy rains, higher-than-high tides, and screaming winds could cause.

"Maybe you should stay here and wait it out," Tim said to Robert.

"I can't. I've got a load of teaching today and tomorrow morning. I don't want to be on the highway in a storm, but where I'll be when I need shelter remains to be seen. I'll call you tomorrow. We'll know better by then."

"Okay. Be safe. Don't take any chances."

"Same to you. You won't be flooded here at the top of the hill, but you might blow away."

The morning air was moist, but calm. The recent rain had come from a different system, not the hurricane. The effects of Felix would show up tomorrow.

Tim decided to drive the short distance to Greene Auto. He knew he'd catch Garland in the showroom, but he might not want to take a call at the moment.

"What's the verdict?" Gar shouted to Tim as he came through the door. "Sweet little vehicle, isn't it? Will he want to lease it, like you did?"

"I don't think a lease'll work. He commutes a lot, and the miles might add up too quickly. He'll take it, though; no sense in pretending he won't. He'll come in late Saturday afternoon to deal with the paperwork, if you're going to be here. If he can get here."

"Good! Good decision! I don't know what's going to happen with this storm. I hate to close early, but if the town's emergency services are called out, I'll have to be Mayor Greene, so let's play it by ear. I'll try to get the paperwork ready, though. Did you bring back that repair estimate?"

Tim handed it to Garland, who ripped it in half.

"We don't need that now. We'll tow his old car to the auction. Did you clear it out? Better do that now. Nice doing business with you again, Tim. Stay off the roads in bad weather. We'll be watching the river and streams and don't want to have to come up there because a tree fell on ya."

Garland handed Tim a garbage bag and went to greet another customer who had come in for service.

Tim filled the bag with Robert's papers and books. He took it home and put it in the foyer closet for Robert to deal with.

"Now, Gloria, my queen, fortify me with your elixir. I have some big thinking to do this morning."

On Wednesday, Elaine suggested that he might be able to group staff members together according to shared criteria. He studied the questionnaires now to refresh his memory of the conversations, hoping those circles would become evident.

It's funny how quickly one forgets, even the conversations that were mostly monosyllabic. Good thing it was a short questionnaire. Let's see: easy questions first. The renovations are generally okay with everyone. I'll ask for their sketches next week so I can tell Conquerall what to do.

"No, I won't. I'll collect the sketches and ask Ed to look them over, *then* we'll discuss them, *then* we'll go to Conquerall. Ed will know what's what."

He marked that down on a sheet of foolscap he entitled OUTCOMES.

Now, that leads me to Ed's workload, which is increasing, and he's not getting time to freelance. His skills are excellent. I wouldn't want to lose him to a poster shop. He suggested that he'd like Helen to take on more of the nitty-gritty work, so let's see how that works.

He made notes.

I've only looked at two people and already there's work to do, and then follow-up work. Is this what I'm supposed to be doing? Someone should, but it's obvious that nobody has been looking into workloads for quite some time, except when some issue bubbles up.

"This calls for coffee and toast," he said to the empty kitchen. "It's plain I hardly know what I'm doing. I've been running the place on smiles and calling staff by their surnames, sometimes. That doesn't impress everyone. Harold, for instance: I might've nominated him to take over personnel duties a week ago, but not now."

He scraped the last of the jam out of the jar, and jotted a note on his grocery list to get more.

So here's a question: which was the real Harold—the nice, smart, compliant fellow, or the irregular, hostile, noncompliant one? And why does he change? I don't know the answer, but there must be one.

Jean Naugler came to his mind as a potential personnel supervisor. She was kind, her previous personal hard times made her empathetic, and her work was impeccable. Would her workload allow time for personnel issues? Whether large, like salary adjustments, or small, like sick leave, or negotiating with their health benefits broker, all such issues had landed on Tim's desk, and he had always bumbled through. Elaine had addressed these with undoubtedly more professionalism this year, but she wouldn't have had the intention of following up next year.

Jean could be the conduit, at least, not to create distance, but to remind me of who needs what. This is another good thought to write down.

He continued through the interview notes. Some were self-contained, but others had hinted at comments made by somebody else, topics they assumed that Tim or Elaine were aware of. He wondered where this was coming from.

But they all relate: they work together in our important enterprise. We've never had departments, per se, just people with tasks. Should this change? That's a good question for Miss Stephanie.

A thought began in Tim's right hand, and eventually reached his conscious brain: he needed to sketch these thoughts out on a large sheet of manila paper. He needed room to write random thoughts in random spaces. Then he could draw those important circles and lines that would lead to clear thoughts and good decisions.

He drove the red SUV downtown. The office was humming along as usual. Some heads that had been down and working lifted up to smile at him as he walked in.

Mrs Rafuse stopped him at the reception desk and showed him a basket of sketches: staff had photocopied the renovation printouts and recorded their suggestions and interests.

"Wonderful! I'll leave these right here for now, but don't let me go home without them."

He went up to his room and pulled off the blank sheets he had taped over the worksheets. He considered the one dealing with the misbegotten Fire Marshall's poster from two years ago.

I don't think I need to bother with this. John did it, didn't he? He probably found it in the cellar somewhere and decided to tape it up, with no thought about the consequences. I don't think he's capable of skulduggery.

The other sheets were more pertinent to the personnel review, which, it seemed, he was now conducting. With all the vertical and horizontal lines covering two sheets, he had the feeling this was going to take awhile. He sat to think.

Tomorrow's going to be stormy, no matter where Felix decides to blow ashore. I should get groceries today so I can batten the hatches and stay out of harm's way, as the mayor advised. If I do that, then I'd better...

He stood and carefully peeled the two sheets off the wall, rolled them tightly, and taped them closed. Before he left the second floor, he checked the windows in the other rooms to make sure they were fastened (one wasn't). There was nothing he could do if there were leaks, though there had been remarkably few over the years.

Downstairs again, he wished the staff good luck during the storm, and asked them to let him know if they ran into difficulties. He said he preferred that nobody come into the office if it was storming.

Ed Garamond beckoned him over to his cubicle, and handed him a cardboard tube with plastic caps on both ends.

"Is this any use to you, boss? That manila paper turns to mush if it gets wet."

"This is great, Ed, thanks! Say, Mrs Rafuse has a bunch of reno drawings over there on the counter, from the staff. I haven't had a chance to look at them, and what's in this tube will keep me busy all weekend. If you had the time to cast your experienced eye over them first, I'd be grateful. In fact, let me get them now."

Tim strode over and returned with the papers.

Ed flipped through them with interest. "I'll take them home and see what happens. Being shut up in a small apartment with teenagers who feel it's my fault they can't hang out in the mall, I will welcome distractions."

"So, there may be some advantages to my being childless? Good to know. Thanks again."

At Elaine's door, Tim said, "Thought you'd like to know that I am inventing a Personnel Department with a staff of twelve. I may revise that, upon consideration. Everything all right with you?"

"Yes. None of it has to do with your grandiose plans. I have made the executive decision to go short by four pages this issue. I heard you telling staff not to come in on the weekend, and I agree, though I remind you that that is my announcement to make, and I had already made it. Ed's working on the advertisements, which we can't omit unless I want to dock my pay, but I think we banked enough columns of print that we can fill the space around the ads without heroics. Agree?"

"Do I *agree* with you? All I heard was angels singing hallelujah. I do apologize for overstepping my bounds. I'm happy you won't be coming in, though. It's scary in this old place in a real storm. Stay home or... wherever you're comfy. Take care."

At the front door, he turned around and went back to Elaine's office.

"By the way, our interviews were very valuable. I'm going to call Miss Stephanie to come and meet with us—" Elaine's shoulders drooped "—and then *she* can take over the file. I don't know where else to go from here. Though you hide it well, you seem slightly reluctant, so we'll let the pro do it. Her suggestion of the questionnaires was a good one. I trust her."

"I don't think I've heard the word 'slightly' used in this context, but yes, yes, yes, call her. I'm glad I'm a journalist sojourner. I can't imagine the quicksand if one were to step in as temporary head of HR."

~

Tim whistled the Spanish carol the choir had begun to learn last evening. Robert had said it was based on a birdsong, so he warbled the notes; not easy, but fun to try.

He was glad he had chosen to shop today. The stores were busy, and supplies of some items, such as toilet paper, were notably quite low. He wondered what he would eat if the power was off for an extended period. Items to be cooked could go on the hibachi, and he had already got charcoal for that. He could retrieve things out of the freezer as they thawed, and then live on canned tuna and bread. Or, as was often the case in previous storms, he could just drive a few miles to where the power lines were still up and humming, and eat there.

~

He thought he should do something with the assorted bits of outdoor furniture in the backyard beneath the trees. They weren't valuable, but they shouldn't be flying around. He stowed them in the spaces underneath the woodshed and the sunroom. The loaded woodshed wasn't going anywhere. It might be difficult to ignite briquettes for the hibachi, but he wouldn't attempt to barbecue while the storm was blowing anyway. It could be nice afterwards, though.

Tim had nothing to fear. He had a strong feeling of *que sera, sera*, and wasn't going to look for reasons why "whatever will be" shouldn't be benign. He had interesting work to do on the weekend, supplies were stowed where he could find them in the dark, and fish and chips were over-baking in the oven. He was ready.

A bottle of white wine called The Mythic Kraken accompanied the dried-out takeout. The label displayed an image of a jolly, rollicking sea monster. Tonight, he thought of inshore fishing boats and ships at sea, fleeing from or turning to face the approaching weather monster, and he toasted to their good luck and good health. He knew that *que sera* meant different things in different situations.

Robert phoned. "I just don't know. They say it's heading up the Bay of Fundy or maybe even over New Brunswick, so maybe we'll just get a windy day here. What do you think?"

"I think I don't forecast hurricanes, Rob. Pretty sure it'll be over by Monday when you'd be driving back to the city, but I don't know about the time between. Decide tomorrow? Call me. I'll be home all day."

September 25: Felix

Saturday

Tim turned the radio on when the alarm went off to hear the latest about Hurricane Felix. Much destruction had already happened along the eastern seaboard of the United States. Even far inland, rivers had flooded, and where there weren't rivers, streets and roads and rivulets ran like rivers, there was so much rain.

"That is definitely not good," he said to himself as he looked out the bathroom window. The morning was dawning much as yesterday had ended. Felix was hours to the south yet. The system, reportedly very wide, was still aiming for the Bay of Fundy, but could wobble east or west. It would dump a lot of weather on South River, whichever way it went.

Immediately following this information, the station played "I Wanna Bop With You, Baby, All Night Long." Tim hit the Off button and went downstairs.

"Nothing we can do about it, Gloria, so let's eat, drink and be merry. I'll have a double espresso to start, please."

He unrolled the papers from the cardboard tube. *That was nice of Ed to give me this. He's a good man. I enjoyed our brief chat on Thursday. Like old times.*

He wondered where to hang the sheets. There seemed to be something in the way on every wall. He settled on using both sides of the swinging door between the kitchen and parlour.

These papers were based on the expanded payroll report he had obtained three weeks ago. Employee names ran down the left-hand side, and he had written the familiar Five Ws across the top, with lines between each, horizontally and vertically, to make a large grid. He had wondered at the time what he hoped to gain from this, but now he had a lot of answers—if these were the right questions.

Perhaps I see things more easily in grids rather than the circles Elaine mentioned. Let's see where this gets me while the winds blow high.

He laid out the staff questionnaires to match the order in which their names appeared on the grid, while singing snatches from a novelty song from the sixties:

> Let the wind blow high, Let the wind blow low
> Through the streets, in my kilt I'll go
> All the lassies say hello
> Donald, where's your troosers?

Mid-morning, Tim took a break from this heavy analysis—which hadn't really got anywhere yet—to try his hand at making cinnamon rolls. He had loved the ones Martha Evers had frequently sent home with him after a visit. He thought fondly of her kitchen in the little rental cottage in Blue Rocks, and the aroma of her baking.

He found the rolls remarkably easy to make. They were ready to put in the oven almost as soon as it had reached baking temperature. He put the baking sheet in, set the timer, wiped his hands on his apron, and picked up the phone.

"Hey, Martha, it's Tim. Guess what I'm doing?"

"Tim, so nice to hear from you. What are you doing, dear?"

"I'm waiting for my batch of cinnamon rolls to bake, whaddya think of that? I was thinking about you as I was working this morning, so I decided to make some rolls."

"You're a clever man, Tim. Did you remember not to handle the dough any more than you absolutely have to?"

"Of course. My mother haunts these cupboards, you know. Whenever I take out a cake pan or baking sheet, she comes out along with it and tells me what I'm doing wrong."

"Well, I'll tell you you're doing everything right, my dear. You're so thoughtful to call. Mort is over at the college right now, the silly old man. I told him I wanted to lay eyes on him by noon sharp. It's going to be a nasty storm and I don't want trees falling on him. Will you be all right down there?"

"I expect so, Martha. The forecasters tend to think the storm will go west, away from you, so it will be someone else's concern. I'm a bit concerned about Robert, though. He teaches until noon on Saturdays, but he'd be heading toward the storm if he drives down then. If it's bad, or the power's off tomorrow, church will be cancelled anyway."

"It's such a worry, isn't it? Tim, do you mind giving me Robert's phone number? If he's stuck in the city, maybe he'd come over here rather than ride out the storm alone. Do you think he would?"

"That's a nice thought. Rob's like Mort: oblivious to the world around him when he's focused on something. He spends as little time as possible in his bed-sit, and might just hunker down in a practice room some-where until the lights go out. Here's his number: do give him a ring."

The timer bell rang.

"Hear that? That's my rolls. Hang on—oh my goodness, Martha, I wish you could see these. They're perfect!"

"I'd love to taste them. Save me one? I made a batch myself yesterday, so I'll offer some to Robert, if he comes."

"He should be so lucky. Well, I won't keep you now. Say hi to Mort for me. Chat later."

Tim smiled. *Who could have predicted that the Everses would be Robert's neighbours? I hope he will make contact with them, and maybe visit them once in a while. It would do them all good.*

The storm was beginning to make its presence known with shots of rain on the windows and sudden gusts of wind. Tim served himself an Americano and more than two cinnamon rolls before returning to the payroll and interviews task. It was peaceful and quite homey inside the house. He thought that everyone should have the aromas of coffee and cinnamon in their surroundings when a storm was approaching.

Another gust reminded him that the power might go off. The weather was relatively warm now, but he might want to add a wood fire to his comforts later. He quickly put on a windbreaker and dashed out the back door to the woodshed, now filled to the rafters with neatly-stacked fire-wood and, he noticed, a few bundles of kindling.

He dashed back into the house with two armloads of wood and a bundle of the kindling and shut the door. He was panting. Running with arms full of wood wasn't easy.

But I did it. I'm not sure I could have done that a year ago. The only ex-ercise I did for years was sitting or pacing at work. Going for intermittent walks must have done me some good.

He placed the wood in the woodbox beside the fireplace. He brought some papers and put them at the ready, along with the box of matches he had bought last week. He towelled his hair dry, put on a sweater, and re-turned to his work and his treats.

~

Tim had been so engrossed in the virtual picture that was emerging on both sides of the kitchen door that when the phone rang and he walked over to answer it, he was surprised at the storm strength outside.

"Guess where I am?" It was Robert.

"Not here, and not on the side of the road somewhere, I hope?"

"I'm at Martha's. We're having soup for lunch. What's it look like down there?"

"It's rotten! It's really nice of you to go over there."

"I had no choice! Martha ordered me to come."

"I did, too!" Martha said in the background.

"Is Mort home yet?"

"Not yet, but he called to say he's on his way. If he doesn't arrive in a few minutes, I'll go out and fetch him. Did you say it's rotten there? It's just raining here."

"Same, and windy, but I don't think we've gotten the real deal yet. I just brought in some firewood in case the power goes off."

"That's good. I wish I knew what to do."

"I wish you would stay there until the storm is over. Nobody'll be at church tomorrow anyway. The handful of faithfuls can sing *a capella*. Enjoy your soup and call me later."

Isn't that lovely! I bet all three of them are delighted to find each other practically in their backyards.

Having stuffed himself with rolls, Tim felt no need for lunch, so he drew a glass of water and continued with his assessment of personnel and payrolls.

At two o'clock, he tuned in to the Met Opera radio broadcast. Today's wasn't one he knew or wanted to learn. He wasn't keen on three hours of atonal music, regardless of what beautiful voices sang it. He was happy concentrating on his work anyway, so he turned the music down and carried on.

Eventually, he noticed that it was getting dark. He turned on the overhead light, and saw that it was only three o'clock.

"Gosh, that's not sunset; that's clouds heavy with water," he muttered. A gust of wind slapped the house and made the old beams creak.

Tim reached for the phone and called the Everses.

"Is Rob still there, Martha? It's looking more threatening here."

"He went out, Tim. He was going to his apartment to pack his bag. He said if it didn't look too dirty he'd set out and see."

"And see? How do you 'see' a hurricane? Either it's good or it's bad, and if it's bad there's no place to turn around on the highway. That scoundrel. He probably didn't want me to worry, and now I'm worried. Did Mort get home okay?"

"Yes, he's here. Now don't you worry about Robert. If he comes back I'll make him call you before he takes his coat off."

"Please do. Thanks, Martha."

A key piece of information was missing in his research. Tim needed it to support a theory that had been percolating as he worked on one side of the door and the other. This key would be in the personnel files in Elaine's office downtown, but he was not keen to run out in the worsening weather, especially since he had admonished everyone else to stay away.

Picking up his mobile phone, he called Elaine's mobile number.

"Good afternoon, Tim. To what do I owe the pleasure of this call?" She laughed. "Are you in need?"

"Must I be? It's getting pretty dark, so I think we'll get a lot of rain very soon. Oops! That was a big gust. The wind's getting up, for sure. It whistles like a train in this old house. Are you snug?"

"I am, thank you."

"Good. I need some critical information—a date—and I don't want to go downtown to look it up. But I know you know it."

"What is it?"

"When did you hire Harold Awalt?"

"Sometime in the spring."

"Yes, good. Can you narrow that down? Do you mean calendar spring, as in late March until late June? Or was it when the weather was spring-like, snow was melting, or—?"

"I see. Let me get my daytimer." She sighed as she returned to the phone. "Why does it matter, may I ask?"

"If you don't mind, I will wait to tell you as soon as I know that answer. But before I spend more of this delightful storm in wild conjecture, I thought a fact might be helpful, and that's the only one I could think to ask you for."

"You know, Mister Brown, you accomplish great things, but you do go about your work in unorthodox ways sometimes."

"Much obliged, Miss Fong. That's high praise."

"Is it? Okay, March three. Wednesday morning, the third of March. So the snow was not melted, if there was any, and it was not spring."

"Oh, my, really? March three? Hmm."

"Is that bad?"

"Yeah…not sure, depends on what I'm looking for. It helps. You may go back to watching the storm now."

"This is my first *bona fide* East Coast hurricane, so that is exactly what I'm doing. It's getting nasty."

"You'll be fine, but stay inside. Call me if you need me."

"Always thoughtful. Thank you, Tim."

The kitchen phone rang, and Tim clicked off his mobile to answer it.

"I'm fine!" Robert announced. "I'm safe! I'm back with Mort and Martha."

"Oh, thank goodness! Martha said you were heading out, and I don't think—"

"The RCMP were at the highway entrance, warning cars not to go farther west than exit five. They hadn't closed the highway yet, but they were asking people nicely not to go, so I turned around. I really wanted to spend a big storm with you rather than sit in the dark in my tiny bed-sit. So I'll stay here."

Tim heard Martha calling in the background.

"Yes, Mama. She says I must be crazy. You're right, Martha, I am." Robert lowered his voice. "There's a nice piano here, Tim, and candles. We're getting things ready in case the lights go out. Martha's making a thermos of tea now. Are you okay there?"

"I sure am. I'll make supper soon, just in case. I have stuff to work on, and I have a piano here, too. I'm glad the Mounties stopped you, you crazy man. You guys have a good time there. Call me later. Hugs to every-one. Bye-bye."

Tim tuned the radio to the local station. Usually, it played a non-stop mix of country and rock music, which did not appeal to Tim any more than it had first thing this morning. Tim did not bop.

Just now, an announcer was talking to someone from the hurricane centre, and the news wasn't wonderful. The eye of the weakening storm was nearing the entrance of the Bay of Fundy, so South River wouldn't re-ceive a direct hit.

"But this system is huge, so the impact will be felt hundreds of kilo-metres from the centre in all directions. To the west of it, rain amounts will be greater. To the east, wind will be greater. Even when the storm drops below hurricane status, it will still be destructive quite far out from the centre."

"Can you time it out for us here along the South Shore?" the announ-cer asked.

"The next twelve to sixteen hours will be the most damaging. While it's passing, and afterwards we should expect downed power lines, pooling rain in low-lying areas, flooding, erosion, all those sorts of things. Residents are advised to stay indoors and be prepared to be self-sufficient for seventy-two hours."

Thank goodness the Mounties convinced Rob to turn back. And he'll stay over at the Everses. Who could have foreseen that? I wish I was there.

The rain was coming down heavier, and sideways now in the increasing wind. Tim went out to the sunroom, expecting to see leaks everywhere. There were only a few at some of the windows, and none where the structure was attached to the outside wall of the house. Corey and crew had done a thorough job of caulking all around there.

It was quite entertaining, watching the increasing storm from this little observation platform.

Tim began to think about supper while he still had full use of the kitchen. Lights were flickering. If the power went off now, he would just eat peanut butter and fruit, or tuna. He wouldn't go outside to try to light the hibachi, currently being pelted with rain. He didn't want to order a pizza, either. They'd be closed anyway, he assumed.

But it was Saturday, and that meant Italian.

He put a pot of water on the stove, then thinly sliced some garlic cloves and put them in a frypan with olive oil. When the water came to a boil, he measured a good handful of spaghettini into the pot.

He grated a generous chunk of Parmesan cheese and set that aside, and pitted some Kalamata olives. Pinching a strand of pasta from the pot, he tossed it against the refrigerator door, where it stuck.

"Perfect! Now, we drain *most of* the water from the pasta, and add the remainder to the browned garlic."

Tim was entertaining himself by narrating as though he were on a television cooking show like "The Galloping Gourmet", which his mother used to watch when he was about ten years old.

"Stir, add *most of* the Parmesan, and stir some more. Add all that back to the pasta in the pot, gently stir. Serve in a pasta bowl, and sprinkle the rest of the parm over top to taste."

Wines were featured prominently on that show, which he had ignored then, but it suited him very well now.

"To accompany this simple and satisfying "Aglio y Olio" pasta dish, I have selected a full-bodied Soave Classico from Italy, called *Tempesta*, which is quite *apropos* for today. *Buon appetito!*"

He took a bowlful of pasta to the sunroom, now an impressive stormroom, and twirled the thin strands between fork and spoon while watching the treetops waving in great arcs. Even the cut grass on the lawn showed the swipes of wind. Water streamed along the paved entrance to the exhibition grounds on his left, and made rivulets down the unpaved emergency exit on his right.

While he was in the kitchen for a second helping, he looked out the front door in the dim light. There were only a dozen cars in the vast parking lot across the street. A service vehicle with the town's logo on the door drove past, orange roof light flashing. Signs were swinging, one crookedly. Streetlights were on, but their light couldn't penetrate the amazing amount of water in the air.

Tim took the pasta and the bottle of *Tempesta* back to his front row seat and watched until the waves of water hit like hail on the thin windows and he prudently chose to come inside. He closed the door to the sunroom, turned on the lights in the parlour, and sat at the piano.

Robert phoned again. "Everything good there?"

"The very best. I made a *delicioso* pasta dinner, with a yummy wine. I'm playing a bit on the pianoforte now, to drown out the racket outside. It's fierce."

"I heard. The television weather report showed that we'll have an ordinary storm here, but it'll be nasty from Hubbards on down, and really bad in Yarmouth. We're playing Scrabble. Martha's too good. She usually beats Mort, so he cheered when I won a couple games."

"Board games? Never did I ever! If the storm's over, and if we haven't lost power here, will you drive down for church tomorrow morning, then?"

"If and if, yes. I'll call the minister around seven tomorrow morning to see what's up, then I'll call you, okay?"

"Yup. I'll drink a toast to all of you. Stay safe."

"You, too, Timo. G'nite."

He considered calling his Aunt Stella, but feared she might take offence at the implications of the gesture, since she considered herself invincible. He'd call after the storm had passed. He knew she did have options.

He found the score for "The Tempest", a Beethoven piano sonata. In imitation of how the storm began, he played in stops and starts. It was a challenging piece, and he had consumed enough wine to impede his uncertain skills. Also like the storm, the music went on and on.

Eventually, he surrendered to both music and storm. He laid some blankets over the freezer in case the power went off, and took his phone and himself upstairs to bed.

His real work could wait for a less distracting day. He believed he had managed to identify and solve one mystery. All he needed now was to decide how to resolve it.

September 26: Who among us?

Sunday

Tim was still asleep when his phone rang.

"Good morning, Timothy, may I speak with Doctor Kirk, please?" It was the assistant minister at Saint John's Church.

"Goom—ahem, excuse me—good morning, Reverend. Robert isn't here. He didn't come down yesterday. He tried. The RCMP were turning cars back. Any damage down there?"

"A few leaks in the usual spots, nothing more as far as we can tell. But we can't carry on without electricity, so the service of worship is cancelled. Can you get that message to Doctor Kirk for me, please?"

Tim fumbled with his bedside lamp to see if he had lost power, too. He didn't want to confess his late lack of awareness to the minister.

"Uh, sure...he said he would call you, but I'll save him the trouble. Thanks for calling. Good day, Reverend."

Tim hadn't been awake to notice that his power was off. He got out of bed and went to the washroom, grateful that the town's water utility kept the water flowing and flushing. People in the country with their own wells and septic tanks were not so fortunate.

Like Aunt Stella. Like Cindy Martin, in her old house on the point. She can't wash or flush without electricity. I hope she still has a roof.

The water was still warm enough for him to shower before he dressed. At five minutes to seven, he called Robert.

"Hello, lazybones. Are you having a nice sleepover? Reverend What's-his-name just called to tell you that church is cancelled. Power's off."

"Oh, for heaven's sake, can they never get it right? The senior minister already called me. Whatever. At least it's the same message. How are things there?"

"Power's been off for a while, but I have running water. And phone. You didn't lose power?"

"No, just some flickers. I slept like a baby."

"I slept like a man who drank a lot of wine. You'll stay there today, then?"

"Should I?"

"Yes, you should, unless you want to come to the woodshed and try to cook a piece of raw chicken in the wind."

"No, thanks."

"I bet Martha is up and making your breakfast already, isn't she?"

"I think she is. This is a nice apartment; a flat, really. Beautiful old house."

"Nice. I'm parched for a coffee. I'm going to take the little red roadster out to see if the power is off everywhere or just here. If I find a takeout joint with the lights on, that'll be all I'll need. Talk later."

Tim drove carefully in the SUV, which was neither his nor Robert's at this point. Tree branches were lying in the street, though emergency services had already pushed some to the side so traffic was not impeded.

As he reached Main Street, he was impressed to see the waters of the South River leaping and foaming under the bridges. It was nowhere near the top of the riverbank, though, so his office building was safe, as was the Daisy Café on one side of it, and the church on the other. No lights were visible anywhere.

He crossed the bridge and drove up the hill to the corner where several fast-food franchises were located. All were lit up and looking quite festive in the gloom. Their drive-thru lanes were full and vehicles were lined up on the street for blocks.

That's nuts. I'm not going to get stuck in that. I'll keep driving eastward until I find a place where I can actually get something to eat.

He found it in Chester. A restaurant there was open and busy, and Tim found a seat at a long table. He eventually got his cappuccino and a nicely-presented wedge of quiche. When he finished eating, he ordered a double-cupped Americano to go.

The storm had passed. Local damage was limited, according to the car radio. A few large trees or branches had fallen across wires, which the power company estimated would be restored by early afternoon, if not some other time. Farther to the west, power outages were more widespread, and at least one wharf was reported to be damaged. The storm was still grinding along, having turned north toward the Acadian Peninsula in New Brunswick.

I wouldn't be surprised to see James Olsen's jeep roaming around town, looking for shots of fallen trees and wires being fixed. People aren't satisfied to merely survive a storm. It isn't really over until they see a dramatic photo in the paper of how bad it was. Fortunate for The Times.

Since Tim woke, his human resources project of the previous few days had been running in the background of his mind. Particularly about Harold.

He liked Harold. He had trusted him right from the beginning, and had taken him along on his first quarterly meeting with the trustees overseeing his business affairs during this year of benign neglect. He had even given him some quasi-personnel tasks last month

Was that real trust, or was I hiding behind Harold's skills because I didn't want to check the details myself? Either way, no harm was done that I know of. He seemed willing and able to take on many tasks, and I let him. We let him. *Elaine has Superwoman's laser vision, and she didn't raise any alarms, though she claims that personnel matters are not her strong suit. If I was going to second-guess everyone, I might as well have stayed right where I was, working all the time.*

He entered his house again just in time to hear it come back to life as electricity was restored. The microwave beeped, and the refrigerator powered on. He hoped its contents were okay.

He zapped the Americano in the microwave, and nibbled on another of yesterday's cinnamon rolls, still perfect. He was glad that he wouldn't have to contend with the hibachi today. He wanted to spend the rest of the day in quiet note-taking so he could hit the ground running tomorrow.

He did wonder how his aunt Stella had fared in the storm, and thought it would be safe to check in now, after the fact. They were due for a visit soon, but it wouldn't be today unless she actually was in need. He called her cellphone.

"Timothy? I thought you were dead!"

"Did you? You missed my funeral, then. It was a good one, too. How are you, dear Aunt? Did your lights go out?"

"Not where I am, thank you very much. I wasn't going to stay in my big house by the ocean and not be able to flush. So I took refuge elsewhere."

"Where is 'elsewhere'? Your condo?"

"No."

"I see. Well, I assume you're safe and in good company, then. Your access to flushing was my main concern. We should schedule a dinner sometime soon."

"I'd like that. My best to Robert."

"He's not here. Church was cancelled because power was off. Take care, now."

Stella seems to drift back to her old habits if I don't check in with her regularly. We've had some very nice encounters recently. She has either cooled a bit, or she's got a man waiting for her to get off the phone. I hope it's the latter.

He set out a small bacon-wrapped tenderloin to defrost, and scrubbed a potato to bake in the oven. Pulling on boots, he walked out to the back gardens to see what he could harvest. Remarkably, most stalks were still standing. He found some late beets that he could reach without stepping on the saturated soil.

By the time his Sunday dinner was ready, Tim knew, without a doubt, what had been behind the undercurrent of disgruntlement at *The Times,* including and ever since Labour Day weekend. Someone was taking steps to sabotage his business, and he knew who that someone was.

What he could do about it was a question for another day. And that day was tomorrow.

September 27: Consultations

Monday

Nervous electricity was buzzing in Tim's solar plexus when he awoke, and it grew as he thought about what he planned to do today.

"Or maybe it'll have to wait a day or two. I don't want to do it wrong, and then have a mess to undo."

He cooked himself a big breakfast, a real stick-to-your-ribs affair. It helped to displace the buzzing anxiety and would keep hunger pangs from jangling his nerves later.

It's not that I'm expecting a physical altercation or anything like that. I just hate to do harm to anyone, even if he is threatening my business. Is that true, though? When Eric MacIntosh was pushing me to sell my building to him, I pushed back, and we exposed his whole crooked enterprise. I didn't mind doing that, did I? No, I didn't. But I was nervous when I did it.

He glanced at the big clock in the kitchen. Elaine would be in her office now, trying to catch up with the weekend before today got too far away from her. He wondered if she ever got nervous.

"Good morning, Mister Brown," Elaine answered his call with a smile in her voice.

"Good morning, Miss Fong. All good there at *The Times?*"

"As far as we can tell. Staff are comparing hurricane stories. John is in the basement, banging on some pipes, as the old boiler has refused to fire up again, and we have no hot water."

"Really? That's great news. Question for you: payday was Friday just past, correct?"

"Yes."

"Excellent. So we have two weeks before the next one?"

"Yes. Why?"

"Wait, now. Have you ever worked for an enterprise, of similar size to ours, which uses a payroll service instead of doing it all in-house?"

"Yes, I have."

"Do they work? I mean, like clockwork? Easy? Low cost?"

"All of that. I forget what they charge, but it has to be much less than paying an employee to do it. They take the funds out of a dedicated bank account, make deductions, print official-looking cheques with a stub, and remit taxes and such payments to the government whenever they're due. I thought about suggesting it to you, but you've been on sabbatical, remember?"

"I do remember. I think of it fondly, like a faraway land that I long to return to one day. So, where do I inquire about this magical service? The bank?"

"That'd be my guess. Good luck."

He might need more than luck. Milton Barkhouse was the manager of the bank that handled all of Tim's personal and business accounts, so that was the natural place for him to inquire. But he had become increasingly uncomfortable that Milton knew so much about his business.

So I'll ask Valerie Coolen if she supports this service at her bank! That's a big leap for me, and a small step away from Milton.

He placed a call to his law firm, argued successfully for a short appointment, and left.

~

Tim parked Robert's car right outside the door of the bank at five to ten, and he pulled the door open as soon as a teller had unlocked it. He asked if he could see Mrs Coolen, just for a moment.

"Good morning, Tim, come on in," she greeted him. "You didn't blow away on the weekend?"

"We're all fortunate that the storm went westerly, so somebody else had the misfortune. I came to see you about changing how we do payroll."

Tim described the situation as briefly as he could: he had always handled payroll himself, then a new hire had taken it over while he was on sabbatical, but the employee in question was going to be leaving very soon, too soon to train a replacement. He had heard about payroll services...

"Do you use accounting software now?"

"Uh, yes. Don't ask me what it's called, as that was implemented after I went on leave, too. I used to do all that with an Eversharp pencil and ledgers."

Valerie smiled. "The good old days, eh? I inherited some accounts like that. You're planning to dismiss the person who is performing these functions for you now, is that right? "

Tim sighed. "Yes. It's a shame, because he seemed to be so good at everything. Computers, too. He kept moving things into the computer, so I can't get access to anything now because I haven't learned how yet. Then he tells us that the computers might fail at year's end, but I don't know if he's doing anything about it or just talking through his hat."

"That is a real threat, but I'm hoping my Head Office will find and correct the bug in time. Is that why you're planning to dismiss him? That alone is not sufficient grounds, is it?"

"I know. There's another issue. I'm seeing my lawyer about it today."

"Good. About your payroll, call this number. They have a representative in this area, so you should be able to get it set up quite easily. Then let me know and we'll set up your account here and the transfer stuff. "

"In time for payday a week from this Friday?"

"I don't see why not. We want your business, and I appreciate the opportunity to show you what we can do for you."

~

Tim had negotiated this short-notice appointment with a junior lawyer in the firm. He didn't need a partner's high-priced strategy. All he wanted was some information about the law as it pertained to the dismissal of employees.

"What are the ramifications if I dismiss an employee with notice, or without notice, or with pay, or without?" were Tim's opening questions.

"Has he passed the probationary period?" The lawyer was wearing a navy power suit, her long chestnut hair pulled back tightly.

"That's the problem: his six months ended earlier this month, and his odd behaviour began at that same time. I don't think it's a coincidence."

"I see. Well, if an employee is guilty of wilful misconduct, disobedience, or neglect of duty—things that have not been condoned by the employer—you may end the employee's employment without notice, probation or not."

"What if he's been meeting with other employees in secret, discussing their pay and possibly other work conditions? It's not just conversation: I think he's been attempting to organize them."

"In a union? It's not against the law for them to organize."

"No, I know, and if they wanted a union, I'd support that. I know my staff, and I believe we have a mutual respect. I've come close to bringing up the subject of unionizing myself, several times. But I've taken this year off, so I was hoping not to get into this sort of thing until next year."

"Perhaps this employee saw the gap in your management, and took advantage of your inattention?"

"I hadn't thought of that. That makes his intentions quite sinister, doesn't it? What I don't get is why—what's in it for him if the staff join a union?"

"Prestige?"

"I wouldn't think so. We're pretty small potatoes, really."

"Prestige is in the eye of the beholder. If he became the union steward, he would have the authority to tell you what you can and cannot do on behalf of the workers, and that puts him at your level. Or perhaps he wants the experience so he can rise in the union ranks at a larger employer later on. Who knows?"

"I didn't think of that. What if we change the job, like contracting out the major portion of what he's doing now? Is that an option for us?"

"We wouldn't recommend constructive dismissal—deliberately changing elements of the job in order to cause the position to disappear. It can be very contentious, and nobody wins."

"But if he's doing our payroll now, and I decide to have it done through a third party? That would save me a lot of money, be more efficient, and what's left wouldn't be a full-time position."

"Nothing else available at his pay scale?"

"No. He has mostly worked himself out of a job, in a way. One of his tasks was to digitize archival files of our newspaper, and that has been going well. I learned that one of our clerical 'floaters' has been doing most of the scanning. I would prefer to promote clerical staff to absorb the work rather than make up work for him that shouldn't be paid at his current rate."

"Well, be cautious, Mister Brown. Say only the words you need to say, firmly and respectfully. If he has been a permanent employee for only a few weeks, then you need to give him only two weeks' notice, or two weeks' pay with no notice, whichever you prefer. But don't give him a glowing reference at the same time. That might encourage him to use it against you."

"Thank you, Counsellor. Good advice. I'll keep that in mind when dealing with my caretaker, too. He has been uncooperative for a long time. He considers his job to be mostly sleeping next to the boiler. I'm changing the heating system to electric, so that'll be the end of the road for him. I suppose that's constructive dismissal, too, but sleeping on the job is just cause, isn't it?"

"Yes. Document everything. And if you'll allow me a bit of extra-legal advice, do be kind. That's not a strictly legal requirement, but I believe it helps. Even if they're at fault, employees don't need to lose their dignity twice. Losing a job does that well enough."

~

It was noontime, but Tim wasn't hungry yet. The jitters weren't so bothersome, either, having been soothed by good advice. He went to the office to see Elaine, hoping that her slimmed-down post-hurricane edition of the paper would mean less pressure for her and a little time for him.

"Would you be able to spring yourself out of here for a brief lunch today, Miss Fong?"

"For food, or for talk? I don't want much food."

"Nor I. Let's go for a little drive in my stolen car, then. I'll show you some nice Nova Scotian scenery while I try to involve you in my schemes."

They stopped at a drive-thru, now without the long lines of yesterday's post-hurricane coffee crisis. Tim mentioned that scene to Elaine.

"I heard. James took a great photo of one lineup. It went around the building and down the street. I don't know if he climbed a pole to get the shot, and I'm not asking. He wants the title to be 'Gridlock in South River'."

"I knew he would find something like that. James has become quite a team player."

"He has. So tell me who isn't?"

Tim talked as he drove on the highway toward the city, turned off at Hubbards and out on the Aspotogan Peninsula, where he had contemplated going last Sunday with Robert.

Elaine loved the scenery. Tim turned into several tiny coves once he saw how happy she was to see the ocean and the fishing boats, some still hauled up to keep them from post-storm tides. In several places they saw piles of rocks on the roadside that had been tossed up by the waves.

By the time they left the peninsula on the Mahone Bay side, they had reviewed the issues with Harold, possible causes, and their preferred resolution.

He pulled up in front of *The Times* building to let Elaine out.

"Not coming in?"

"In a moment," he said. "I just realized that I took you all the way out to sea and back without checking the tank. I might have to push it the last hundred feet. I'll fill up and then I'll be in. I'll have that little chat with Ed Garamond, as you suggested."

~

"Hi, Ed. Did you get a chance to cast your eyes over those reno plans yesterday?" Tim was phoning him from upstairs.

"Hi, boss. Yeah, I had plenty of time after the power went off. My notes are here in the envelope."

"Would you mind bringing them upstairs so we can look at them together for a few minutes? Won't take long."

Ed came up and knocked on the open door.

"Thanks for this, Ed. Is there anything here that you think I won't understand?"

"I don't think so."

"Good. Have a seat for a minute, would you? Close the door. I want to ask you some questions about Harold."

"I wondered if you would...or when you would."

"Really? Because he's been sowing dissent amongst the staff?"

"Something like that. Acting strange. Saying something one day and something different the next, and saying it came from you or Miss Fong."

"Is it only with you, do you think?"

"Gosh, no. I don't know if you've noticed how he calls us on the phone, like you called me just now? You won't see him standing at our desks. But he calls to tell me I shouldn't be working that hard to prepare all the new advertising without asking for a raise, or that I shouldn't be working after hours without extra pay. He had just made one of those calls that day when you came over and made that crack about lingerie ads. I was already annoyed, so you got the wrong side of me. Sorry about that."

"I didn't know, of course, but it's water under the bridge now."

"Anyway, I don't need him niggling at me. I can negotiate my own remuneration, though he has let it be known that he will soon be in charge of that."

"He will not. Did you tell him to leave you alone?"

"Yes. He says I'm a bad example for everyone else."

"Yikes. Is he trying to get staff to form a union?"

"I don't exactly know, but I think so. Unionizing doesn't appeal to this old art school free-thinker. Some of the others are quite disturbed by his calls, criticizing what you do, what Miss Fong does, what we all do. The clerical staff don't feel as secure as I do, or James or Cindy, too, and they're feeling edgy."

"I didn't know about this, Ed. How long has it been going on?"

"I guess he started while you were over on the Island in July, just a little, and it sounded like he was pitching in at first, you know, just interested in helping. Then a little more. At the Labour Day picnic, when you and Miss Fong didn't arrive, he really ran with it. Kinda spoiled our fun a bit. I wasn't sure if you knew about it or not. What do you plan to do?"

"I have plans, but I think it's best if I don't tell you right now, Ed. I won't tell Harold what you've told me. I am grateful that you did, though. It must have been hard to know what to do."

"I was getting close to telling you. I just want to play with pens and ink and paste and be left alone."

"I think you want a little more than that, but without the sneaky phone calls, for sure. You'd better get back to your work now or Miss Fong will give us both her dead-eye look."

"Not today. That's her Tuesday specialty. You know, she has the whole layout in her head, down to the line, and moves pieces around like one of those three-dimensional puzzles. She's something else."

"So are you, Ed. Thanks for giving me your confidence. And thanks for reviewing those renovation sketches."

"Anytime, boss."

Next, Tim phoned Stephanie Duplessis-Lachance. He told her briefly what had transpired, and what was about to transpire. He said he had consulted a lawyer, and was confident of his standing.

"You are telling me this for my information?"

"Not entirely. I need your help. I signed your contract already, but I still have it. I guess the hurricane distracted me. Will I mail it, or..."

"Would you like me to attend the meeting at which you dismiss your employee?"

"I would, very much. When can you come?"

"This Wednesday afternoon is possible. At three-thirty? We will require a private room."

"You've been in the only one we have. We'll work with it. Thank you so much."

After hanging up, Tim wasn't sure if he was feeling nervous again, or finally hungry. Before he went home to medicate his nerves with food, he called Conquerall Services.

"Hi, Amanda. I have an envelope full of my staff's comments on Tyler's designs, and I'm going to take them home to review tonight. Can I bring them to your worldwide headquarters tomorrow morning so Tyler and Corey can take the next step?"

"Our worldwide headquarters has a huge, muddy lake in the front yard, Tim. It's not deep, but it's nasty, so take care. I told Tyler that you wanted to add electric heating, so he put that in. The computer spits out a parts list, too, right down to how many feet of wire and board feet of lumber. That program will make estimates accurate to the inch, and that saves you money."

"Could you use it to sketch up my weekly newspapers every Tuesday? Writing stories is easier than figuring out how to build something, isn't it?"

"Might be, someday. Computers are pretty neat."

~

He'd had a very large day. Still reluctant to do what needed to be done, he was pleased with how he had gone about preparing for it. If Harold simply had acted strangely once in a while, he might have deserved counselling, or a new probationary period. But making secret calls to agitate the staff while they were trying to do their work wasn't strange behaviour; it was harassment.

Harold needed to go.

Tim carried two beverages to the sunroom: a tall tumbler of water, and a balloon glass of *Tu peux le faire* for sipping while he looked over what Ed had given him.

Elegantly and simply, Ed had incorporated his coworkers' wish lists into the overall plan, on both floors—or gave reasons for why he couldn't. The computer program was a useful tool, but Ed Garamond had revised the sterile printouts to accommodate workflow, based on his coworkers' comments. He had drawn friendly work spaces for friendly humans.

Tim's eyes filled to see it.

As he poured a second glass of wine to go with supper, he noticed a second label, painted on the back of the bottle but visible only inside it. As the level of wine diminished, the interior label was revealed.

It read, *Tu l'as fait*

September 28: Helpers

Tuesday

"A double of your darkest this morning, please," Tim said to Gloria.

The machine built up pressure, but it seemed to take longer. He wondered if it needed to be cleaned or serviced. He and Robert had given it to themselves last Christmas. As with all household appliances, once Tim learned how to run the functions he wanted—which hadn't come naturally—he had put the instruction book aside.

He rummaged in a kitchen drawer, found the multi-language book, and laid it on the counter, in case.

"We wouldn't want you to get clogged arteries, Gloria. Leave that for the humans."

Tim phoned Robert, but he didn't answer. It was a bit early for him to be at school, but maybe he was making up lessons lost during the storm.

"Hi Rob, just me. Sorry I didn't call to update you yesterday. I've been immersed in a bunch of staff things, and I uncovered some employee troubles that needed my attention. It'll be resolved by the time you arrive for choir. Stella sent her love. She was hunkered down somewhere during the storm, wouldn't give me a clue where, so I'd say she's dating again—-or still, who knows? It's great that you spent the storm with Mort and Martha. I'm going to try to catch Garland Greene tomorrow to settle the business about your car. If he has the paperwork ready, I'll give it to you on Thursday and then you can do whatever you need to do at your bank. I like driving it, so—"

The automated voice butted in with a warbled "Recording has ended."

He made another coffee and toast and considered his day. He had an errand, a visit, phone calls, and decisions to make.

Don't sit around worrying and dithering. Finish your toast and get on it.

He had made one photocopy of Ed's drawings yesterday, and he wanted to display it at the office. He dropped it off at the small print shop at the four-way stop in Blockhouse for enlargement and laminating. This wasn't exactly on the way to Conquerall, but it pleased him to use the small shop when he could, and to take the cable ferry across the river.

The river was still swollen with weekend rains. The current was too strong for the cable ferry to cross, so he had to drive back to South River, cross over the bridge, and drive back down the other side to Conquerall Bank.

Amanda wasn't kidding about the pool of water at the front of the building. Heavy trucks and machines had worn a depression in the dirt yard, perhaps only a few inches deep, but the murky water seemed bottomless. He slowly navigated the little SUV to a spot on the perimeter where he could park, and from where he could walk on dry land to the door.

"I told ya to wear your boots," Amanda said when he entered.

"I forgot." Tim looked around warily. "Where's your big dog—Laddie, was it? I bet he's a regular mud mop, if you even let him in."

"It's nice of you to remember him. My Laddie's gone. Some kind of tumour, the vet said. I miss him every day, except he isn't knocking everything over with his big tail any more."

"I'm sorry for your loss, Amanda."

"Thanks. Let's see what you brought."

Tim unrolled Ed's drawings, and proudly spread them out on the counter.

"Ho-lee! You went and got an architect anyway? They must've cost a bundle. Looks nice, though."

"Not an architect. Our own art director drafted these during the hurricane. Some of the staff had submitted notes or sketches of what they'd like to see happen, based on Tyler's presentation. Ed incorporated them all into this, which doesn't disagree with what Tyler did. He grouped the work spaces by task, which Tyler wouldn't have known about, and I wouldn't have thought to do. I love it."

"Me, too. I'd like to work in a place like that instead of this metal cavern, ha-ha. But it's my metal cavern. I'll give this to Tyler and Corey when they come back, and we'll get back to you soon about costs and timelines."

"Why don't I just send you all the money I have and hope that'll cover it?"

"I think you'll be pleasantly surprised. The space being open like that, I think the biggest job will be the new stairway, which I heard them saying could be a prefab steel frame. Then maybe portable walls where your fella marked them on this." She tapped Ed's sketch. "Couple million should cover it, ha-ha."

"Yikes!" Tim responded with mock fright. "I'll leave it with you. Thanks, Amanda."

As he left the building, Tim noticed a worn dog collar and leash hanging on a nail at the door.

~

Those curvy roads along the riverbank were less charming when he had to negotiate them for the second time in the same hour, due to no ferry. He reached Main Street in town, crossed the bridge and continued out to the highway. He drove back to the print shop at top speed, for entertainment, just to put the SUV through its paces.

Gar said he'd put new snow tires on it, so that'll be done for the winter. I worry about Robert driving in snow and ice, but I'm glad he does it. I could go to the city more, but we still need him here to direct the choir and play the organ. Funny, I didn't miss choir this summer, but now that we're back at it, I really enjoy it.

He whistled the Spanish carol when he picked up the laminated drawings from the print shop, and again as he drove back to the office.

"Mrs Rafuse," he said to the receptionist, "would you kindly set up the easel somewhere and put this on it?"

"Oh, my!" she said, admiring the enlarged, laminated sketch, "will this be us? I thought the fresh paint we got last spring made a big difference, but this'll be over the top!"

"What's going on?"

Staff gathered around to look at what was on the easel. There were exclamations of admiration, pride, and pleasure. "I got what I wanted!"

Tim stepped away from the easel and went over to Ed Garamond's cubicle. "Go take a bow, Ed. You've earned our gratitude, not just for your skill at architecture, but for incorporating what your coworkers wanted. That's a big deal."

Ed did go to take credit for his handiwork. Even Elaine withdrew from her deadline-induced trance long enough to focus on the sketch, and she patted Ed on the back for his work.

Harold went over to glance at what was on the poster, and quickly returned to his desk. Tim saw him catch Ed's eye and point at him. It didn't seem like a friendly gesture. It looked like a warning.

~

Up in his private room, Tim phoned the payroll company that Valerie Coolen had recommended. He spoke with a representative and asked him if he could come Thursday morning at nine.

"Let me check." He put Tim on hold for a long time. "Thanks for waiting. If nine-thirty Thursday is okay, I can make it then. I'll ask for you?"

"Yes. How long does it take to set this up, usually? Our next payday is Friday, October eighth."

"That's tight, but we can get it set up on our end. The auto-withdrawal from your bank account might not be ready, though. It takes a bit of time to set that up."

"I'm not concerned about that. Between me and my new bank, we'll get the funds to wherever they need to be, even if I have to carry a bag of cash there. Would that work?"

The service rep laughed. "You're keen. I like that. Just remember: Friday next week is the beginning of the Thanksgiving long weekend, so if there's a hitch, we won't be able to address it until the following Tuesday."

"Duly noted. Seems like we just had a long weekend, doesn't it? Oh well, let's give it a shot. The person who has been doing our payroll is, uh, is leaving...on short notice, so we'll be in a squeeze. Let's assume it will work. See you Thursday morning."

Tim wrote down the next two days' important arrangements. When he finished, it looked like this:

WEDNESDAY
3:30 - Ms D-L here to help dismiss H: need your support and your office
- meanwhile, I will get Jean N to type up H's official Notice of Dismissal, eff. immediately;
- H will receive two weeks' pay in lieu of notice (only one wk req'd) by registered mail
- the above is pending receipt of H's keys to building, file drawers etc, + H's portable computer

THURSDAY
- 9:30 - Payroll Experts rep to set up new paycheque svce: fingers crossed!!!
- suggest we appoint Jean N to temporarily supervise payroll transition
- suggest we appoint clerical staff with most computer skills to

handle archives until - -

OCTOBER:
- discuss: computers, life choices (☺)

He made a copy, tucked the original in his pocket, sealed the copy in an envelope, and took the envelope to Elaine's office. He wrote WEDNESDAY & BEYOND - VERY IMPORTANT on the outside of the envelope, and left it on Elaine's desk.

He would have spoken to Jean Naugler now, but he was aware that Harold had a clear view of all employees, and he didn't want to raise any suspicion. As he passed Elaine, who was drifting amongst the desks, possibly looking for something small to insert in the paper, he quietly said, "All good," and left.

He stopped at the bank in the plaza, and asked the teller if he could have a quick word with Miss Coolen. This bank manager hadn't established the pretentious protocol of asking him to state his name and wait to be announced. If she was busy with someone, of course, he'd wait, but she wasn't.

"Did you want to come in, Tim?"

"Actually, I think I want to go home. I've had a day. I just wanted to let you know that I called your payroll firm and their rep will come to see me Thursday morning. What will happen after that is unknown to me, but I'm trusting that they and you can make it all work by next payday?"

"Don't worry about that. We've done this a few times. Can you come by tomorrow afternoon? We'll have papers for you to sign, funds to transfer. Then we can set things up."

"Gee, I'm not sure if I can get here before you close tomorrow, as I have a very important meeting at half-past three. It could be long or very short. I'm seeing the payroll fellow at nine-thirty Thursday morning. Hmm. Let's say I'll get here as early as I can Thursday morning. Okay?"

Valerie laughed. "I know you'll do your best. So will I!"

~

Tim thought he was never so glad to get home from work.

Oh, come now, I've come home from work before, just as befuddled as I am today. Maybe the difference is that I rarely came home if there was still work left to do. This is a nice change.

"Come on, Tim, let's go for a walk and cast off our cares of the day.

There'll be plenty more tomorrow."

He drove to a part of town he rarely saw, since it wasn't on the way to anywhere he had to go. It was mostly smaller homes, some a little run down, but they were largely hidden from view by the huge oak and chestnut trees that towered over them. He really enjoyed walking here. Trees had lost leaves and branches in the hurricane, and he breathed in their woody smell.

The street ended at a wooded area, so he turned around and meandered back, taking every side street on the way, and singing as he walked: "Begone, dull care, I prithee be gone from me...la-la...and feign thou wouldst me kill...thou never shalt have thy will."

Instead of obsessing about Harold's disruptive behaviour or second-guessing his own actions, what he feared he'd be doing, Tim found himself thinking about all the helpers that were available. Whether for a fee or for free, it seemed he just had to ask. A solution was always near.

Is that my real job, I wonder? To uncover what needs fixing, and ask the universe for the fix, the solution? To be Mister Seek, but just for the newspaper? When I go back as editor after Christmas, I won't be able to steer the ship and be the lookout in the crow's nest at the same time. Once the new offices are built, will I just go back into mine and continue where I left off?

He strode along, imagining himself entering his new office, opening the door to it...but there was Elaine—in his imagination—sitting at his desk.

That's my new office, Elaine. But you're still here until January, maybe even February...and we can't share one office. Maybe I should hang on to my upstairs hidey-hole. I wonder if there's a spot available? Must ask Ed about that.

Home again, feeling invigorated, Tim made a ground beef and rice casserole for supper. There was enough for leftovers. He would appreciate not having to prepare supper following tomorrow's events.

There was some wine left from yesterday, so he poured it. It didn't match the casserole, but that rule wasn't mandatory on Tuesdays.

Anyway, it wasn't the wine he liked as much as the message *in* the bottle.

September 29: One for all

Wednesday

Tim's mind had been busy all night, reviewing and rehearsing. He was as confident of his decision to dismiss Harold as he could be without holding a hearing with witnesses, and he was not going to do that, for many reasons.

He was less confident about getting next week's pay into the hands of his staff.

And not just in their hands. Pay is automatically deposited in their bank accounts. Their rent and mortgage and car and credit card payments are withdrawn automatically, too. If their pay doesn't get in on time, things'll be bouncing all over town—including my head!

He got out of his bed of second guesses and took a long, hot shower. While his coffee poured from the shiny spout, a comforting question came to mind.

What if we just run last week's payroll again at our regular bank next week, worst case? We can take care of the pluses and minuses later. Good question, Mister Seek. I'm not the expert in this, or in most things. I'll ask the first expert I run into.

He decided to call Elaine's office phone. Unless she were seriously ill, or even if she was, she'd be in by now.

"Good morning, Tim. Do you like today's front page?"

"Oh, yes, it's great! Great photo!"

"You haven't looked at it yet, have you?"

"Guilty. But I didn't want you to think I'm not interested. I have other things on my mind this morning. But I'm sure it's fabulous. James' photo of the cars at the take-out, right?"

"You'll see. In other news, I received your to-do list, thank you. May I make a suggestion?"

"Please."

"If you draft the letter now and bring it with you in advance of the event, I can get Mrs You-Know to type it up so it'll be ready to present and sign. Mademoiselle would approve, I'm sure."

"Great idea. I'll get on that now, since I'm just sitting here, fidgeting. Will you be in the office all day?"

"I'll be back by one o'clock if I go out. Bring the letter in then and we'll take it from there."

"Okay. Much appreciated."

He stepped out onto his front porch to retrieve *The Times* and other papers from the box. He waited until his breakfast was ready before he opened the paper.

The front page was a huge colour photo of all the cars lined up for coffee, as he had guessed. The headline didn't use the word 'gridlock', though the caption did. The headline said "HURRICANE EXHAUST-ED. More colour photos in centre fold-out."

The byline gave credit to James Olsen, photojournalist. The photos did indeed tell a story. James had not only captured the many cars and trucks that had lined up for coffee, but also the empty parking lots, and the empty tables inside the places. Plus the great shot of the huge tree that, in falling, had stolen electricity from the west side of town.

The slant was definitely about unnecessary running of engines and emitting of exhaust. The short column next to the interesting photos used terms like "greenhouse gases" and "global warming". These had begun to appear in *The Daily* from the city, but had not, to his knowledge, been used in *The Times* before.

Tim sighed. *This criticism is aimed at the drivers of those vehicles, and at the drive-through places, too. Fair enough. I know other towns have complained in the winter when the lines are backed up into the streets and the snowplows can't get through the clouds of exhaust. Let's see if our mayor supports the clean-air movement while continuing to sell cars.*

He called Elaine again.

"Am I fired?"

"Keep trying," Tim said. "It's very clever, running a climate story alongside attractive colour pictures. Everyone will be looking to see if they know anyone in the cars. I'm glad I wasn't in them."

"We were careful not to show license plates or faces of drivers. I think it's great. By the way, in case you're worried about losing advertisers over this, Cindy Martin says the franchises are the worst advertisers, so she's given up on them."

"Ooh, a personal vendetta, too! Y'know, if you find an attractive position somewhere in the Yukon…"

"Yes?"

"...maybe I'll take it and you can stay here?"

"I'll keep that in mind. But remember, controversy sells. See you later."

He spent the remainder of the morning composing Harold's Notice of Dismissal letter. He only needed to state the facts, no need to tell a story, especially one that Harold could argue with. Even so, it wasn't an easy letter to write.

[*The Times* letterhead]
To: Harold Awalt
From: Timothy Brown, Publisher
Date: September 29, 1999
Subject: NOTICE OF DISMISSAL effective September 29, 1999

~~I regret to inform you that~~ This letter is to inform you that ~~I am terminating~~ your employment with *The Times* is terminated effective this date.

~~While~~ ~~you began~~ ~~Your work with us was~~ You ~~were~~ seemed a ~~willing and~~ ~~enthusiastic~~ capable employee during your six-month probationary period. However, ~~in the past month,~~ both your work and your ~~attitude~~ demeanour have dropped below our standards ~~since you became~~ ~~since the beginning of your seventh month,~~ recently, causing distress and mistrust amongst ~~your fellow employees~~ staff and management. This is unacceptable.

In lieu of the one-week notice required by law in Nova Scotia, we will send you two weeks' pay at your current rate, and other documentation as required by law, by certified mail, on or before Friday, October 8, 1999.

The above is subject to receipt of the following items today:

- all company keys in your possession, including, but not limited to, the office building, your desk, file cabinets
- all passwords to computers and programs
- all property of the employer, including the laptop computer

Please sign below to acknowledge that you have received and accept this letter:

____

Harold Awalt Signature, Date

____

Timothy Brown Signature, Date

Tim considered re-writing the letter so Jean Naugler would have a clean version to type from, but he knew he would only continue to revise it. It had already taken a large mug of tea and a banana, sliced lengthwise and wrapped in a slice of bread spread with peanut butter. It was the comfort food that enabled him to keep at it until he was satisfied.

"I can't make it nicer. I can't say 'You're a swell guy and this hurts me more than it hurts you.' It's Harold's malfeasance that brought this on, so the sooner and the cleaner we cut him off, the better."

He folded the letter, put it in a white envelope, sealed it and took it to the office.

~

Of course, Tim had disciplined and dismissed staff in his time, but it had been either for some obvious breach of company rules or due to insufficient work to keep them employed, though he had kept old GB on the payroll for seven years longer than his natural retirement date.

But today's dismissee was a different kind of human resource. Tim had never encountered a disruptor before, and it had been a shadowy situation to identify.

It wasn't until he and Elaine went for that drive on Monday that the penny had dropped about the Fire Marshall's sign. Elaine had asked him if he had found who put it on the front door. They had looked at each other and said "Harold" at the same time.

It made sense, now that they knew more of what Harold had been doing. John was too lazy to have done it.

The receptionist phoned him: Stephanie Duplessis-Lachance had arrived.

"Thank you, Mrs Rafuse. Please take her to Miss Fong's office. I'll be right down."

Tim entered Elaine's office and closed the door. Both women were standing.

"We don't need all of us in here, do we?" Elaine asked. "Why don't I step out?"

"I was going to suggest that," the HR expert said. "If you like, you may explain to your staff what is going on, once your employee is in here, so they will know to give him privacy when he comes back to his desk to retrieve his personal things."

"Perfect. I'll take a box to his desk and be there when he comes out. I know what to get from him; it's listed in Tim's letter you have there."

"Will I get him now, then?" Tim asked, wanting the answer to be no.

"Allow me. The element of surprise deters outbursts. He knows what he has done and why he has done it, but he does not know what you have decided. It will be a shock. We will address him firmly, with respect. When your other employees see how you deal with him, they will feel comforted, as they will see you acting on their behalf."

"All right, let's go," Elaine said.

She opened the door and went to the paper supply closet, where there was always a stack of empty boxes.

Tim stood just outside the office door so he could observe the coming interaction. He couldn't entirely let go of his responsibility in this.

Stephanie walked directly to Harold's desk. "Hello, Mister Awalt, my name is Stephanie Lachance-Duplessis." She extended her perfect hand.

"H'lo," Harold replied, and hesitantly shook her hand.

"Mister Brown and I would like to speak with you in private. Would you come with me, please?"

As she made this request, Stephanie smiled a friendly smile that said not to mess with her.

Tim ducked inside as Harold followed her toward the office.

~

When Elaine heard the door close, she brought the box to Harold's desk, then looked around. All eyes were on her. She wasn't smiling, but she made eye contact with each pair of eyes that she saw.

"This box," she said, very quietly, "is for Harold. He will take his personal things home today. Please show him respect when he comes out."

At the back of the room, Elaine saw the two sisters briefly put their heads together and then silently clap their fingertips and grin. She put her fingers to her lips and looked around again. Ed Garamond responded with a firm thumbs-up.

Not many minutes later, the office door opened and Harold emerged, red-faced, followed by Tim, who gave Elaine a nod. Harold returned to his desk.

"This is for your personal things, Harold," Elaine said, gesturing toward the box.

"I don't need that," he said abruptly. "I just have to give you my keys."

He pried the keys off his key ring, and tossed them on the desk. Elaine beckoned to Jean Naugler to come over.

"Jean, would you check these keys for me, please? It's not that I don't trust you, Harold. I just want to make sure we know what opens what. So many keys look the same."

Harold was writing down passwords.

"Please indicate which is for what, Harold. Now, I have to ask you to please shut this computer down and reboot it, and I'll log in just to make sure I understand which password is for what."

"Keys are all good," Jean said. "I'll take the front door key over to Rachael, all right?"

The receptionist, being the farthest away from the scene, had been watching with interest, surmising what was going on. With Jean's manoeuvre, she'd have the news delivered.

"That it?" Harold's earlier meekness was hardening toward hostility. He pulled his jacket off the back of his chair and put his arm in one sleeve.

"Not quite," Elaine said. "What about this computer?" She pointed to the laptop bag that had been covered by the jacket. "This belongs to the company too, correct?"

"It's mine."

"I don't think so. I authorized the purchase, if you recall. You insisted that you needed it, so I approved it. The password, please. Or we can inventory all our computers right now."

Harold wrote the passwords for the laptop log-in and the various programs in it. Elaine started up the laptop, carefully entered passwords, and waited until she saw that they worked.

She pointed to an icon on the screen that wasn't familiar to her. "What's this for, Harold?"

"I don't know. It just showed up."

"You didn't put it there? You don't use it?"

"That's what I said. That's everything, right?"

"Yes, thank you, Harold. Good luck."

Harold walked toward the door. Without turning around, he raised his fist in the air and shouted, "So long, losers!"

He pushed hard on the crash bar at the door, making a clatter. He tried to slam the door, but the pneumatic arm resisted.

Then he was gone.

Tim said, "Thank you, everyone. I know this must be disturbing. If anyone wants to talk about it now, I'm available."

He wasn't prepared for what happened next; the staff, by ones and twos, stood and broke into applause and then cheers. Someone started to chant, "Ding-dong, the witch is dead," but Elaine quieted that with a look.

"I guess you feel we've done the right thing today," Tim said. "I assure you, dismissing any employee is a sad day for me, and I'm very happy that all of you are still here. I'd like to introduce you to Stephanie Lachance-Duplessis. She has guided us through this process today, and will continue to share her expertise with all of us as required, on a contract basis. I, for one, am very relieved to have found her. Please welcome her, and then you might as well go home—if Miss Fong agrees. Tomorrow's another day."

Computers were powered down. Staff greeted their new HR associate as they left for the day.

"I will leave now," Stephanie said to Tim and Elaine. "I want to congratulate you both for how you handled everything today. You were firm and respectful, and all your employees appreciate it, except the one who was dismissed, though he may see it differently when he has time to reconsider."

"I'm going to run, too," Tim said after Stephanie left. "Today has been a stressful week, ha-ha. You've been a brick, Elaine."

"Just doing my job, sir," she said, giving him a mock salute.

"The heck you say. Have you seen enough of me today, or could I entice you to join me in a leftover casserole and some tra-la-la-ing? I've heard it helps to dispel the cares of the day. Who told me that?"

"I did. I am available...and I don't have any leftovers..."

"Let's get out of here, then! It's early enough that you can have a second glass of whatever poison I was planning to pour before you drive home."

"Poison? My favourite! I have to make just one short errand first. I'll see you at your mansion."

~

Tim bypassed the *Plonk de Mercredi* he might have opened. Instead, he took out a top-shelf burgundy more suitable for this special occasion. He removed the cork and poured two glasses.

Elaine arrived with a large bouquet of roses. "You earned these today, Tim. I've been working with you long enough to know that confrontations are not in your nature, but you're no shrinking violet, either. You wade right in with courage and more skill than you give yourself credit for."

Tim cleared his throat, said, "Thank you," and handed her a glass.

She raised the wine. "To you, Tim. Well done!"

They clinked their glasses and sipped.

"Oh my, what's this?" Elaine exclaimed. "Elixir of the gods?"

"I haven't had it before, but I liked the label, which often influences my purchases. This is one of a series of French wines named after famous French authors, Alexandre Dumas in this case. He's the fellow who wrote, "All for one—"

"'And one for all.' An appropriate choice."

"As are those flowers. I don't think I've ever received a dozen roses. I like them. A lot. Let's take our wine to the sunroom, if it's not too chilly. And since I know we need to, let's debrief before we eat. Afterwards, we shall sing like birds. In fact, like Spanish birds."

September 30: Angels unawares

Thursday

I know how today goes.

Tim had come downstairs in his dressing-gown for an espresso prior to starting the known day.

It has all the elements I like. Mrs A will come to clean whatever mess I've made—

He stopped his musing to peel the two sheets of manila paper from the kitchen door and lay them on the kitchen island.

Glad I didn't leave those there, though Mrs A wouldn't know what they're about anyway.

He went upstairs to shower and dress, then came down and unlocked the door before Mrs A arrived. If she saw his car in the yard but the door was locked, she would not unlock it, in case there was a man in a state of undress anywhere inside.

—and then I will go to the Daisy Café, where Evelyn will sass and serve me according to her mood, which is always warm and friendly. Later, Rob will arrive for a quick supper, and we will go to the church and sing for ninety minutes. And then, finally, we'll catch up. I like Thursdays.

He greeted Mrs A and reminded her that he would "undo" the garden whenever she would tell him what to do there. He rolled up the sheets of paper, put them back in Ed's handy cardboard tube, and set out for downtown with them in Rob's new car.

"Oops! It's not Rob's car yet. I must go over to Greene Auto after breakfast and get the papers for that transaction."

Evelyn was in a great mood this morning, laughing and teasing customers. She even asked the regulars to "please welcome" a pair of customers who said this was their first time in. When she got to Tim's booth with a mug and the pot of dark roast coffee, she slid in the booth opposite him.

"You're joining me for breakfast? I'm honoured!"

"I wish. Busy, busy, that's me."

"How come you're smiling, then?"

"Payments, hon." She was whispering.

"What about them?"

"We're makin' them—easily! Remember? You set me and Kenny up with Art, that accountant investor guy? We thought that'd be the ruination of us both, truth be told. But here we are, after just a few weekends with that new fella at the grill, and we're covering our payments, Timmy! If you have any more great ideas for us, just say the word—but maybe not right away. Mama might like a new dress or new shoes first, you know?"

She left the booth then. He hoped it was to get him something to eat.

~

Tim pushed open the door to the newspaper office, and held it for a man coming in. They exchanged "Good morning"s and "Thank you"s. As Tim proceeded past the reception desk he heard the man say, "Steve Urquhart to see Tim Brown, please."

Tim turned around and tried not to sound like he had forgotten all about the payroll service representative coming to help him figure out how to make payroll a week from tomorrow. "Ah, Mister Urquhart, I wondered if that might be you. I'm Tim Brown. Pleased to meet you." He glanced at his watch. "Right on time, too. Come in, please."

Elaine had someone in her office and the door was closed.

"I'm just looking for a place for us to discuss your service," he said. "Our only private office is in use. Will you need to see our payroll setup?"

"I'd like to take a look at it, sure. Did I understand you to say that the employee who was looking after it was leaving?"

"Left. Yesterday."

"Is his or her computer accessible? That will tell me all I need to know, if we can get into it."

"That I can do. Follow me." Tim led his guest to Harold's open cubicle, which caused several heads to rise and glances to be exchanged. "Sit right there, Mister Urquhart, and turn it on while I see who has the passwords."

To the room at large, Tim said, "Good morning, folks. I invited our visitor to tell me about outsourced payroll services, rather than doing it in-house." The heads lowered. "Mrs Naugler, do you still have the passwords?"

Jean Naugler came over. "Miss Fong has them. In the safe, I believe."

"Good. Do you know who's in the office with her? I don't want to interrupt if it's—"

Elaine's door opened, and her guest left.

She noticed the three people looking at her. "Can I help?"

Jean went to tell her and they went inside to retrieve the passwords sheet.

When Steve Urquhart had logged into the computer and was looking for the file that he needed, he pointed to an icon on the screen and asked Tim if he knew anything about it.

"I don't know anything about anything in computers. Mrs Naugler, are you able to sit here and help Mr Urquhart with this, please?"

Jean came back and leaned over to look.

Elaine had wandered over as well. "I asked Harold about that icon yesterday," she said. "He said he didn't know what it was; thought it might have come with the computer."

"Nobody else here has it," Jean said.

"Well, I would advise you to get rid of it," Urquhart said. "It looks vaguely familiar. Might be some kind of spyware or cloning thing."

"What would that do?" Elaine asked.

"It would likely track what anyone does in this computer, and transmit it to another one. Did this employee have a computer at home?"

"Wait a minute."

Elaine went quickly to her office, returning with Harold's laptop. "He used this."

"Let's hope that's the only one he connected it with. I guess we'll proceed, because I need to get data out of this one, but once I'm done with it, I strongly suggest that you take both of these to a computer shop and ask them to remove that software or device or whatever it is. Your employee was spying on you, looks like."

"I'm not surprised," Jean said.

"But why?" Tim asked.

"I don't think he did anything bad," Jean said, "not yet. But we could all see that he was getting more and more weird, more secretive. I thought I saw him loading something into the computer a couple weeks ago; maybe that was this thing. Maybe he was planning something."

"Like duplicating himself in the payroll," the payroll specialist suggested. "We've seen that a few times. The fake name mightn't show up on a printout, but the money goes to their bank account."

"Didn't happen when I was doing payroll in the ledgers," Tim said.

"Okay, I said it, now I'll shut up. Can I ask you to look over his shoulder, Mrs Naugler, and ask good questions? When you're finished, Steve, please come upst—no, just call me, Mrs Naugler, and I'll come down. We'll go over to the café to talk business."

What a ridiculous building this is! No meeting room on the main floor, and no access to the second floor unless you don't mind climbing a ladder. I can't wait to get the renovations done. Urquhart's a big man; I don't want to embarrass him by making him climb the rigging.

He drew the manila sheets out of the cardboard tube and looked at them. Along with the employee interviews, they had given him a good picture of some remuneration gaps and inconsistencies.

I hope Mademoiselle will find this useful when she begins consulting with us. I think the staff will love having access to her, too. If they have a concern, it'll be a lot more satisfactory to discuss it with someone who knows how things can and should go, than it would be with me. I'll always listen, but my solutions are amateurish and suspect—to me, anyway. I nearly forgot the payroll guy was coming today, so that proves I'm unreliable.

He took the ENTRANCE FORBIDDEN sheet down.

I'm glad we didn't pin this on John. I'm convinced this was another of Harold's attempts to sabotage us. John will be another showdown, but there are upsides. We'll have better heating, and we'll hire a cleaning service specializing in offices. Amanda can send someone over if a lightbulb needs changing, and sure as shootin' it'll be done faster than John ever did. And all of that will cost less.

He rolled up all the sheets and taped them together. He wrote *September: Sabotage* on the roll and placed it inside the cabinet on top of the growing pile of rolls.

Jean Naugler called to say that Steve Urquhart was ready for him now. He locked the door and went nimbly down the stairs.

He led his guest to the Daisy, where Tim asked Evelyn if they could please have the "executive booth."

Steve was amused. "You have your own board room here. That's fantastic!"

"People treat me well," Tim replied, as Evelyn brought two porcelain mugs, not the usual heavy crockery, and all the trimmings on a tray.

"Dark or regular brew?" she asked the guest, and gave Tim a saucy look when Steve asked for regular.

"So, tell me," Tim asked finally, "can it happen?"

~

Ever grateful for the expertise of others, Tim took the forms the payroll specialist had given him and delivered them to Valerie Coolen at her bank. Tomorrow, the bank and the payroll service would exchange whatever information was required, and Steve and Valerie assured him that they were "reasonably confident" that it would work in time.

They would notify Tim's present bank, using forms he had signed, to terminate the payroll transactions, effective immediately.

Their "reasonable confidence" could only be about what was within their control. What Milton Barkhouse would be able or willing to do was up to him, but the worst-case scenario seemed to be that staff of *The Times* might be paid from two sources next Friday.

As Steve Urquhart said, that would be a mess, but the best kind of mess if it didn't put his bank account in the red, and it was fixable. He suggested that Tim advise everyone of the possibility, so they wouldn't "accidentally" spend the double pay, mistaking it for a Thanksgiving bonus.

All good. Wheels are in motion. Changes will be made. I think we're in a better place. We might have done all this a year ago, but I didn't have the mental or emotional capability then. This only proves that my sabbatical was necessary and worthwhile.

At Greene Auto, Robert's papers had been set aside for him, with sticky arrows indicating where he needed to fill in blanks or sign. They needed a copy of his driver's license, which Tim said he would get before Robert drove back to the city tomorrow morning.

That was everything. He could go home now, and have a pleasant evening with Robert, sharing him with the choir, and talking afterward. He felt good. The stress had been worth it.

~

The simple, tomato-based fish soup he made for pre-choir supper was a hit with both of them. They discussed whether a light red wine would go best with it, or an oaky white. They had neither, of course, because Robert wouldn't touch a drop before playing, and Tim didn't want to press wine-flavoured air from his stomach while breathing from his diaphragm. This was not a sacrifice. Music took precedence in its allotted time.

It was nice to sing familiar pieces and learn new ones, too. The choir thought the Spanish carol was easy after Robert introduced *Stille Nacht*, in German.

"Don't think you know this piece," he said. "You know the tune, of course, but I don't want to hear English speakers singing German. I want the audience to wonder where we found the German choir to sing it, got it? It's not 'sssstil-la not', it's 'schtill-eh nacchhtt. Try that."

Tim took his copy of the score home to practice later, and a second copy in case Elaine would learn it with him on Wednesdays. He was surreptitiously hoping to keep her familiar with some repertoire in case she decided to join the choir late in the season. Neither she nor Robert were aware of his hope, but he knew that hope worked better with some preparation.

After choir, they relaxed with a tasty Newfoundland port and some savoury crackers shaped like twisted sticks, and shared stories of their week. Robert's teaching was going well. Two students had dropped out of his composition class because they found it too difficult.

"Remember I told you that I made them begin at the beginning, with whole notes and four-four time in C Major, and some thought it was beneath them?"

"Yes. Did they see the wisdom of your method?"

"Most came around to it. But the ones who complained the most were the two who dropped out. As always, music is not poorer for their loss."

"Funny you should say that. We hired an employee last March who seemed to be good at everything, or he took on whatever we asked him to do, anyway. Then something went awry and he just…I don't know… malfunctioned, like. So he's gone, and already I can see how we'll be better off."

"Are you back at work full-time now?"

"I nearly was. That issue had to be dealt with, and Elaine couldn't fire him without my say-so. Meanwhile, the office building is in desperate need of renovations, so I've been leading that file, too."

"I thought you did that already, last spring or sometime?"

"That was all paint. We painted the interior, which made a huge difference. And then the whole stink with that crooked developer led to all the 'Gem District' façades getting painted. Now, finally, I will get some interior walls and doors and a legal stairway put in. Staff are quite excited, I think."

"Costly?"

"Yes and no. Seems everything I think is going to cost money ends up saving money somewhere else, so I think I'm still in a good position."

"Good. Well, we'd better turn in." Robert said, without moving to get up. "Early start tomorrow."

"Yes, and don't you dare leave in the morning until I get a copy of your license for Garland."

"Okay, I'll put it in my shoe."

"I was thinking, Rob...I might go in with you some Fridays, and come back on Saturday. What do you think of that? I could window-shop, or shop-shop if I see something good. Or visit with Mort and Martha. I miss them. Maybe the four of us could go out for dinner or the symphony sometimes? What do you think?"

"It's a terrific idea, and I know they'd love to see you, too. They talk about you all the time. I think Mort especially misses you. Martha has taken up the position as my chief cook and mother."

"Do you mind that?"

"Are you kidding? You've seen the state of my little pad. The rent's going up. It isn't worth more, except that it's near campus, and that puts all the rents up in that area. For the Everses, too. And now I'll have new car payments. Anyway, Martha is soothing me with soup and rolls, as you know."

Robert had shifted his position in the chair to face Tim. Something in his pose attracted Tim's attention.

"Yes, I know about Martha's soup and rolls. Are you winding up to tell me something more? I can't guess."

"Ahem. Yes, I am. They asked me...they suggested that it would work well for them and me..."

"Spit it out, man. They suggested what?"

"They invited me to move in with them, in their big flat. To share in the rent, proportionally, you know. It would help them out a lot, I guess, because Mort's pension doesn't nearly match his title. It'd be wonderful for me, too. Martha can hardly contain herself. My room is very large, too, with a real queen bed. I think it used to be the dining room in the original layout."

Robert paused.

"Sorry. I'm giving you the tour before I've even asked you."

"Asked me what?"

"What do *you* think?"

"It's not my decision, Rob. If you and Mort and Martha are sure about it, then you have my blessing, of course. Just be sure. If it doesn't work out, you'll be moving to the suburbs and taking the bus to work, or living here and parading with all the other poor commuters on the highway."

"You think it's okay, though? I have to give a month's notice or more, so there's time."

"I think you couldn't find better flat-mates anywhere. I'm almost envious."

"You don't have to be, Timo. You're included in this arrangement. As you just suggested, you can travel with me whenever you like, and stay over, too. Martha already suggested it. You can walk to lots of places from there, maybe see a play, drive them around while I work my fingers to the bone."

"This is exciting, Rob. You never know, do you? I suppose all this came about because of Hurricane Felix. There are some famous phrases that apply to this situation."

"It's an ill wind that blows nobody good?"

"Yes, that, and the Biblical reminder to welcome strangers, because you might be entertaining angels unawares."

"I'm the angel?"

"Without a doubt. Come on, it's time for lights out."

THE END

Tim's wine list for September, 1999

Here is Tim's (and sometimes Robert's) wine list for the month. You may seek these at an exclusive purveyor, but your search will be fruitless. Neither will you find them in your local wine outlet or 7-11, more's the pity. They are produced in very limited quantity.

September 2:   *Terre à terre* - down to earth
September 4:   *Buona fortuna* - good luck
September 7:   *Hombre Trabajador* - working man
September 10: *Nezměňujte* - don't change
September 11: *Un bel di* - one fine day
September 12: *Cari Amici* - dear friends
September 14: *Bois de Chauffage* - firewood
September 17: *La pêche aux compliments* - fishing for compliments
September 19: *Mother Julian* - Julian of Norwich
September 22: *Trompe-moi 2 fois* - fool me twice
September 25: *Tempesta* - storm
September 27: *Tu peux le faire* - you can do it
                    Tu l'as fait - you did it

Sneak Peek into *October: Underground*

Book ten in the Tim Brown series is due to appear in the spring of 2026.

October 7: Regular day

Thursday

When this sabbatical year was gaining traction, after Tim had detached himself from the regularity of work, he had felt quite untethered. So he had come to develop a fondness for Thursdays. They always began and ended with pleasant events, and he found them comforting.

He was also grateful because nothing today required stealth.

First was the arrival of Mrs Aquino, his Filipino housekeeper. He had discovered this summer that she was not only the enemy of dust and dirt, but a skilled gardener as well.

"I noticed that you've been weeding in the garden, Mrs A. Should I do some?"

"I do it. Still growing. No frost yet."

"Well, okay, but let me know if there's any, you know, work to be done. Robert will be here this weekend, and we'll have a guest. For sure we'll show off our garden. Your garden, I should say. Anyway, take whatever veg you want, remember."

As he reached his car in the driveway, Mrs A opened an upstairs window to bring fresh air in and let out the whine of the vacuum cleaner.

To escape this all-day cacophony, his habit was to go to the Daisy Café for breakfast on Thursdays.

"Whoopsie-daisy!" Evelyn called when he came in. "One sec, hon, gotta clean your table."

He waited for the second, and then she waved him to his favourite booth. A mug of black coffee was sitting on an envelope.

"What's this?" he said, sliding into the booth.

"You got mail," she said, and disappeared.

The envelope contained a Thank You card, of the kind sold in boxes with flowers and butterflies on the front. Inside, Evelyn had written:

> Dear Tim: We're glad to see you every time you dine at the Daisy! Thanks for your business. See you tomorrow!

It was signed by Ev and Kenny.

"Thanks for the card, Ev, that's really nice of you."

"Kenny, too. He was in favour of doing it right away. Silly fool really surprised me. But anything that lets him stay back at the grill suits him. Anyway, I thought it wouldn't hurt, y'know? People have choices."

"We do? Where else could I go to get food as good as Kenny's, and sass like yours?"

Evelyn feinted a swipe at his head with the menu. "No place would treat you as well as I do. D'you want to see this menu, or will I decide for ya?"

"Whatever you like, just not too much, please and thanks."

Tim stood the card up on the table.

A card with a note and two signatures. So simple, but very effective. I should mention this to Elaine. Maybe we'll do this for our subscribers for Valentine's Day. Too hokey? She'd tell me if it is.

Then he remembered. Elaine would be leaving South River in the new year, moving on to her next locum. She might distribute Valentine cards somewhere else, far away.

I'll ask her about it before she goes, then. Darn it.

As he ate the standard serving of eggs, bacon, and toast that Evelyn brought, Tim considered a possible menu for next Tuesday's Round Two.

It can't be steak again. What, then? Those men seem like the type who go hunting for big game, but what would I do with the rest of the rhino, and how would I cook it, anyway? Stella has a gas barbecue, but I'm not comfortable using it. They'd love that roast with the chocolate wine sauce that Robert served last month, but that required too much hands-on prep. I just want to serve the food and disappear.

He drew a fresh napkin from the dispenser on the table and attempted to write on it, but the lead in his sharp mechanical pencil tore the thin paper. He patted his pockets in search of a better method.

Passing by, Evelyn dropped a ballpoint pen and a scrap of manilla paper towel on the table. That worked.

He wrote three headings across the top, and drew two vertical lines between them:

FISH | FLESH | FOWL

By the time he was done, he had designed a meal fit for robber barons, and also for Thanksgiving dinner on Monday. He'd be able to test his meal plan on Robert and Jeremy. They wouldn't need to know he had an additional top-secret dinner in mind. They might make some useful suggestions.

He folded the paper and tucked it into the envelope with Evelyn's card. He paid the small bill, left a large tip, and headed out.

Now, he thought, *it would be okay to drop in at the office.*

Enough time had passed for the dust to settle, literally and figuratively, since last month's encounters with a recalcitrant employee. There was just one action remaining—a rather large and important one. He wasn't needed to accomplish it but he would be needed if it went wrong at the last minute.

"Good morning, Mrs Rafuse, how are you today?"

"Oh, Mister Brown, good morning to you. I'm so glad to see you."

Tim's insides considered tensing. "Why is that? Something wrong?"

"Gosh, no, everything's fine. It's just that we see you here, and then we don't. Personally, I like to see you here."

He sighed with relief and his insides concurred. "I like to see you, too, Mrs Rafuse. No messages for me?"

"Oh, no. I would have let you know if there were. Miss Fong takes care of everything, and Mrs. Naugler's doing a great job, too."

"Jean Naugler? What's she—?"

"You know, the computer stuff. She's got quite a team over there." She nodded toward the back corner. "I guess more staff knew more about computers than we knew, if you know what I mean."

"It's amazing, but I think I do. Thank you, Mrs Rafuse. I just came in to check on tomorrow's payroll transfer, speaking of computers."

"Isn't it great? Steve's been in a bunch of times to check with Miss Fong and Jean—Mrs Naugler. It's not my responsibility, but I think they're all pretty pleased. Excuse me."

She answered a call on her switchboard, and Tim took the opportunity to slip away.

I didn't know that October seventh was my lucky day, but so far, so good.

He tapped on Elaine's half-open door.

"Enter!"

"You neglected to tell me that everything was going smoothly vis-a-vis Steve and the payroll switcheroo."

"Nothing to tell. Yes, Steve, your payroll specialist, has been hovering like we were his only client, which is very reassuring. Mrs Naugler is assisting, very capably, too. Your new bank manager has been in twice to check. Everything's done, as far as anyone knows. Tomorrow is payday, which means the funds will be deposited in staff bank accounts overnight tonight, including mine, thank you very much."

"Mine, too. I might have actually earned it this time." He sighed. "Well, then, my work here is done, I guess. Nice to see you last evening. I hope you got some rest. I crashed."

"I did, too. Sometimes things just creep up on you, don't they? All good now. And another long weekend approaches. We can't print a skinny issue this time because there's no slowdown in ads. Do you realize how much money we make, indirectly, from the sale of candy alone?"

"Candy for Thanksgiving?"

"Not Thanksgiving, though we advertised turkeys and squash last issue. But Hallowe'en approaches, and the pharmacies are spending a fortune to make sure we buy everything made of sugar."

"Ah, yes, everyone benefits from All Hallows' Eve. I suppose I had better shop for a turkey, too. Will you be having a festive dinner somewhere, or should I ask?"

"You may ask, and yes, I believe I will. Go away now."

"Happily. I will drop in tomorrow morning. Just in case, payroll-wise."

"Good. Bye."

~

Tim went upstairs to make calls. First, to Stella.

"Yes?"

"'Thomas' here. Confirming Tuesday."

"What in particular?"

"I'm going to mortgage my house to buy the food."

"Go ahead."

"Did you get a locksmith?"

"What? No. I'm in the city. Can you look after it?"

"Install a lock? No, I can't. Anyway, I don't have a key to get in."

"I'll send Spencer to your house with an envelope. He won't know what's in it. I must go."

Stella hung up.

"Well, that's not very helpful, Aunt Stella," Tim said to the disconnected phone. "What am I going to do with the key to your house?"

I bet she's never given the key and code to anyone before. Well, it's all about security. If she's secure in her bedroom, I won't have to stay on guard all night, which I will sincerely appreciate.

The next call was to Conquerall Services, the construction firm which would transform his inefficient old office building into comfortable working and living space for all, and soon.

"When?" he asked Amanda, Conquerall's friendly more-than-receptionist.

"The plans are with the town now, Tim. Corey thinks it'll be soon, that's all we know. We did a presentation of the computer design program for them, and they were very impressed with it, which sure helps."

"Nice."

"The long weekend's coming up and Corey's working flat out, so don't expect to hear anything tomorrow. He sees the building inspector all the time, and he checks on all our files whenever he's there. My guess is the end of next week, or close. We're hoping to start your work toward the end of this month. That's all I can tell you now."

"Okay. I'll have to be patient. Thanks, Amanda."

That completed his business calls for now. Next task was to find a way to keep Stella secure inside her home.

It seems so unfair that a smart, powerful, influential, petite, attractive woman like Stella feels insecure around the men she dates and does business with, whose interests she's planning to promote, for goodness' sake. If I don't find a lock I can install myself, given my lack of skills, maybe I'll buy a baseball bat. Not for her. For me.

He spent a long time in the hardware store looking at door locks, but he knew he wasn't able to cut through a door with a hole saw, if he even had such a tool.

"What else is there?" he asked the salesclerk.

"What are you trying to accomplish?" the clerk asked him.

"I'm not sure I know how to answer that question," Tim said, laughing. "What am I trying to accomplish with a lock? Isn't that obvious?"

"Maybe not. If you want to prevent entry, then a deadbolt is the answer. If you want an alert or alarm to warn that someone is trying to enter, that's a different item. Would one of these help?"

He gestured to a rack displaying what looked like key holders that realtors hang on doorknobs. Instead of providing or preventing access, according to the writing on the package, this motion-sensing device would emit a warning strobe light for five seconds when disturbed, followed by a high-pitched alarm. It would alert everyone around that someone wanted in.

"All you have to do is put a fresh battery in it, hang it on the knob and set it."

Tim bought one of those, and also a sturdy rod with a foot at one end and a fork at the other, to prop under the doorknob from the inside. It would be nearly impossible to dislodge, he hoped, but easy for his petite aunt to put in place, should she feel the need.

She'll be protected with these, even better than with just a deadbolt. With all that commotion, any creep would pack up and run off. Problem solved. At least, neither Stella nor I will have to confront anyone, or even stay awake.

Tim stopped on the way home to pick up ingredients to make chicken stew for supper. He and Robert usually ate sparingly prior to choir, but he added dumplings anyway, because they both loved them.

When Robert arrived, he smiled at the aroma, and cheered when he lifted the lid and saw plump dumplings floating in the broth.

~

As choristers gathered in the choir loft, Spencer, one of the few tenors, came over to Tim and surreptitiously passed a sealed plastic envelope to him. There was no To or From on it.

"I was requested to hand this to you, Tim. By hand."

"Oh, right. Thanks, Spence."

"It's from—"

"I know, Spence. Got it."

Disregarding the instructions printed on the outside of the envelope not to bend it, Tim tucked it into the inside pocket of his jacket. He didn't need it now. He'd return the envelope to the sender unopened.

The choristers were proud of themselves, having a famous pianist coming to play in their church on Sunday morning. Word was out. The pews would be full. Fuller, anyway, not easy to do these days, as Thanksgiving mostly meant a holiday, not a holy day.

"Our guest pianist has very good ears, as you might expect," Robert said, "so please sing pretty for him. And don't let yourselves be distracted. Your task is to lead the congregation in singing the hymns, so focus, please, especially when we sing 'Now Thank We All Our God.' Jeremy and I will improvise a prelude, then first verse organ, piano second, and everything we can throw at it in the third, when you will sing in unison. Gosh, I wish we had a trumpeter. It's just great fun to raise the roof sometimes."

"That was a terrific rehearsal, Rob," Tim said later as he poured some of yesterday's By the Bay wine. "Everyone's sure fired up. I like it when we end rehearsal with a quiet vespers hymn, but tonight's cheers were fun."

"I enjoyed it, too," Robert said, ladling stew into a bowl and topping it with a dumpling. "Want some? I thought about this all through rehearsal."

"It didn't seem like that's what you were thinking about, somehow. Sure, I'll have a little more stew. Whatever's left is for you to take back to the city. Have you been in touch with Martha and Mort? When are you moving over there?"

"We're waiting on you. Martha says I can move in any day, and bring my stuff over whenever."

"I'll check the calendar...maybe next Friday? I could go in with you on Friday morning with a load of cartons and garbage bags, and do the dirty work while you teach. We should get it all done by the time we leave to come back Saturday afternoon."

"I appreciate that, Tim. Moving is not my strong suit. Cleaning, either."

"Oh, pshaw. It'll be easy, and a chance to visit with the Everses."

As they put the house away for the day, Robert asked, "How are things going with you, Tim? I know you were concerned about stuff at work. Is that all behind you now?"

Tim glanced at his watch. "It should all be behind me in about three hours. If it isn't, I'll address it tomorrow."

"You're very calm in the face of uncertainty, Timo."

"Oh, you don't know the half of it."

"Should I?"

"Nope. All good."

Jan Fancy Hull

Acknowledgements

I am grateful for readers who follow the goings-on of South River's assorted residents, Tim Brown in particular. Writing a series requires that things change in every book even while they remain familiar. Knowing there are keen-eyed readers out there who might spot inconsistencies makes my work more challenging, but better.

As always, my Dear Readers help me with this task, which is becoming more difficult in many ways as Tim Brown's year of delving wears on: Janet Barkhouse, Judi McDonald, and Catherine Walker have all pointed out important ways I can—and do—make the book better. And now, Kathy Mac has joined their ranks.

After I integrate their wisdom, the manuscript goes to Andrew Wetmore at Moose House Publications for his final layer of "betterments".

My name's on the covers, but gratitude for these wise folk is in my heart.

Read all the Tim Brown Mysteries!

Order from Moose House Publications (moosehousepress.com)
or your favourite bookseller.
Follow Jan and see all her books here:

amazon.com/author/janfancyhull

or use this QR code with your smart phone:

About the author

Jan Fancy Hull lives in a log chalet beside a quiet lake in Lunenburg County, Nova Scotia, where she has written non-fiction, award-winning poetry, short stories, and novels.

In former lives, she worked as a radio broadcaster, arts administrator, sailing tours skipper, and employee benefits broker.

During the winter, Jan watches snowflakes fall as she writes. In warm months, she enjoys the occasional round of golf, and drifting on the lake in her little boat, which she claims is a great place to edit.

In 2022, Jan received the Rita Joe Poetry Prize for her poem, "Moss Meditations."